Pam of Babylon

Suzanne Jenkins

ISBN: 1-4611-3592-3
ISBN-13: 9781461135920

Pam of Babylon

I

Jack Smith was thinking, *I am the luckiest man alive.* Sitting at a white-linen-covered table on the sidewalk outside of his favorite restaurant, he was gazing at the perfect face of his mistress of nine months. This place was "their" place. They had spent a rare night together, and now, in the early morning, they could sit here and have a leisurely breakfast, enjoying the perfect weather of late May in New York. Being with her was one of the few problem-free areas of his life.

"What do you have to do this weekend?" Jack asked, knowing this could be a dangerous topic. Sandra was sipping her coffee, head bowed, but eyes on him. She slowly put her cup down and straightened up. He really wanted to know. He was interested in her life outside of where it meshed with his.

"After you leave, I think I'll start getting ready for the week, and then I can relax tonight and tomorrow. Monday I am having lunch at my sister's. My schedule next week is fairly packed, so the more I can get done now, the easier it will be." She thought of her messy apartment, the empty refrigerator, the pile of laundry, but didn't mention it. Jack's solution to it would be to say, *Pay someone to do those things for you so you can do what you want. Your time is worth more than what it would cost.* "One thing I would really like to do is get back to that gallery on Houston and see if there isn't a deal I can work out for that piece we saw last night." She smiled at Jack, and they both nodded their heads, remembering the vibrant painting of the Riverside Gardens. It was so colorful, the yellows and reds and blues exaggerated, the flowers oversized. They both loved it.

"You should have said something while we were there!" he said, smiling at her. She knew he would have bought it then and there for her. But she really wanted to buy it for herself. She knew it was wise to keep things like "community property" out of their relationship.

They ate the rest of their breakfast in silence. Soon, Jack would start fidgeting, pushing his chair back slightly, looking around him, and fighting the urge to look at his watch. Their time together would be over for now. Sandra would try to beat him to the punch; it was easier for her to be in control of this aspect of their life. His schedule would dictate when they could see each other, but she could be in charge of when it would end. She hated those last minutes while they waited for the check to come, feeling like she was sitting in a vacuum. Today was a little different, maybe because of the night before. It was so special having the evening together and then spending the night with him. The hotel was the same one they always used. It was clean and comfortable and—impersonal. But she didn't allow herself to think of that.

He suggested early on that they go to her apartment, but she didn't know how long they would be together and didn't want those associations in her home. It would be hard to end the relationship without memories of him permeating where she lived. No thank you. Having to see him at work every day would be awful. Besides, he was wealthy enough to afford a hotel, and she was worth it.

He would not have argued if he knew what she was thinking. On one hand, he was wondering what was taking so long to get the check, as he had a lot to do at home today, but on the other, he would miss her terribly. It took all the strength he had not to pout like a child when he was away from her. He thought of his home, close to the sea, the smell of salt air. He imagined the two of them sitting on the veranda overlooking the beach grass. But the face of his wife kept popping up on Sandra's body as he thought of this, not allowing anyone to take her place, even in his thoughts.

She walked him to the subway, refusing to have him walk her home first. He preferred the subway over taking a cab all the way downtown. She would shop on the way home, and he had a long commute, over an hour, to his home on Long Island. They walked arm in arm, a striking couple to look at. He mature, graying at the temples, and in good shape for his age; she young, model thin, and beautiful. Heads turned to look. Were they famous? The attention they got when they were out in public together pleased them, and they became even more animated, laughing, standing up straighter, happiness radiating from them both.

On Broadway, another observer took note of the radiant couple. Jack's sister-in-law, Marie, waited in the Saturday-morning bagel line at H&R. She happened to be uptown because of having gone to the theatre the night before with her friend, Arthur, and then staying the night at his apartment. Marie stood there with her mouth open,

3

heat spreading through her body, shocked and furious. The man behind her tapped her on the shoulder; it was her turn already.

"Never mind, go ahead," she said as she moved out of line. Her body turned toward her brother-in-law as his back and that of his companion continued down the street toward the subway. She inched along the pavement staying close to the storefronts, not wanting to be seen, but dying to see. When they reached the subway, the woman, a girl really, didn't go down the stairs with him. Marie found it incredible that Jack was going to take the subway. What the hell was that all about? The couple stood at the entrance to the stairs talking, his arm around her shoulder protectively. It was clear that they were a couple, not just work associates, not just friends.

Standing out of sight in a doorway, Marie could barely tolerate the physical sensations she was experiencing. Her entire body was vibrating. It was a combination of disgust, shock, and excitement. She had loved Jack as her brother. She was certain her sister, Pam, had no idea her husband was cheating on her. Pam would have said something. Marie didn't yet think of the implications this would have on her relationship with her sister. If she didn't know, it would remain that way because Marie wasn't going to tell her. She would confront Jack and insist he tell Pam. That was the only way. Let him do the dirty work. Her patience paid off; Jack took the girl into his arms. He didn't look around first to see if they were being observed, although this was a neighborhood in which many of their relatives lived. Then they kissed. He kissed her passionately; she reached up and, with her arms around him, kissed him back. They parted, reluctance obvious to all who looked upon them, intimacy flourishing in a public place.

Jack went down the subway stairs, looking behind him and smiling. The young woman stood there smiling down at him, waiting to move away until he was out of sight.

Marie watched as the young woman, beautiful in a white sundress, turned her back to the stairs and starting walking up Broadway. Marie didn't have all day to play detective, but she knew that for her sister's sake, she would need to find out as much as she could about this person. So she followed her, supposing she was headed for home, but having no way of knowing. She stayed about half a block behind her. Watching her from the back, she made mental notes: tall; slender (of course); long, dark hair. Marie thought the woman should be blonde, but that didn't make any sense. She told herself to just keep walking. When they got to Eightieth, the woman crossed the street and went into Zabar's. There was no way Marie was going in there. She would wait outside for a few minutes. She didn't have all day. If the woman were doing a big shopping trip, Marie would leave. She stood across Broadway, watching, not wanting to miss it when she left the store. Looking up at the sky, she could see blue between the buildings, sunlight peeking down from the east. It was going to be a beautiful weekend. Memorial Day was Monday. Marie was going to her sister's house on Long Island for a picnic. She had been looking forward to it all month. Now this.

The young woman stepped out of Zabar's with two bags of groceries. She turned left and started walking up Broadway again, with Marie following closely behind.

When she got to Eighty-second, she turned left, walking toward West End. *It figured*, Marie thought, remembering her own apartment in no man's land. About midway, she made another left and walked up to a lovely, beige-brick mid-century. She went to the door, turned the key in the lock and disappeared. Marie stood in the center of the sidewalk, disappointed. Well, she had an address, just in case.

She walked back to Broadway, thinking all the way. She wanted to call Jack's cell right there and tell him off. Suddenly, she was overcome with nausea. She moved to the curb and threw up in the gutter.

2

Pam Smith was puttering around her light-filled kitchen early on Saturday morning. Jack had spent a rare Friday night in the city. He loved to get home after being gone all week. Once in a while, he would even come home midweek in spite of the commute. She had all week to prepare for his homecoming. She went to the gym every day, had her hair and nails done, and stocked the fridge with his favorite foods. The house was in good order. There was rarely anything that he needed to attend to; she tried to make it an oasis for him. They could rest, play tennis, go for walks on the beach, and have a mini vacation.

This weekend would be spent in preparation for the annual Memorial Day picnic they hosted. Friends and family would come from all over the tri-state area. Pam had the cleaning lady air out the guest quarters above their garage. Their nieces and nephews could bunk in the kids' rooms; Lisa was in L.A. for the summer, doing some kind of internship, and Brent was staying at school until July, doing extra work to make next year a little easier. Her kids would be missed on Monday.

Marie would stay over, as would both Mom and Jack's mom. The house would be full. Pam had arranged for the bed-and-breakfast down the beach from them to take the overflow from the house. Everyone would come the next afternoon and stay through Monday night. Marie and Mom might stay through until Tuesday evening.

Pam had planned what everyone would eat down to the last crumb. She loved that sort of thing. She did all her shopping on Friday morning and would pick up fresh vegetables and fish on Sunday. She couldn't wait for Marie to come; they would run all over town looking for things together.

Pam was ten years older than Marie. Marie was there for her while Jack was in grad school, during the lean times, through two pregnancies. She was her mother's helper when the kids were little; never turning down an opportunity to stay with Pam and Jack when school was out for the summer. When they moved to the Upper West Side, she moved with them, eventually getting her own apartment in Midtown. When they left the city for the island, she wept. She knew she would be welcome to visit every weekend and holiday, but there was something so nice about being able to drop in for coffee in the morning or run to a last-minute movie.

Pam rarely came into the city. Although her friends told her she would probably be in every weekend for shows during the fall and winter, the truth was that she never really enjoyed the nightlife, and once they moved, the apartment became Jack's private domain while he worked during the week. He left for work on Monday morning and stayed in town unless he got homesick for the beach house and his wife. In that case, he would come home once or twice during the middle of the week and leave early the next morning.

He never asked Pam to visit him in the city. Their relationship had lost that urgency of needing each other. Once or twice when they were first separated during the week, she had woken in the night crying, reaching out to his side of the bed. If that had happened in their youth, he or she would have picked up the phone for reassurance and connection. When had that stopped being necessary?

Lately, Pam had been a little worried about Jack. There was a tiny, itsy bit of doubt, a niggling worry, an insecurity in the back of her mind. He was disconnected from her. He still seemed eager to get home and reluctant to return to the city, but that stemmed more from his love of the house she had made for him and the peace and quiet of the beach. He never reached out for her anymore, didn't hold her in bed at night, and hadn't initiated sex in months.

She didn't notice it at first. She made love to him when she needed to and left him alone when she didn't. That was where the worry came in. Unless she reached out for him, they didn't do it. At first, she thought it might be his age. They were both nearing fifty-five. She didn't dare complain to him. What man's ego could take that from a middle-aged wife?

Those worries were then buried in the busyness and anticipation of his return home every Friday night. She made mental lists of plusses and minuses; it was enough that he came home to her. And then she noticed another change. He started being very picky about what he ate when he was home. In the past, a big steak, a baked potato, and a salad with blue cheese dressing would make him happy. He loved her home-baked bread and pies. Now, he seemed to be counting calories. He didn't come right out

9

and say he wouldn't eat something she had prepared, but she noticed he watched the size of the proportions, ate more salad, and used less dressing. He skipped dessert. Then he requested more vegetable dishes, even fish.

He started working out on the weekends; one day he just showed up while she was there. That should've been enough of a warning sign. But when she said something to him about it, teasing him because of all the years she invited him to come to her gym, he told her that their family doctor recommended he lose some weight, that he was a walking heart attack. She was frightened. She had always been a healthy weight and in shape. Watching him eat a veggie burger was a contradiction.

The day before, he had called her after lunch and said he was staying in town that night because he had a late meeting. He had stayed before on Friday if the weather was horrible or the train wasn't running for whatever reason, but rarely for business. She didn't suspect a thing until she tried calling their apartment at eleven that night, right before the news came on. There was no answer.

It was so strange that she thought she had dialed the wrong number and hung up the phone to dial again. But the second time, letting it ring and ring, she wondered if maybe he was in the shower, or worse, if he had fallen. Not knowing his cell phone number by heart, she dug through her purse to find her own and hit his number, letting his cell ring until the call answer picked up. She hung up without out leaving a message, not having anything to say to him other than that she was thinking of him and suddenly missed him. There was that seed of doubt.

So as she puttered around that morning, expecting him any minute, she wondered if she should say something to him about the unanswered phone call but decided to let it go. If there were anything to learn, she supposed she would find out soon enough and was more than willing to let things remain as they had always been—peaceful, content, and happy.

3

Jack took the subway to Grand Central and hopped on his train home. Once he was in his seat, he pulled out his cell phone to call Sandra and make sure she had gotten home safely after her shopping expedition. When he opened his phone, he saw he had a missed call. Thinking it was from her, he pressed the button and saw it had been from Pam at eleven-ten p.m. A sick feeling washed over him. He needed to think of what to say to her, to call her right away and apologize.

"Oh my God, I just saw you had called. My phone was off, and I went right to sleep. I'm so sorry."

"Okay. That's okay, Jack. I didn't really have anything to say anyway."

Was she buying it? He could never tell with her. She was so patient, but she was cool, too.

"When will you be home?" she asked, her voice neutral.

"I'm on the train now, so by noon. See you then." He put his head back on the headrest. He remembered he wanted to call Sandra. He keyed in her number, but there was no answer there. He put the phone away, closing his eyes once again. It would be good to be home.

Sandra let herself into her apartment. It smelled musty, closed in. She put her bags of groceries down and went around opening windows. She was on the ground floor of the building and had a door that lead out to a concrete slab, which she and her neighbor used as a patio. The only drawback was that it faced the back of a commercial building on Eighty-first. There wasn't much privacy during the day. But after five, the building was empty. Sandra would make herself a cup of tea and go out there to sit. It was about as relaxing a place as you could get in the city. There would be no relaxing now, however; she had to clean her apartment and get ready for next week so she could play the rest of the weekend.

She loved her apartment. It had a galley kitchen on the first floor with a big window facing a brick wall, a small sitting room, a full bath, and a bedroom. On the lower floor, there was a huge room that she used as a combination den/guest room and another full bath. This level also had a door that lead out to the patio. She realized how lucky she was to have a two-bedroom, two-bath place with outdoor space in New York City. She would hold on to it as long as she could. Her rent went up every year and was now hovering at three thousand a month—a steal in the city. But that was half her salary. Soon, she would either have to leave and move to Brooklyn, or worse, New Jersey. She didn't mention her dilemma to Jack; he'd surely offer to pay the rent, and then she would have to allow him admittance. No, she wasn't ready to be kept.

She changed out of her white sundress into black spandex shorts and a sleeveless T-shirt—her outfit of choice for cleaning sprees. She went from room to room, hour after hour, homemaking. At three, she stopped for a bite to eat, just a piece of fruit and a cup of coffee. By five, she was finished. She showered, debating whether or not to put her nightgown on or get dressed and go out.

An unexpected phone call from a nurse at St. Vincent's Hospital made that decision for her. A man had had a heart attack on the train. And if that weren't bad enough, thugs had taken his wallet. The only thing left on him was his phone, and she was the last person he had called. The nurse asked Sandra if she knew who he was hoping she could verify his identity.

Once she caught her breath, she said she would be right there, not thinking of the consequences, not caring about being discovered. She dressed, pulled her wet hair into a ponytail, grabbed her purse, and ran out of the apartment.

4

By the time she got to the hospital, Jack had regained consciousness long enough to give them the name and phone number of his wife. Then he died.

Sandra was not a drama queen. She was composed in the worst of circumstances; her father's death was just such an example.

Her mother had suffered with breast cancer for ten years. The first six or seven years were spent taking rounds of chemotherapy, radiation, and experimental drugs. Finally, she couldn't take the punishment of the drugs and succumbed to the vileness of the disease. It spread to her bones first, causing agonizing pain and debilitation, and then it went to her brain. She was a dynamic, aggressive woman in her day, but the brain tumor reduced her to a meek and passive mouse.

She began to waste away, growing thinner as the days pasted until she was skeletal. And then her body began to die. Her strong heart continued to beat, her brain stem working to maintain her breathing and heart rate, while, gradually, her circulation shut down. First the tips of her toes turned black. Slowly, death worked its way up, her legs turning purple, then blue. Finally, mercifully, she died in her sleep.

Sandra thought it would be a huge relief when she finally died. How wrong she was! The family was devastated. Sandra's father couldn't control his sadness. He cried for the first few days and was unable to get out of bed or get dressed, refusing to eat. She missed feeding her mother, tempting her with her favorite foods, plying her with sweets, anything to get her to eat. At the time, it was the most frustrating experience she had, often thinking, *God, please take her.* And now all she wanted was one more chance to feed her, to serve her in some way. Her mother. Gone.

Preparing for the funeral was hell. Sandra knew her mother hated pomp and circumstance, but her sister, Sylvia, was hell-bent on throwing the biggest party they could afford for their friends and family. Sylvia interviewed the priest; her mother would have hated a religious ceremony, being a passionate atheist. She rented a banquet room at the Bentley in Bergen, an over-decorated monstrosity of a place that reminded their mother of the Palace of Versailles. Now, the final indignity was having the wake luncheon there. Sandra did what she could do to try to dissuade her sister from the plans, but it was hopeless. She prayed that something would happen to change Sylvia's mind.

The evening of the viewing was cold and windy. Sandra struggled to get her father up and dressed. He was still despondent, begging her to allow him to stay home.

"Just tell everyone I am ill," he said. "Mother would have hated all this fuss."

"I know, Dad. But it will help us to go, to see it through. I miss her, too. I hardly know how I am going to look at her."

In addition to the expensive funeral, Sylvia had also insisted on an open casket. Sandra thought of those black toes, that almost dead body. Maybe she should have insisted that Sylvia help with the caregiving. She may have had a different perspective if she had.

Sandra pulled the car out of the garage and drove to the front of their building to pick him up. He stood under the awning waiting. She was shocked at how frail he looked, bent over, shaking. He was only sixty-one years old, yet he looked like he was ninety. She wondered if they should bypass the funeral, do as her father said and just stay home and pretend they were sick. Sylvia would never have allowed it; she would come and drag them out.

The rain made the air in the tunnel stagnant and toxic. Of course, traffic was backed up, and they were forced to sit there breathing exhaust fumes and who knew what else. Coming out the other side, they pulled onto the turnpike and started heading north toward Bergen. Sandra would ask Sylvia if Dad could stay with her tonight; the trip back into the city would be too much for him.

They got to the funeral home right at seven p.m. The parking lot was crowded with cars displaying New York State license plates. Sandra thought about how ridiculous it was to have to come here for the viewing tonight, come back during rush hour the next morning for the funeral, drive upstate for the burial, and then back down for lunch. She got tired just thinking about it.

She had dropped her dad off at the door and parked the car. Running to the door to avoid getting wet, she stepped in a puddle of icy-cold water, ruining her shoes and splashing dirty water up her legs. *Could this get any worse?* Sandra wondered.

When she reached her dad, he was surrounded by sympathizers and, she saw with regret, was crying again. He had someone on either side of him, assisting him as he walked reluctantly into the building. He looked so old; Sandra was choking back tears herself.

She excused herself to the helpful friend and took hold of her father's arm. She wanted to be with him when they approached the casket. Sylvia was standing there already, glaring at them for being late, greeting guests as they lined up to view the body. Sandra wished there was a way they could avoid this public viewing, thinking it would be too emotional and too private a thing to share with all of these people. But having seen the casket, her father was propelling himself along, now wanting to see his wife one last time.

Those who were standing there looking at her stepped aside when they saw her husband of forty years being led by his daughter toward the body. Sylvia came up to them and took his other arm, as it was important that the three of them see her body together. Sandra gasped when she saw her mother. Sylvia had done well. Her mother looked much like she did prior to the worst of the disease, with chubby cheeks, perfect makeup, and her favorite suit. Sandra and her father were both relieved at what they saw.

She could see her father visibly relaxing as he stood and talked with their guests. Many people told him stories of what she meant to them or anecdotes of their experiences with her. It had a great effect on him. For the first time in five days, he smiled.

Sandra took her sister's arm and said, "Thank you, Sylvia, this is perfect."

Sylvia smiled back at her and said, "Told you so."

Sandra remembered the favor she wanted to ask Sylvia. "Would you take Dad home with you?" she said. "I don't think he can handle a trip back home tonight and then back here in the morning."

"That's fine," Sylvia said. "I'll go get his coat."

Sandra turned to yet another friend, someone who had known the family since before the girls were born, while Sylvia retrieved her father's coat and helped him into it, the two of them saying good-bye to the lingerers. Sandra looked up in time to see her father, his eyes seeking her out, give a feeble wave, smile at her, mouth "so long," and then drop to the floor. By the time she reached him, he was dead.

Now, seeing death again, another man she loved, she was numb, frozen in place. She was told she could view the body if she wanted. Remembering the peace seeing his wife's body had brought her father, she said yes. He was so peaceful that he died on the spot. Perhaps that would happen for her too, because she truly did not know how she was going to go on. Talk about a trite cliché. She realized why it is cliché, because it is true. *Let me die, too.* The nurse took the young, distraught woman by the arm and led her into the room. If there had been any heroics to save his life, all evidence of it was gone now, except for a thin, shiny, pink snail trail of dried mucous in the corner of his mouth.

"Oh, Jack," she said. She took his cold hand in hers and bent down, putting it to her cheek. She felt the familiar texture of his skin, with its wiry hairs on the back of his hand tickling the side of her face. But that was all. He was gone. She couldn't help herself, couldn't prevent the tears from coming. The nurse, compassionate and concerned, led her out of the room and toward a private office where she could be alone for a moment before returning home. As she was being lead, head down and weeping, another woman—attractive, middle-aged, worried—was being lead into the room by a nurse, but not before noticing the beautiful young woman who had just exited the same room crying. Jack's wife had made good time.

Seeing his body lying there with the sheet pulled up to his shoulders, looking so normal, his hair neat and combed, his face shaven, Pam burst out, "Oh my God! He's dead!" without thinking, not remembering that someone had told her on the phone that he was dead. *Or had they? Didn't they just say he had a heart attack?* "He's dead!" she repeated.

The nurse said, "Yes, he's dead. Right before he died, he awoke and gave us your phone number. You see, his wallet had been stolen on the train."

"Who was that woman who just came out of the room? Did he tell you her number, too?" She knew she sounded like a tired child, querulous, whiny.

The nurse, with years of experience in matters of death, made the snap decision that taking Mrs. Smith to the same room where the "other woman" was recovering would not be wise. "Come in here with me, Mrs. Smith." The nurse had her by the hand. Pam wasn't pulling away, but she was reluctantly being led. There might be a problem. As they were going into the room, Marie came running down the hall, having received the message when she came in from spying that Pam was on her the way to the hospital.

"Pam, Pam, for God's sake, what happened?" She grabbed her sister and they held each other, both sobbing, until Pam could get it out. Jack was dead. He had a heart attack on the train, and someone had stolen his wallet. Another woman had come to see Jack, too. No one would tell Pam how she knew to come to the hospital. When the nurse returned, she was with a social worker. The woman, a Miss White, gently lead the two crying women into a small anteroom just off the nurses' station. It was cluttered with papers and stacked cardboard boxes, but there was also a desk and a chair. The nurse grabbed a chair from the nurses' station and wheeled it in, directing the women to have a seat.

"Who's the other woman here?" Pam repeated. She understood how inappropriate this must seem. For God's sake, her husband was lying dead in the next room, and all she seemed to care about was this woman. But she had to know. She had to. Marie, stony silent, thought she knew, but would sooner die herself than be the bearer of this tiding.

"Mrs. Smith, when your husband was brought in, the only personal item he had was his cell phone, so we called the last person he called. I'm sorry, but we aren't allowed to divulge any more information than that."

Pam stood up, fuming. "That is ridiculous! What if the last person he called was the trash collector? Would you have let them come into his hospital room?" Both the nurse and the social worker tried to calm her down while they waited for the director of nursing to call them back. Marie left the room. She would find the woman herself and confront her. She spotted her walking quickly down the hall toward the exit.

"Miss, wait! Wait, please!" she called after her.

Sandra walked faster at first and then decided it was fruitless—she might as well get it over with. She stopped and turned, not replying, just waiting as asked. Marie quickly walked up to her. She stopped then, looking at her face. She was the same girl who she had seen earlier on the street, only now she was without makeup, and her eyes were swollen and red from crying, clearly brokenhearted.

"Please, I am sorry to disturb you, but we have to know who you are. Jack was my sister's husband." She repeated, "Who are you?" The young woman hung her head down and began to weep again. Marie led her over to the side of the hall, out of the way. "I saw you with him, with Jack, this morning," she whispered. "I was at the bagel place on Broadway, and I saw you walking hand in hand to the subway. I saw you kiss each other. I was going to confront him tomorrow. They're having a Memorial Day picnic for the family—were having a picnic. I would never say anything to hurt my sister, but she needs to know the truth now or it will kill her."

Sandra heard what was being said to her, but she couldn't respond. She didn't know what to say. If they had been discovered, so be it. There was nothing else to tell.

They had nothing together that was tangible. It was fleeting, an illicit affair. A momentary encounter that brought two people who were attracted to each other together for just a few months, not even a year.

"What do you want me to say? I'm sorry? Will that do it? Okay then, I am sorry. I am sorry I had an affair with your brother-in-law. I'm sorry he died tonight. I am sorry they called me to come to the hospital, that my number was in his phone." *No*, she thought, *I take that back. I'm not sorry they called me. If they hadn't, how would I have found out he was gone?*

She realized then the travesty of what had just taken place—that the mistress was called first, before the wife. No wonder she was angry! The mistress should only find out about death by reading the paper, the final indignity, the obituary. *New York Times*, page thirty-two. Jack Edward Smith. Born Nineteen fifty-five. Died Two thousand ten. Husband of Pamela, father of Lisa and Brent, son of Bernice. Lover of Sandra.

Yes, thank God for the cell phone. Without her number, she would have waited to hear from him for three days. Then the final horror—going into the office on Tuesday and being surrounded by their coworkers and having to hear it from one of them.

Her revelry was disturbed by Pam, her voice echoing down the corridor.

"Marie, what's going on? Who's that?" Sandra watched her as she scurried toward them. She remembered Jack using a similar term when describing his wife; everywhere she went, she scampered, he had said. She was always in motion, always doing something. She couldn't go to a movie or the theater without taking something like knitting or it would drive her nuts.

Pam was as gorgeous as a fifty-five-year-old woman could be. Although hardly at her best now, you could tell she took good care of herself. In addition to good genes, she worked out daily, stayed out of the sun, and spent a small fortune on her hair and skin. It showed.

Now they stood face to face. Marie needn't have said a word. Pam was no slouch. She knew who this young, attractive woman was. She could see immediately why Jack was attracted to her, why he would betray his wife for her. It must have been uncontrollable.

She stood there looking at Sandra and put out her hand, not to shake hands, but to grasp Sandra's.

"I'm Pam Smith," she said. "Please, who are you?"

Sandra started to weep again unattractively, snorting. She could barely get the words out. "Sandra. Sandra Benson. I am so sorry." The tears cruised down her face, dripping off the end of her nose. Pam took a step toward her, and Sandra looked up startled, fully expecting her to haul off and slap her across the face. Instead, she placed her hands on the young woman's shoulders and pulled her to her bosom. She had to stand on her toes to hug Sandra.

Then she started to weep, too.

"I'm sorry, too. Poor Jack. I'm sorry, too."

5

Pam had to get home. She needed to call the children and get them home safely. Jack's mother—*oh God, how was she going to tell the woman that her son had died? Who does that?* The parent should die first. She didn't think she had it in her. She would have someone call Jack's brother, Bill. Let him do the dirty work. She had a party to cancel; it would be a funeral picnic instead. But, first, she had to see this young woman home safely. There would be plenty of time later to sort it all out, and she said as much out loud.

"I wish we could go to the coffee shop across the street from our apartment. I could sit there all night with the both of you, talking, sharing stories about Jack," Pam said, with Marie thinking, *My sister is really an asshole.* Pam continued, "But I have to get home. Promise me you will rest tonight, and tomorrow, or Monday, we must get together, okay? I have two children who don't know their father is dead yet, and I must contend with that before I do anything else."

The three women got into a cab together. Pam held Sandra's hand until they reached her apartment uptown. She asked Marie to see her to her door. She did as she was asked. Marie remembered to get her phone number, although she now had Jack's cell phone, which housed the number, along with text messages, voicemail messages, and only God knew what else.

Faced with an hour's cab ride home, Pam made a mental note of whom she needed to call. When Marie got back inside, she told her she was going to call the children and then Bill. The calls to the kids were the worst. Lisa became hysterical, screaming, "No! No!" into the phone over and over again. Pam faced that it was not going to be easy to hang up on her teenage daughter, so she gave the phone over to Marie and, using Marie's phone, called her son, who had the same reaction. Fortunately, both children where at places where public transportation was abundant, and no one would have to get into a car to come home. They both promised to wait to try to get home until the morning. *Things wouldn't seem so bleak then*, she thought.

Then she had Marie call their mother. She just couldn't do it. She couldn't say one more time tonight, "You need to brace yourself, Jack is dead." Or worse, "Your father is dead."

She was sure the shock of his mistress, the girlfriend, would come, although she hoped it would be sooner rather than later because, magically, she needed her. She needed someone else who knew him intimately. She was happy with the knowledge that it wasn't so much that he was tired of her and that was why he no longer asked for love-making; he was simply spent from doing it with Sandra. That somehow, oddly, made it easier to swallow, the idea that he had someone else, someone who he might have liked better than her. But that would be dealt with later. She was in shock. People in shock were expected to make wrong decisions. She didn't want to make any mistakes.

The rest of the ride home passed in silence. Every once in a while, Pam would remember and start crying again in choking sobs, already lonely for him. Marie, crying too, would take her sister's hand to comfort her.

When they got to the house, Pam suddenly felt empty, saying she would like a cup of tea and something sweet, like cookies, or toast and jam. She put the teapot on and went to their room to change into pajama bottoms and a T-shirt. She washed her face, the makeup streaked and blotchy, and felt better for it. Maybe she would go without for a while. Give her skin a break. But she knew she wouldn't. Putting on her makeup and doing her hair was so much a part of who she was that it would be like going without a bra, or her bridgework. Not possible.

Marie was waiting for her, having poured the tea. They took their cups out to the veranda. The salt air was soft and moist, enveloping them with its gentle caress. Pam felt like she needed a shawl, her grief magnifying the cool air. Marie went into the study and got it off the desk chair, trying not to look at Jack's desk.

Putting it around her sister's shoulders, she said, "I love you, Sis," and hugged Pam. They could see the grasses swaying in the breeze. The moonlight was yellow, its beams falling on the water almost still as a lake. The echoes of the little waves reached them, sounding sad and melancholy.

Pam wondered out loud if she would be able to stay in their house.

"You love it here," Marie said. "Why would you leave it?"

"I don't know if I can afford to stay here now," Pam said, not ready to share her real feelings with Marie. "We will have to see what happens. We'll have to see what kind of financial shape we are in." Pam didn't want to think of that already. Jack wasn't even to the funeral home yet. He was still in the morgue. She thought of his body, not on the metal table or still in the hospital bed, as she had last seen him, but she thought of him the weekend before, in loose shorts and a sparkling white T-shirt, lying on a bench at the gym doing chest presses. She thought at the time how proud she was that he was her husband, wondering if anyone knew that information. *Had he greeted me when he came in?* thought Pam. It was her gym first, after all. He had finished with the weights and then got on the treadmill. She watched him out of the corner of her eye. He started slowly, walking, adjusting the earpiece on his iPod, and then, after a brief warm-up, started running. She hadn't seen him run for ages. He used to be fast. He stayed on the treadmill for half an hour. She estimated he ran three miles. And later, questioning him, she found she was right. He was still fast.

That afternoon, both home from the gym and showered, he in his study going through some papers and she gathering up items for a rummage sale her book club was having, they passed each other in the hall, brushing arms. He paused, looking down at her. She smiled up at him. She could smell the deodorant he used, a strong, herbal scent, and it went from her olfactory nerve to her crotch. It was the weirdest sensation; she could almost feel the pathway. She reached out for his arm and ran her hand down the length of it, feeling the soft, spongy hair; he reached for her hand when it came to stop on his wrist. They stood there, holding hands, smiling at each other.

"So, wife, what do you say?"

She was willing him to say something sexy to her, to proposition her, but he seemed unable, or unwilling, to do it. But, what the heck, she was only punishing herself if she didn't engage him.

"I say we should hop into bed right now. You game?" She smiled again, looking up into his eyes, sticking her tongue out so the tip of it ran around the corners of her mouth.

He let her lead him to their bed. It was the lovemaking of two people who had been together all of their lives. It was slow, it was tender, but at the end of it, it was explosive. He always remarked afterward, "Wow, for a couple of old people, we can really hang one on." She laughed. "You are such a romantic," she would reply, and he would laugh. So if she was satisfied physically, and she always was, there was something lacking in the emotional end of it. They weren't connecting any longer. There was no "I love you," anymore. He didn't comment about her appearance as he used to, no "God, you look good."

Now she understood why. He had betrayed her. She would find out later what had really happened, the depth of his feeling for this young, beautiful woman. Was it a new, superficial romance? She didn't think so. But she wouldn't waste one second thinking about it. She had no facts to back up her doubts.

They sat in silence, the two sisters, one thinking about what she had seen that morning and wondering when the time would be right to tell the story or if she could get away with never revealing what she knew—that Jack had loved this young woman. You could see that from clear across Broadway.

Suzanne Jenkins

Finally, Pam spoke. Rather than speaking of the pain that had transpired that evening, she talked about how Marie had impacted their lives. There were two other sisters in their family, born between Marie and Pam, yet it was the two of them who would bond completely, as close as could be. Pam spoke of how she wouldn't have survived her early marriage without the support of Marie, only ten years old at the time. She cried, inconsolable, when Pam left home. She was promised that each weekend, every holiday, she could visit her big sister and new brother-in-law. And they kept that promise, either Jack or Pam taking a cab to pick her up, or after the kids were born, Marie old enough to come alone.

Pam remembered the excitement of having her baby sister coming to visit on a Friday night. They would walk to Big Nick's or Broadway Pizza and then get ice cream. Saturdays would be spent doing crafts, either painting some piece of furniture Pam had found at a secondhand shop or knitting something for one of the babies that was due to arrive soon. They would walk in the park or find something free to do, a gallery opening or a concert. Saturday night was always movie night. Pam would fix dinner, something fun like burgers or homemade pizza, and they would watch whatever Marie wanted. Jack would take her to the video store, and they would spend at least an hour choosing a movie for the night and one for the next morning.

On Sunday mornings, they fixed a big homemade breakfast. Pam made wonderful pancakes; Jack could handle the waffle iron like a chef. They divided the Sunday paper between them and spent hours reading, eating, and talking. They would walk around the city, sometimes staying out until dinner if the weather was nice or coming home for hot chocolate and an afternoon nap if it wasn't.

The years flew by, and Marie never left. The kids grew, and she became part of their lives as well, there for the triumphs and the childhood dramas, the maiden aunt who could be depended on for companionship, advice, or a bedtime story. If the times had been different, Marie would have been a nun, Pam thought. She was devoted to the task of whatever was put before her, never asking herself if this was all life was supposed to be—living through someone else's dream.

Jack was Marie's male figure, the person she sought if she had a bad day at work or needed advice about investments, buying a new car, going on a fishing expedition, and so much more. He took her to her senior prom, went to shows with her, and taught her how to ski and change a tire. After their father died, he became a father figure to her as well.

She, in turn, stood in for Pam doing those things she couldn't bear to do; sitting in a theater to watch plays, attending any sporting event, going fishing or hunting, Marie loved that sort of thing. She stood in for Jack, too, going to antique shows, festivals, the farmers' market, all things that bored him to tears. She was a real companion.

Marie wept when Pam thanked her for her devotion over the years. Pam secretly wondered if her marriage would have lasted if not for Marie. She acted as a buffer between Pam and Jack. There was always someone willing to do something, allowing the other partner to do his or her own thing. In that regard, no one had to make too many compromises.

They chatted about their life together until the sun peeked up over the horizon. They gathered up their shawls and blankets, cups and plates, and went into the house. The day stretched before them, with sadness and tears, reliving the night over and over again for family and friends. Pam had to get some sleep. She would shut off her phone, and Marie would field calls. She would get someone to pick up the children from the nearby airports, Brent from Newark and Lisa from JFK. Indispensable Marie. In the meantime, they would go to their rooms and get a few hours of rest. It was too early to get anything done anyway.

Pam got into her bed with the same gratefulness she did each night. The cool, clean sheets and their wonderful mattress were heavenly. Physical comfort overpowered the sadness in her heart. She lay on her back, looking up at the light coming in over the top of the closed drapes.

He was gone. She would never see him again, never hear his voice, never wait for his car to pull in the garage, never smell him, touch him, or feel him. How would this become real to her? There would have to be a point in time that it would hit her, smack her in the face. Right now, she didn't feel too much besides her bed. They would never resolve their problems. He had gotten away with his infidelity. Sometime that day, after funeral arrangements were made, she would find the strength to call Sandra Benson and ask her to come to the funeral. They would have to decide how to handle her appearance there, surely someone knew of her existence in their circle of acquaintances. The only thing she would ask is that the children be spared this information about their father. They would take it personally, if she knew them as she thought she did.

She finally fell asleep around six a.m. Marie tip-toed around the house when she got up at nine a.m. Lisa had called to say she would be in at three that afternoon, followed by a call from Brent that he'd be there at four. Marie was relieved that Pam would have that time to herself until the kids came home. She wasn't sure what their response to this was going to be. *Would there be thrashing about, screaming? Or would they be adults, offering to help out in some way to lighten their mother's burden for the day?* She would know soon enough.

Their mother, Nelda, was planning on being there by eleven. She would take over the logistics of the guests. She was a whiz at party planning. Thank God for the bed-and-breakfast down the beach; Jack's family could stay there. Nelda was going to make the calls as well. She had started last night. There were at least a hundred people who needed to be personally called.

The *New York Times* had written a small article about his death on the second page: "CEO Mugged on LI Train, Suffers Fatal Heart Attack." They used an old, but sufficient picture of him from the days before his graying hair. People who knew him would be okay with that. It was an attractive picture, him smiling at an opening of some play downtown, the sort of activity he loved. Marie was worried about the headline. *Did he get mugged first?* She thought the hospital people had said he was mugged after he went down. Added to her list was to make a call to the police precinct. They needed the truth. As soon as the paper was read, she was sure the phone would start ringing.

Quickly walking around the house, she turned down all the phone bells, thinking it would help her sister to not have that incessant noise.

Marie thought of Jack's mother. She picked up the phone to call Bill just as she heard the front door opening. It was Bill; his wife, Anne; and Bernice, Jack's mother. She had aged overnight. Marie explained that Pam had been up all night and that she was determined to let her sleep as long as she could. The funeral home had not called yet, so no plans for the burial had been made.

They moved to the kitchen, pulling out the chairs to sit around the table. Thankfully, Anne took over the role of hostess so Marie could repeat the details of the tragedy to Jack's brother and mother, who were both in shock and in need of some information to make sense of what had happened. They talked in low tones, trying to keep it quiet for Pam. *Poor Pam, what would she do, how was she going to get through this?*

It was just like Anne. She had a way of sliding into whatever space needed to be filled. The youngest of six girls in a big Irish family, Anne was used to serving her family. In spite of marrying into the wealthy family of the Smiths of Manhattan, Anne still never sat and waited to be served. The expression 'rolling up her sleeves and getting to work' described Anne to a T. When they received the call last night from Pam's mother, Bill left the room and went into his office where he remained for the rest of the night.

Bernice called right after Nelda, hysterical, needing her son, but Bill had locked himself into his office and didn't respond when Anne tapped on his door. She ended up lying to Bernice, telling her he was so upset that he had left the apartment. Bernice wanted to come over right then. Anne could feel the hysteria building in her chest; her mother-in-law was mildly annoying when in the presence of her sons; without, unbearable. No, there would be no late night visitation no matter how horrible the circumstances.

"Mother, please stay right there. I am going to look for Bill; for all I know he is on his way up to you right now. I have a bugger of a headache and would be of no earthly use to you." Bernice ignored her.

"Oh, my God! I can't stay here alone!" She cried into the phone.

"Isn't Mildred there with you?" Anne asked, thinking of not only poor Mildred, but Alice the cook and that brow-beaten driver of hers. "Bill could be walking up your steps this very minute, Bernice!" Anne's voice had gone up an octave, along with Bernice's. Now, they were both yelling into the phone.

"I need my family with me at a time like this," she yelled. "Not a maid, not a cook! I want my son!"

Oh, for God's sake. Anne almost gave in. And then, resolve renewed, calmly replied to her mother-in-law,

"Mother, I think I hear Bill. Hold on." Putting the phone on mute, she walked to the back of the apartment where her husband's office was, and no longer caring if she woke their children up, or if Bill was furious with her for disturbing him, proceeded to pound on the door with her fists, yelling at him.

"Bill, open up the God-damned door! Your mother is on the phone and wants to come here now!" The door swung open with a bang. Bill, red-faced and ready to kill, yelled,

"No fucking way! No way! She can't come here!" Anne released the mute button and spoke softly into the phone;

"Here's Bill now for you, Mother Smith." And thrust the phone at him.

6

An hour before, at just half past ten, Pam awoke. Her feelings had returned, and she was angry. She knew that anger was an important step in the grieving process, but she was pissed! She muttered obscenities during her shower and while blow-drying her hair. She stomped around her bedroom, slamming her closet door, throwing shoes across the room. *How dare he do this to me? To not even have the decency to let me fight with him over the girl? To go and die and leave it in my hands to resolve?* By half past eleven, she was exhausted, spent. The anger had dissipated. She put her makeup on, taking particular care with her eyes—everything waterproof, not too much mascara, and light on the powder—to reduce the appearance of those crow's feet, which were deeply etched that morning from lack of sleep and too many tears.

The numbness had returned. She would be the gracious Pam, allowing those closest to her to express their sorrow, and she would be strong for them. It would all be fake, though. Her life partner was dead at only fifty-five years old. She was still young. It wasn't fair. *Oh God,* she thought, *don't let too many people say that to me today.* None of that "God's will" horseshit; I beg your pardon. No "You have to be strong for your kids." She prayed that she could keep her mouth shut and not fake swooning to give the masses something to talk about. *Pam fainted she was so upset*, she could almost hear her cousin Nancy saying.

Thankfully, both Marie and Nelda kept the crowd under control, asking people to keep the family in their prayers and telling them that the children would be home that afternoon, when they would need time alone, to be together, to mourn.

Throughout the day, well-meaning friends and neighbors stopped by with cakes and pies, baskets of fruit, trays of cookies, and hors d'oeuvres. There would be no need for much food preparation. Anne did a great job organizing the dishes, refrigerating what needed it, keeping some food out for the family to snack on, and throwing away that which appeared indigestible.

When Pam appeared at last, she repeated what she knew about the tragedy to Bill and Bernice. Bernice seemed to shrink. Pam asked her if she would like to watch TV. They went into the den, and Bernice sat in Jack's chair. His afghan was there, still smelling of his aftershave. Pam put the remote in her hand and shut the doors. Bernice would have some down time.

After the door closed, Bernice buried her face in the afghan. She breathed deeply of the scent, a combination of something fragrant, herbal, and chemical, like a man's deodorant or aftershave. It was her son's scent just after he got out of the shower. She recognized it from the time he was a teenager. He would come in after a day of roughhousing with his buddies and head for the shower. He would then come down to the dining room, just in time for dinner, with clean sweatpants, a white T-shirt, and a towel around his shoulders to catch the drips from his just-washed hair. She loved seeing him like that, relaxed, sitting around the table with his brother and father, talking sports and school. *He was so vibrant as a teenager!*

Harold worried about the boys. With so much written in the press about teenage suicide, drug use, and high school dropouts, he was vigilant, always inquiring about their activities, asking them if they needed anything or if he could help them in any way. He sat through more awful rock concerts than any parent could be expected to endure, and he drove the boys and their friends anywhere they wanted to go at any time of day or night. He made himself available to his sons. It paid off. Both boys were happy and successful, married to wonderful women, and devoted to their families.

When Harold died the year before, it was Jack who took it the hardest, even more so than she did. He was inconsolable. And now this. Two of the three most important men in her life were dead. Just Bill and Anne and the kids remained. She knew she must be in shock, the unrealistic event of her son's death hovering at the periphery of her thought. *But was it a dream? How could Jack be gone? Jack, who was larger than life, the maker of dreams, always strong, always on top of it, always dependable, wouldn't he walk into the den any minute now and say, "Mother! Stay right where you are! I'll pull up a chair here"?* And he would do just that, pull his desk chair over while she sat in the recliner, his chair. He would take her hands in his, gaze into her eyes, and make a horrible joke or ask her if he could pass gas, or some other inappropriate comment, all the while with the most holy look on his face. They would laugh, she almost screaming, her sons the only ones who had the power to make her relent her poise long enough to laugh at a joke.

She bowed her head, the afghan waded up in her hands, and started to cry. He would never walk through the door of this den again or come to her house unannounced, yelling as he slammed the door of the regal entryway, "Mom, where are you?" She would never again run into him at the hardware store on Amsterdam, suggest they have a cup of coffee together, and walk arm and arm to Columbus Circle, going into their favorite coffee shop and sitting there for hours, forgetting the time, talking about everything. He used to ask her opinion of different political figures in the city, so she made sure she read the papers every morning and checked the online news stories. She thought he might have done it on purpose to keep her on her toes. She would never know.

He told her one time how proud he was that she was his mother and that she looked so good for her age. After that, she went to the gym every single day, even on Sunday. She must write all of these things down somewhere, have something to show for her relationship with him. *His own children, those two fabulous, intelligent beings, they would want to know someday, wouldn't they? To know what kind of son their father had been?*

She tried not to think about the past year, how her relationship with Jack had changed, unspoken events that would change them forever. No unpleasant memories would be allowed admittance that day.

She shook out the afghan and folded it into a neat square. *How long would this scent stay in it? A week? A month?* It would grow stale before long, and Pam would take it and throw it into the washing machine. She would ask her daughter-in-law if she could have it. It still had traces of his DNA on it, maybe a stray hair, a dried tear, or a skin cell. She thought of the sheets on his bed in the apartment. *Oh God, the apartment.* Pam had to deal with that as well. If she were smart, she wouldn't sell it. She would keep it, just in case. But that was not her business. She must say nothing but loving comments. She thought Pam silly, shallow. But Jack had loved her, and she loved Jack. Her daughter-in-law must be feeling about the same way she did last year at this time when Harold died.

She worked her way to the end of the chair and struggled to get up. *When did I get so old?* She wanted to be with the rest of the family now, to hear what they were talking about. There was plenty of time to be alone. She had the rest of her life to be alone.

7

Sandra struggled with the key, willing the woman to leave, to get back to her cab and be gone. *How much could one person tolerate in a day?* She stumbled to her own door after slamming the hallway door shut. Once inside her apartment, the terror of the moment subsided. She took a deep breath. Here was safety. She smelled the clean smell of the house. The order around her brought her peace.

What could be worse? Jack was dead. Thank God we had last night together. "Thank you, God. But why? Why now?" she said out loud. Her momentary peace escaped her, and she fell apart. Sliding down the door to the floor, she crossed her legs and put her head in her hands. She was alone in the world. There was no one on earth who she could call right now and say, "Jack is dead," who would understand, who would care. The impact of it brought her to tears again. No one knew. Well, not exactly no one. Those women who she had earlier wished be gone might know. They cared.

How lucky am I that the woman, Jack's wife, was so lovely! Could it be she was under medication? Was she in shock? Sandra certainly didn't expect that sort of greeting, that much caring. Jack never bad-mouthed her, but he also didn't go into a lot of detail about the kind of woman she was—a gracious, giving woman. One who could put aside her own feelings and embrace the woman who had been sleeping with her husband. Her grief, compounded by guilt, paralyzed her. She lay on the floor in front of her door in the dark for the rest of the night.

The next morning, stiff from the hard floor, Sandra got up, put her purse in the closet, and walked to her bedroom. She pulled the shades up. It was a bright, sunfilled day. Picking up the bedside clock, she saw that it was eleven already. *How'd that happen?* She felt lightheaded, strange. She remembered that she hadn't had dinner last night. But, first, she would have a shower. She gathered up clean underwear and a robe.

The hot water felt good on her skin. She couldn't shake the lightheaded feeling. Hurrying to get finished, she went into the kitchen and put the kettle on. She was concentrating on the mundane tasks of her morning. It was Sunday. She would take care of herself and wait for the call. Her life would be in bondage to the funeral of her lover. That much she could do for him. There would be nothing else as important, nothing as eternal, as going through this process of burying her lover. Pam Smith was going to make it possible for her to have the experience, to be part of it—at least she said she would.

Sandra put a tea bag in a cup. She reached into the refrigerator and pulled out a plastic container of orange-frosted rolls she picked up the day before at Zabar's. *Was it really just yesterday? Saturday morning?* Her life had changed overnight. The small tasks of her daily routine were comforting. She arranged a sliced apple on a plate and took her tea and roll to the small table set up in her sitting area, positioned so she could look out the window at the alley while she ate. The disadvantage to being on the ground floor was the lack of view. But seeing the way the sunlight shown on the brick and the tree of heaven, with her bird feeder in it swaying in the breeze, made her feel a sense of peace. Most things were out of her control. She was at the mercy of everyone else. *Just go with the flow.*

She had made a poor choice. Getting involved with Jack was wrong, and she knew it, resisting it from the onset. So did he. They should have taken drastic steps, asked for a transfer for her, anything to get them out of the same office. But the chemistry and the tug between them was more than either of them could ignore. They were human, after all. Flesh. The spirit is willing, but the flesh is weak. They didn't even flirt with each other. It transcended that sort of behavior.

Now she realized that he was just lonely. He was at that dangerous age. He should have moved home with his wife or insisted she come to the city with him. It would have been worth it to protect their marriage.

She first saw him three years before. Prior to that, she was working in the Bronx office. It was closer to her home than Wall Street. She could walk if she allowed enough time, but usually hopped on the subway. She loved working that far uptown. The shopping and the restaurants were fabulous. She tried so many different ethnic foods. Picking up something unusual for dinner each night got to be a habit, so much so that she actually put on weight!

When she was summoned to the Wall Street office, she figured that someone there wanted her to do research that couldn't be done from the outside. Jack was in his office talking on the phone. She was standing in the hall just a foot from his door. Pete Andrews was talking loudly to her, explaining what he needed. Jack walked to his door, smiled at her, and closed it. She wished Pete had shut up.

"Do you think we could go someplace and sit down while you tell me about the project?" she said. "I want to take notes."

He led her to an empty office and, pointing at the desk said, "Welcome to Wall Street."

It was a long commute downtown. She had to leave the house earlier than before, giving herself an hour to get downtown and then walk to the building. The atmosphere wasn't the same down there. It was darker, as the surrounding buildings stood tall around their office, blocking the sunlight. She really didn't like it. Maybe having the interest of a man helped her settle into her new position. She may have used Jack to feel less lonely, less unhappy about her new digs.

It started innocently enough. They just worked together. He never asked her to lunch, never flirted with her. He seemed eager to get home on Fridays, occasionally going midweek. Sandra wasn't attracted to him, either. She had never dated an older man, and he was twice her age.

And then her parents died within a few days of each other. He was so nice to her, so concerned, that they began talking, and a real friendship developed. It wasn't a father-daughter relationship, although there were enough years between them that it could have been. They were just coworkers.

Last year, Jack's father died. He was devastated. He turned to her for advice about how to grieve, how to come to terms with the loss. Three months later, it began. It wasn't one pursuing the other, but more of a mutual need to be together. They started walking at lunch. He said his doctor warned him about his heart, high blood pressure, and cholesterol. He hated working out. His wife was a gym rat, going there daily for years. But she was in great shape, he had said. He didn't want to leave her a widow.

The funny thing about it was that once they had sex, it wasn't a big deal. They just did it. He was okay at it, but there didn't seem to be any passion. That bothered her. She felt passion, but didn't express it; it would have been too one-sided. She wondered if it was his age. They didn't go to hotels during the day or anything tawdry like that. Very rarely, he would ask her if she would be able to spend the night with him. He asked to go to her apartment, but she refused. They got a hotel room. She wasn't sure that staying all night was wise; coming into work together in the morning would raise suspicions. People were already talking.

So it wasn't the sex; it was just Jack. There was just something about him that drew her to him. She knew it would be short-lived; he would never leave his wife. He made that clear from the beginning. He was madly in love with her. They had two grown kids together. His mother worshiped him. He thought his in-laws did, too. He would never disappoint them by divorcing his wife. He didn't even know why he was doing it, having this affair, except that he loved Sandra. He told her that. "I love my wife, but I love you. I need you in my life," he would say. She remembered their last night together. After they made love, Jack lit a cigar, his one concession to vice, and sat against the pillow smoking. She was curled up at his side. The ash fell from the cigar, and they let it scatter on the sheets.

Laughing, she looked up at him and said, "I don't date men who smoke."

"You do now, my dear," he replied.

She finished her tea and roll, and as she got up to put the dishes in the sink, the phone rang. She picked up the receiver and looked at the caller ID, and her heart started pounding right away. *Jack Smith*. Of course, it wasn't him; it was his wife. Seeing that name, she had to take a deep breath to pause for a moment before she answered.

8

Marie was bored. Anne had efficiently taken over the kitchen, so there was nothing for her to do until two that afternoon when she would accompany Pam to the funeral home. They had picked out a suit, his most beautiful spring suit made of silk, cut close to the body to show off his new physique.

They still had to choose the casket. Would that make it real for Pam then? Marie thought she was acting a little strange. Granted, she was grieving, but she was not your usual grief-stricken widow. Marie found that she was avoiding her sister. Strangely, her Hell's Kitchen apartment was where she really wanted to be at that moment, not here, not in this foreign place she had once loved so much. Maybe it was she and not Pam who was acting strange.

For one thing, this house no longer held a single atom of Jack, not his den, his bedroom closet, or even his clothes. It was as though he was spectral dust, and with a strong wind, all traces blew away. Had Pam foreseen this day and systematically removed all traces of him, little by little, so even he didn't notice? Marie found it hard to believe that she was ever comfortable there. She felt a combination of rage at his betrayal and deep, profound grief at his loss. *Who am I feeling this about?* she thought. *Was he betraying me or Pam? Oh God, there are so many issues to sort out now.* What had been just simmering under the surface had been exposed to be dealt with, at least as far as she was concerned. If he were still alive, she could have dealt with him in her own way, forcing him to confront his wife, exposing the truth. With him dead, it was a nonissue. The years she spent in servitude to her sister and her brother-in-law would go unpaid. She brought this on herself, and now the price would be paid in her wasted life.

Anne and Nelda took some of the food gifts and made lunch for everyone. They all encouraged Pam to eat something. They noticed Marie and tried to get her to sit down and eat, too. But she just couldn't. All accepted that she too, had a broken heart. But the extent of it, the depth, was known only to her. She would have to fake it or risk devastating her sister and their relationship.

At one-thirty p.m., Pam and Marie left for the funeral home together.

Getting into her car, Pam sighed and said, "I need to go to the train station and pick up Jack's car."

"Do you want me to get the key and we can go get it on our way home? It probably shouldn't sit there over the weekend," Marie suggested.

"Oh, do you mind?" Pam said. Marie's heart rate increased just thinking about getting behind the wheel of Jack's beloved Lexus. No one ever drove it but him. "It would save time, I guess, since we are already out. I hate to impose."

"No, I'll get the key." She tried to hide her obvious nervousness, her hands shaking and voice trembling. This may be the thing she needed to purge her sadness, to let the tears flow. She wasn't sure what would do it for Pam, but this might do the trick for her.

She went through the garage to the back landing. There, on the wall just outside the laundry room, was a rack with ten hooks. There was a hook for each of the cars, plus spares. The kid's car keys were there, an extra for Pam's car, a key for the lawn tractor, one for the utility truck, and then a large leather triangle with a silver L, Jack's keys. Marie reached out for it, grasping it with her hand, bringing it up to her lips. Her eyes were closed. She knew she better get out there before Pam began to wonder what was taking so long. She would have time to love the key once she was in the car.

When she got back in the car, Pam was looking at her with concern.

"Are you okay, kiddo? I mean, the obvious, right? But will you be okay to go with me? I really appreciate it. I know how much you loved Jack, and he loved you."

Pam was the most generous person Marie knew, but she didn't know how much Marie loved Jack, no matter what Pam thought.

"I'm okay. I was just think in a few hours, Sharon will be picking Lisa up in Newark."

Sharon was the middle sister, second to last, born one year to the day before Marie. She and her family were coming up from Cherry Hill for the weekend; they were going to come anyway for the picnic, but now instead for this tragic event. They would swing by the airport and pick up their niece.

"Thank God we don't have to worry about airport pickups. I know that must sound crass, but I think having to drive into Newark or to brave the traffic to JFK would have pushed me over the edge," Pam said. "Jack always did the driving to the airport."

"How are you doing, Pam?" Marie said.

Pam didn't answer at first. She was unable to repeat what was really in her heart, the resignation that her marriage was a farce, that she felt more empathy for a stranger, a young woman who had been involved with her husband, than she did for her own children. She was hopeful those feelings would be resolved when she saw the faces of her kids. She knew the calm now, the numbness, would soon give way to the angst of young adulthood in turmoil.

"Do you remember when Daddy died?" she asked Marie. "All I felt was guilt and anger. Guilt because I had been mean to him the day before he died, and anger because he allowed his daughters to be taken care of by other men without putting up a fight. I was mad about that for a long time. Mommy would say that I was still mad at him. I'm not sure."

"Were you mad at Dad because he allowed me to live with you and Jack?" This was news to Marie if it were true.

"Not mad, because Lord knows I needed you so much, but confused, like why are you letting your baby daughter live with us? Are we fit parents for a twelve-year-old? I don't know."

"I can't imagine what life would have been like if you hadn't allowed me to come to you and Jack," Marie said. Silently, she thought, *It would have been unthinkable.*

They pulled into the driveway of the funeral home, driving under the portico. A pale, thin man in a black suit, the funeral home director, was waiting for them. Another man came around and opened Pam's door. They were greeted with a solemn but friendly "We're sorry for your loss."

The first man lead the way through double doors in to a strangely decorated entryway. There was a bust of George Washington in an alcove. Marie sneaked a glance at Pam. She tried to contain her laughter. Pam felt the hysteria rising in her throat.

"Don't make eye contact," Pam said. *How inappropriate.* She had to pull herself together.

They followed him into an office with upholstered chairs, where he offered each woman a seat. Pam forced herself not to look around. She hadn't noticed before, but the place was horribly decorated. She hoped Jack didn't mind, if that were possible. *He was already here for whatever they call it. Embalming, that was the word. They cut your vein and drain all the blood out. You are laid out like roast beef on a slab, naked, exposed.*

The next thing Pam knew she was lying on the dirty carpet of the office. Marie was crying and patting her hand, her cheek. Someone in a powder-blue suit was holding a glass of water to her lips.

"Pam! Pam!" Marie shouted. "Pam, wake up, for God's sake!" Pam could hear her sister say, "Maybe we should call nine-one-one."

Pam struggled to wake up, to let her sister know she was okay. "I'm here," she whispered. There was a lot of commotion as people around her assisted her to stand up. She said she would like to use the bathroom, if possible. She had to wash her hands, at least. Get some of the germs off her clothes.

Suzanne Jenkins

Marie led her to the bathroom, the lady in the blue suit guiding them, leaving them at the door.

"Are you okay?" Marie said to her sister for the tenth time that day.

"I think so. Can we hurry this up? I regret using this place. We could have gone to the one on Main Street. Jack golfed with him, I think." She was pale, shaky. She washed her hands and, wetting a paper towel, asked Marie to help her wipe off the back of her pants and jacket.

Marie giggled through her tears, saying, "What do you think you picked up from that rug?" They laughed, but Pam was not taking any chances.

They made their way back to the office, and Pam was all business.

"Let's get this over with," she said.

All pleasantries stopped then, and questions about Jack's last wishes began. Marie had a list of things they wanted put in place, like a picture easel, a guest book, and a string quartet, as well as things they didn't want, such as a video, taped music, and ushers.

Marie went out to the car to get the suit in addition to the other necessary items—polished black shoes and a silk tie with frogs printed on it that the kids had gotten him for Christmas the year before.

When she returned, Pam had picked out a casket, a dark walnut piece. He would have approved.

The earliest they could do it would be Tuesday morning. They would have to wait two days. Pam wasn't sure how the kids would hold up. She looked at her watch; Lisa was just landing, and Brent was an hour away. Once the kids got home, she was hoping some feeling would return to her mind and body. She also wanted to be alone with them. That would be tough. Sharon and her family were staying for the funeral. She could hardly ask Bernice to leave. She'd have to find a way to let them know she needed time with the kids.

They pulled up to the house just as Lisa and Sharon's family were getting out of the station wagon. Lisa saw Pam and ran to her, crying. They embraced. The others walked away, giving them privacy. Marie, hesitant, decided in favor of her own well-being and went into the house. Mother and daughter stood there, holding each other, while Lisa got her emotions under control.

"Oh, Mother," she said, "I feel so horrible for you!" Pam led her over to the car.

"Let's get in, shall we? There is a house full."

"I really am not in the mood to have to deal with anyone else's emotions right now," Lisa said.

"I think they know that, honey. They've been leaving me alone."

"Mom, what happened? I just saw Dad last month, and he looked great! I kept saying, 'Gosh, Dad, look how thin you are!' Did he know he had heart trouble? Aunt Sharon said someone took his wallet while he was on the train. Did that cause his heart attack?"

Pam willed herself not to decompensate. Her daughter needed her questions answered. Maybe she should have invited Marie to stay, dividing the answers between them. She knew she had used her sister for just such issues in the past. Marie acted as a buffer in so many ways for the family. Maybe now was the time to end that. Jack was gone. It was just the three of them. She reached across the center console to embrace her daughter. Lisa started to cry again.

"I think his heart simply gave out. It was his time to die. Poor Lisa, I wish you didn't have to suffer through this! You are too young to lose a parent."

Pam thought of the ages she and Jack were when their own fathers had died. It hadn't been easy at any age.

"Was it hard for you when Grandpa died?" Lisa asked.

"You cope somehow," Pam told her daughter. "There is an inner strength that rises to the surface. I'm not sure how. I feel like the other shoe will drop soon, but right now, when I have to be out there in front of everyone, I can be strong. Dad's mother, for instance, what must this be like for her? Oh, how horrible." Pam lowered her face and started to weep. "I go up and down like this. One minute I am calm, and the next, crying like a baby."

"I love you, Mom!" Lisa said.

They sat and regained their composure, drawing strength from each other, so that they could enter the house and not have a torrent of sympathy flood their way. The thought of it was intolerable.

Inside, Bernice was looking out the kitchen window at her daughter-in-law approaching the house with her granddaughter. She had not seen Lisa in months. Neither was a good letter writer. *What would we say to each other now?*

Lisa walked through the door first, and seeing her grandmother standing there, dressed to perfection, hair and nails done, just the slightest red around the eyes, she flew to her, crying out, "Oh, Bubby! Oh, I am so sorry!"

And they grabbed each other and began weeping, loud, mournful sobbing that brought the rest of the house to join in.

It was probably the most therapeutic moment, because after just a few minutes, Bernice stopped and, laughing out loud, said, "Oh, for God's sake! Let's pull ourselves together!" She took Lisa by the shoulders and, at arm's length, said, "What do you suppose your father would have said if he walked in on this scene?"

In unison, Bernice, Pam, Marie, and Lisa all said, "Who died?" Anne, Bill, Nelda, and the rest of them laughed.

"Okay, so what news do you have?" Bernice said.

Marie had waited until Pam came in to let her make the funeral plans known. She had also neglected to tell the group about Pam's fainting spell, either out of protection for her privacy or some other, less noble, motivation.

"The viewing is Tuesday morning, and the funeral is at eleven a.m. The burial will be private. The little cemetery in Amityville can't handle more than six cars at a time." Pam looked around at everyone. They stood together, looking to her for direction. It was five. Brent's plane would have landed by now and he on his way home. She had to lie down for just a bit before facing that emotional meeting. "I'm sorry, I know I haven't been much help to you, but please, if you don't mind, I would like to rest for a few minutes before Brent gets home."

The family rushed toward her, encouraging her to go, making sounds of empathy.

The shaded coolness of her beautiful bedroom had the desired effect. The moment she stretched out on her chaise, she fell asleep. It felt like no sooner had she closed her eyes that she felt a hand on her shoulder and a kiss on her cheek. *Jack?* She opened her eyes upon her beautiful son, her oldest child.

"Brent," she said, sitting up and swinging her legs over the side of the chaise. He sat down next to her and, with one arm around her shoulder, lowered his head on her other shoulder. And by the shaking of his body, she surmised that he was having a good old-fashioned cry. She knew that to lose it at this point was to doom both of them to an afternoon of misery. He was so like his father that she better keep it together or suffer the consequences. "Smith men cried at a good steak," it was said.

"Brent, I am so sorry!" she muttered the same words to him that her daughter had said to her. "What a thing to happen to you."

"What about to you, Mom? God! He was only fifty-five!"

She reached over to her table and pulled a tissue out of the box. Handing it to him and soothing his cheek with her hand, she said what she had said to Lisa. "I am still numb. Probably, after the funeral it will become real to me—the loss." She wanted to say, *Our life stretches out ahead of us without him.* Then she remembered another person who was suffering, who needed validation. When she had a chance that evening, she would call Sandra. She stood up and, taking his hands, attempted to pull him up to his feet. They both laughed, he being over six feet tall and close to two hundred twenty pounds like his father. "Come and see your grandmothers," she said.

"I already did, Mom. I've been home for two hours."

"What time is it?" she asked. "I must have been sleeping for hours!"

"It's almost seven-thirty. Come on, Bubby is making dinner."

"You've got to be kidding me! She hasn't had to cook in fifty years!" Pam said. They laughed together, once again. He took her by the elbow, leading her out of the room as though she were a queen or a bride. Her heart did a somersault. She felt guilty for dreading the homecoming of her two wonderful children. "I have to make a phone call, okay? Tell everyone I'll be there in a minute." She went back into her room, quietly closing the door behind her.

She dug through her purse for the scrap of paper that contained the phone number of Jack's lover. She still felt no animosity toward Sandra. If anything, she needed to talk to her. She felt that, having done so, she would be stronger for it, that they were allies. She keyed in the number and waited it for it to ring.

After six long rings, it was finally answered by a quiet hello.

"This is Pam Smith, Sandra. I'm so sorry that I am just calling you now about the funeral. Both children came home in the interim since going to the funeral home, and this is the first chance I've had."

Sandra didn't know what to say. *How do you thank the wife of your lover for calling you?*

"Thank you. I appreciate it."

"The viewing will be held at nine on Tuesday morning, with the funeral to follow at eleven. The burial is private, but of course you'll come to that. If you don't mind, for the sake of the children, I will introduce you as Jack's very close friend." She realized how inane that must have sounded to Sandra, but she didn't know what else to do. She felt her nerves faltering. She decided to throw caution to the wind and go at it. It was better than hanging up. "Sandra, please help me. Help me understand. I feel like you are the only one who can possibly understand me or what I am going though. You are going through it, too—alone. You don't know how I wish you could come here and talk with the family, share your memories, your observations. If you can figure out a way to do it that won't hurt you or anyone else, it would be wonderful." She was out of breath. And then, sadly, she started to cry. "I don't understand. Why did he die? What earthly purpose did it have to take him so early?" She was crying out loud now, snorting into the phone. She reached for a tissue, and several came out of the box at once, stuck together. She blew her nose.

There was silence, and then Sandra spoke. "I don't know. I just don't know. I've asked myself the same question again and again. Mrs. Smith, I wish I could tell you everything. There is so much you should know about how much he loved you, how screwed up he was. His being with me didn't have anything to do with you. You know that, don't you? It was just a lapse of moral judgment." She was crying, softly, then into the phone. "I think he had a premonition that he was going to die. I think he knew."

Pam was shocked at that comment. "We have to meet, Sandra, somehow before the funeral. I have a house full of people here, but I could come to you. I could come to the city." She thought of their apartment on Madison

Avenue. She could go there, look through it, and see if there wasn't some evidence of what Sandra just said. She had made up her mind. The next day, Monday, she was going into the city to see Sandra. Of course, she wouldn't tell anyone. Marie might suspect, but she wasn't telling her, either. She wanted an untainted perspective. "I've decided. I am coming tomorrow to our apartment. Do you know where it is?" She gave Sandra the address. "I'll call you again when I get in, okay, dear? I feel so much better all ready."

Sandra agreed, somewhat reluctantly. *What did this woman have in mind?* Sandra felt like she had done enough damage already.

Pam put down the phone, feeling at peace.

The rest of the night was spent with the kids going through old photo albums. It turned out to be the best idea yet because, starting with his hippie look in the seventies, to leisure suits, to vests, the metamorphosis from funny, young person to gorgeous businessman was a wonderful review of where their dad had been and where he ended up.

Marie suddenly said, "We forgot the car!"

Brent said he would go with her to pick it up. She hid her disappointment; he would most certainly drive his father's car home from the train station.

9

Across the East River to the north, Sandra was sitting at her table looking out the window at nothing and sipping a hot cup of tea. It was a warm night, but she didn't care. The tea was relaxing her, clearing her head.

The call from Pam Smith was nerve-wracking. She was specific about what she expected from Sandra, but it just didn't ring true. She didn't understand what Pam was going through. She was the wife, with the kids and the history. All Sandra was, in addition to a work buddy, was a girlfriend, a dinner date on lonely nights. They loved each other, but now, seeing the devastation of his family, knowing the loss the children would suffer, the relationship revealed what it really was—an immoral affair between a married man and a woman young enough to be his daughter. No matter how much she rationalized what they had, it was wrong. And it couldn't be taken back.

Monday morning dawned gray and rainy. Pam woke up early after a sound, dreamless sleep. She rolled over to face Jack's side of the bed. *Had he ever slept there? Had his impact on her life diminished to the point that she was over it already, after two days?* "Stop it," she said to herself. She rolled over and got up to begin her day, going through the steps she always took, carefully bathing, doing her hair and makeup, preparing for what she did not exactly know. She thought in the past that she was doing it for him, for

Jack. He said how proud he was of her, how she looked so nice all the time, and how in good shape she was for her age. *What did that really mean? It didn't keep him from being unfaithful. Well, too bad*, she thought, *I'll continue doing this for myself.*

The house was quiet. Pam didn't feel like making excuses for going into the city. Marie or Lisa would want to go with her, and she was making this trip alone. She would take Jack's Lexus. He called it their "city car." It would make a final trip in to Manhattan; this time without him.

She wrote a note in her neat hand saying she wanted to go in to look at the apartment alone. Propped on the coffee pot where no one could miss it, it looked furtive, but she didn't care. This was her house; it was her husband who had just died.

As she got into the car and pulled out of the garage, she realized that she was looking forward to this being over, for everyone to be gone, so she could begin her life. The kids would be gone soon enough, and that might be difficult. She missed them all of the time, never getting used to their absence.

Traffic wasn't bad on the Long Island Expressway. She got into town quickly, getting to the apartment and pulling into the garage at eight a.m. sharp. She would have plenty of time to putter around before Sandra arrived.

Going up in the elevator, Pam's resolve started to whither. *What am I going to find there? Was it Jack and Sandra's love nest?* She hadn't come in over a year, so he might have felt safe to take another woman there.

She stepped off the elevator into the dimly lit hallway. Their apartment was on the fifteenth floor, not high enough to escape the shadows of other buildings. Her hand trembled as she put the key in the door. She pushed the door open as it scraped on the carpet. She always hated having carpet right there; tile or stone should be at the entrance. But Jack argued that your shoes would be cleaned off and dry by the time you rode up fifteen floors.

She was surprised at what she found. Everything was exactly as she had left it the last time she was there. There was a year-old *House Beautiful* magazine on the coffee table right where she had put it down. She stood in the middle of the room and slowly turned around. *He had lived here, alone, five days a week. Shouldn't there be a sweater thrown over the back of a chair? A pile of mail, the top piece with an opened envelope? A used coffee cup with cold coffee?* She wondered if perhaps Sandra had come in right after talking last night and cleaned up.

Pam turned around and walked into the kitchen— completely cleaned. The cleaning lady came on Friday she finally remembered. Opening the refrigerator, she saw milk for his cereal, bread, margarine, a jar of peanut butter, pizza slices wrapped in saran wrap, and a lone orange. On the counter was a bowl with two ripe bananas in it. She would take them home or throw them away.

She entered the first bedroom Jack used as a study. There on the table that held the television was the mail she was looking for. There was a big pile. She took the pile and shoved it in her purse. She suddenly knew that she couldn't spend too much more time there. The walls were closing in on her.

She turned around and left the study and went into their bedroom—Jack's bedroom. The bed was made, but it had a rumple where someone had sat. Maybe Jack sat down to change his shoes for the trip home. She went and sat on the spot. She could feel him there. His presence suddenly filled the room. Her purse slid down her arm. She lowered her head into her hands and began to weep. She lay down on the bed and pulled the cover up over her body. She cried until she fell asleep.

The ringing phone woke her up. She sat up and picked the phone up, looking at the number on the caller ID. It was home. She wasn't going to answer it. She was an adult woman. If she wanted to spend a week here, she would.

The emotion had gone. Now she was just sad. Her husband had lived his life here, away from his family, so they could be comfortable. He had provided a wonderful and abundant life for them. *Did I ever say thank you?* Her heart was beating wildly in her chest. She supposed this was the feeling she was waiting for. She had to come into Manhattan to find Jack. He wasn't there at their house after all.

She got up and went into the adjoining bathroom. She looked in the mirror. *What a mess!* She opened the right drawer in the vanity, and to her surprise, all of her cosmetics were still there. She supposed he would have thrown them out. He was always waiting for her to visit him on her own. She sat down and touched up her makeup, the cover stick almost hard from a year of disuse. She would have to get rid of the stuff eventually, but was glad it was here now.

She got up and went into the closet. He was a real neat nick. He saved everything, but it was organized. She could smell him in the closet; the scent of his aftershave and deodorant combined with that of dry cleaning fluid. Her side of the closet was empty except for a robe and a pair of slacks. There was also a pair of her sneakers on the floor.

She went back into the bedroom and opened the drawers in the bedside tables. On her side, there was nothing. On his, she found a pair of reading glasses and a pair of binoculars for spying. She remembered nights looking down at the street with those things. They often had laughing fits at what they saw. "This is an invasion of privacy!" she would warn. "Oh, just come and look," he'd say.

This was just a place where he hung his hat. There must be more of him at home, maybe in his desk or the garage. A thought occurred to her. There was a closet between the bathroom and the den that she didn't check. She went down the hall and opened the door. There on the shelf above the empty clothes bar was a clear plastic container. She couldn't reach it, so she went back into the den and dragged the desk chair over to the closet.

Carefully, she stood on the chair and grasped the container. It was heavier than it looked. Hoping the people in the apartment below were out, she let it drop to the floor with a thud. She hopped down from the chair like a teenager. Dragging the box back into the bedroom, she decided she would unpack it and spread everything out on the bed. She didn't know what she was looking for, but there had to be something in there that would shed some light on the man her husband had become.

Checking her watch, she noted that it was nearing lunchtime and she better call Sandra by one. Quickly, she took the lid off the box and lifted out the first sheath of papers. They looked to be mostly receipts he was keeping for next year's taxes—gas, tolls, paper supplies, and that sort of thing.

Under that was a manila folder that had seen better days. She set it on her lap and slowly opened it. What lay on top looked to be a birth certificate. It was yellowed with age and bore a stamp on the lower left corner that certified that it was from the State of New York. She picked it up and carried it over to the window.

At first, she didn't grasp what she was looking at. It was for a male baby named Franklin Albert, born September Thirtieth, Nineteen Fifty-five. She skimmed the weight and length, then the father's name, Bertram Franklin Albert, and then the mother's name, Bernice Paula Stein. *Jack's mother.* Confused, she thought Jack had a brother who was born on his birthday with a different father. How could that be? It didn't take long, however, for her to figure it out.

"Oh, for God's sake!" she said out loud. Jack was Franklin. Jack's beloved father, Harold Smith, the man whose death a year ago knocked the wind right out of his sails, wasn't really his father.

She stood up and began to pace. *When did he find this out? Was it right after Harold's death? Or was it later?* She went back to the folder. The next paper was a letter from a woman, a Beverly Johnson, telling Jack that she thought he may be her half brother and asking if would he consider meeting. There wasn't a copy of any reply. But she had included her telephone number, so maybe he called her right away. Knowing Jack, that is probably what he did. She could almost hear his voice. *Beverly! What a damn surprise! You are the child of my mother, Bernice? Or my father Harold?* Neither, Big Boy.

She sat on the bed again, numb. Checking her watch yet again, she dug through her purse for Sandra's phone number. Picking up the phone, she keyed in the number for the second time that weekend.

Sandra picked up on the first ring.

"I wasn't sure if you were going to call," she said.

"I'm sorry. I got here early but fell asleep! I guess I must be more stressed out than I realize," Pam confessed. "Can we get together?"

"Okay. Where do you want to meet?" Sandra asked.

"Do you want to come here, to Jack's?" Pam asked. "I thought you might like to be here."

"We never met there, truly," she said. *Was this woman for real?* "But I would like to see it if it is okay with you," Sandra said.

Pam gave her the address. Sandra said she would leave right then and would take about fifteen minutes to get there. Pam used the time to go through the rest of the papers. She found copies of Bertam Albert's birth certificate, his death certificate dated August 1955, and more communication from Beverly Johnson with copies of Jack's. There were copies of all sorts of legal documents about Harold—his discharge papers from the army and a marriage license to Bernice dated two months after Jack's birth. Jack had done his homework. There was nothing to reveal whether or not Jack ever confronted Bernice. She would think he had died none the wiser.

The door buzzer downstairs sounded. Pam didn't bother speaking, just pushed the button to open the door. Hopefully it was Sandra. She was suddenly shy, like meeting a date for the first time or interviewing for a job. In five minutes, the buzzer on the hallway door rang. Pam went to open the door.

She couldn't help herself. When she saw Sandra, she reached for her as if she were an old friend, embracing her. She felt all of her tension releasing, her body almost folding, and she began to cry. Sandra returned the embrace and held Pam while she cried, doing for her what Pam had done the night of Jack's death—offering comfort.

Finally, when Pam could support her own weight, she stepped back from Sandra and smiled at her through her tears.

"I feel like you are on old friend. I know that must sound ridiculous because of our age difference."

Sandra didn't think the age difference was what made it strange. But she was glad that Pam felt that way about her and said so. "I'm glad you don't hate me" was all she could get out.

Pam took her by the arm and led her into the living room. Sandra looked around at Jack's home. She couldn't picture him there. It was so not what she thought of Jack. She thought he would live in a more cluttered, homier environment. This place was as sterile as a hotel room.

"Are you thinking it doesn't say anything about Jack?" Pam asked.

Sandra nodded her head yes. "We worked together," Sandra said, waiting for Pam to respond. She just nodded her head. "His office was always a disaster. Books and papers piled on the floor, file folders sliding off his desk, junk like radios, gifts for you and the kids, just chaos. So, yes, this is surprising." She laughed.

Pam offered her a seat. "His cupboards are bare," she said. "I can offer you a banana. It is the only thing in the house to eat."

"I feel a little claustrophobic. Do you have time for lunch?" Sandra said.

Pam nodded yes. "I have to call home first. I left without telling them I was coming here, and this phone has been ringing all morning." Pam excused herself and went into the bedroom and dialed home. Lisa picked up.

"Mom, I would have gone with you. Everyone is concerned here."

"Please tell them I am fine. I had some business to take care of, Lisa. I really wanted to be here in the apartment, alone. I hope you understand. I'll call you when I am on my way home." They said good-bye, and Pam hung up. Lisa would be her advocate.

She went into the bathroom and reapplied her lipstick for the third time that day.

"This crying garbage has really taken a toll on my makeup today," she said. They left the apartment. Pam made small talk on the way down in the elevator. She told Sandra how they found the apartment. "We had a place on the Upper West Side when the kids were little. We loved it there. When we moved out onto the island, Jack wanted to be closer to work. We were eating dinner at the place in the basement here—Grendels, I believe it was called—and the man who owned the apartment was eating at the table next to us, eavesdropping on our conversation. 'I just heard you say you like this building. My apartment is for sale. Right here on the fifteenth floor,' he said. Just like that. We went up to look after we finished dinner, and Jack bought it right then and there."

Sandra smiled politely. She wasn't in the mood for small talk, but was grateful Pam was keeping the conversation going. It would be easier to talk about important matters if they could keep talking.

They stepped outside. It had stopped raining. The air was cool and the sun was peaking out from behind the clouds. It would be a good day after all.

"Do you mind if we walk a while?" Pam asked.

Sandra said, "No, that would be nice."

As they walked down Madison Avenue, passersby gave admiring glances at what they thought to be a lovely young woman and her mother. Both attractive, they got the same kind of attention that Jack and Sandra used to get. Pam didn't notice.

They arrived at a coffee shop and found a table for two at the window. Pam was starving. The waitress brought coffee and menus. Usually a light eater, she ordered a burger and fries. Sandra got a salad.

"I haven't had a burger in years. My husband died, so I guess I can eat a burger if I want." She looked up at Sandra. "That was tacky, I'm sorry. I don't know what's gotten into me," she said.

"Don't give it another thought," Sandra said, thinking, *How bizarre can this get?*

"I feel like I can be honest with you," Pam said. "My family is waiting for me to fall apart or do something dramatic. I have to be careful what I say. Evidently, I fainted at the funeral home yesterday. Oh, yes, I was quite a spectacle." She paused, careful about how she approached the next topic. "The man who we thought was Jack's father wasn't his father at all." She picked up her coffee cup and took a sip, looking over the rim at Sandra. "Did Jack ever mention that to you?"

"No, but I knew that something life changing had taken place shortly after his father died. He kept saying things around the office like, 'Make sure you know who your parents really are,' and 'I wonder if we are related,' to one of the black men who worked with us. No wonder!"

"Well, I have to decide to keep it a secret or confront my mother-in-law. What do you think?" Her food had arrived and she dug in like a truck driver.

"Don't ask me! I'm terrible at that sort of thing. I mean, look at us. What would Jack say if he could see us together like this?" Sandra was still unsure of the reason for this meeting. She hoped that Pam would say whatever it was that needed saying.

"We never have to worry about Jack again, that's one thing for sure. Can I ask you a personal question?" Pam said.

Oh, here goes, Sandra thought to herself. She nodded yes.

"Did you love him?" She was looking up at Sandra, not with dread, but really interested. "I mean, it is clear why he was with you. You are beautiful. You're nice. What's not to like? I can't be angry about it, at least not now. At first, I was hurt. For about ten minutes, I thought, 'He found someone he liked better than me.' But then I rationalized that maybe he needed both of us for some reason."

"I think I did," Sandra replied. "I mean, it wasn't real, if that makes any sense. It was all wrong, and we both knew it. Plus, it wasn't what you think an affair is. All sexual, I mean," she started to stammer, but Pam put her at ease.

"You can speak of sex without incurring my wrath, if that is your concern. I know you slept together. Okay?" Pam smiled at her, but Sandra noticed she had gone pale. She hoped Pam wasn't going to faint in the restaurant.

"I'm no expert psychologist, but I just think he was lonely. He may have thought it was expected of him to sleep with me. He...well, he didn't really seem like he was into it." She thought she had blown it for sure now and waited for the firestorm that comment was sure to start.

Pam heard the words spoken and was eternally grateful. She reached across the table and took Sandra's hand in hers.

"Thank you, Sandra, for trying to preserve my pride. I will always be grateful for that."

"No! It's true! Oh, this is so weird, talking about it to you. But you have to believe me. He loved you. He loved me, too, but in a different way. We were playing. It wasn't real. I didn't come to your apartment, and he never came to mine because we both knew it wouldn't last. We were already getting bored. I hated the sneaking around as much as he did. He was too old for me, or I too young for him." She bowed her head and fought the tears. *Really, why the hell are we here—together?*

Pam pushed her plate aside and started rummaging through her purse.

"Let's go, dear. You'll feel better when you get out of this stuffy place."

Pam put some money down on the table, and they got up and walked out. Pam took Sandra's arm. They walked like that for a while, an attractive middle-aged woman and her beautiful companion.

"I would like to be your friend. For more than the obvious reasons, not just that you understand something about my life that no one else on earth does, but because I like you," Pam said.

Sandra didn't know what to say in return, so she just smiled at Pam.

"I was thinking, if you want to come over and stay the night, it would be easier for you to get to the funeral home by nine." Pam knew she was on unexplored territory here. Inviting her late husband's lover to spend the night in their home was probably not the best plan. *How would I explain it to Marie, who knew all the details?* She would have to get tough, tell her sister that it is was her house, her husband.

"Thank you for offering, but really, I'll be fine. I don't drive, so I will take the train and then a cab."

"Okay," said Pam, hiding her disappointment. She was hoping that they would have a better opportunity to talk in the comfort of the house. They walked in the direction of Jack's apartment.

"You don't have to walk me back, Sandra," Pam said. She stopped and turned to face her, having to look up to see her face. "I enjoyed being with you today. It is the first time in twenty-four hours that I felt relaxed." She dug through her purse and came up with a pen and a grocery receipt and started scribbling her address on it and then added her cell phone number. "If you get stuck or can't get a cab, call me. I'll send someone to pick you up from the station."

Sandra took the scrap of paper from her. Then she bent over to kiss Pam on the cheek. Pam stood on her toes. Sandra felt genuine affection for her.

"Thank you, Pam. Thank you for validating me. I don't deserve it, but thanks anyway."

They said their good-byes and then parted, Pam walking east one block to Madison and Sandra going south toward Seventy-ninth. She would walk across the park.

As she walked along, Sandra felt a moment of rare and unexplainable joy. Her boyfriend was dead, she had a job she hated, both of her parents were dead, and her sister couldn't stand the sight of her. *So what is going on?* Having lunch with Jack's wife was probably one of the strangest experiences she could have had at that place and time, but it left her with a feeling of contentment. She would have to think about this for a while, figure out how to make this moment last.

Everything was green in the park. The trees full and lush. The freshly cut grass smelled wonderful. Children were playing, running after each other and throwing balls, while couples sat on blankets and read the paper. She and Jack never did that. She couldn't think of a Sunday or holiday they had spent together. She had her own routine on the weekends and didn't mind that he was unavailable. She didn't miss him now.

She'd have to take tomorrow off for the funeral; the whole office would be there. She didn't think of that. Suddenly, she wanted, or rather, needed, Pam Smith. She needed to talk to her. Turning around, she ran up Fifth Avenue to the cross the street to Madison. She turned the corner just as Pam was walking into her building.

"Pam!" she called. "Wait!" Not caring if she looked foolish, Sandra ran toward the building. Pam walked back out onto the sidewalk.

IO

Marie was in a quandary. On one hand, she was happy her sister was adjusting so wonderfully to the news that her husband was screwing some tramp and then dropped dead without being able to explain himself. On the other hand, she was furious that something was going on and Pam wasn't including her.

When she got up that morning and found the note, she knew right away that her sister was going to the city to see Sandra. She felt left out, unappreciated. If Pam only knew, if she had known what Marie saw Saturday morning, she wouldn't be so damn accommodating to Sandra Benson. She knew that somehow she had to pull herself together, that she was being irrational. It was moments like this that destroyed families and relationships. She mustn't lose control. She must try to understand her sister and show her some respect.

She poured old coffee down the drain, rinsed out the pot, and filled it with fresh water. Her favorite routines would help pull her out of this mess. The kids needed her to be strong. Making coffee and busying herself in the kitchen would be a panacea to madness.

None of the food gifts looked appetizing, so she would bake muffins. When the family got up, when Bill and Anne came in, she would prepare whatever kinds of eggs they wanted. In the meantime, she would fry bacon, too. Those aromas would surely get everyone up. If she were surrounded with people, she would have purpose. Then the fears that were tormenting her, fears that she would no longer be useful in this house, would abate for a while.

She took flour, eggs, and butter and measured out the correct portions, washed a quart of fresh blueberries, and put those in. Greasing muffin tins drove the demons back. Pouring the creamy batter with soft, juicy berries into the tin, Marie began to relax. The smell of the coffee made her mouth water.

Once the muffins were in the oven and the timer was set, she poured herself a cup of coffee, suddenly grateful for the morning solitude. She decided to hold off on cooking the bacon. She took her coffee out onto the veranda. The rain had stopped for the time being. She wiped the chair down with a kitchen towel. A freighter, probably loaded with trash, was visible in the distance inching along toward Staten Island. *What am I going to do now?* She never felt so alone. Being needed had filled a void so big and so obvious that now she almost couldn't bear it. She set her cup down on the table and put her face in her hands.

Whispering, although no one was up yet and there wasn't anyone around to hear her, she prayed, "God, please take me, too. Please don't leave me here."

Pam left Manhattan at four p.m. She would be home in time for dinner with her family. Right before she left the apartment, she called home, and Marie answered the phone, laughing. She was playing cards with Lisa and Brent and Sharon's family.

Marie confirmed that everyone would be there when Pam got home and told her to drive safely. Pam was glad Marie was okay. She was worried that going to the city without inviting Marie to come along would have been an issue.

She turned the radio on and switched the tuner until something familiar came on. It was Vivaldi. She didn't want to think about the day while she was driving. Traffic was horrendous, and the music helped her to stay focused and keep up. At the speed everyone was going, she would get home in record time—if she didn't crash first.

When she pulled off the expressway, the back roads were deserted, a sign that dinner was being served. She remembered the weekend before. Jack had stopped at the farmers' market in town on his way home from golf. He got freshly caught flounder and the makings for a salad. They prepared dinner together, grilling the fish out on the veranda. Pam made a huge salad and opened a bottle of wine. They sat outside, eating and then drinking, until the sun disappeared behind the house. The sky was clear that night, and the stars were so bright you could see them all the way down to the horizon.

Jack had said, looking at her, "I never want to forget nights like this." It was as close to a confession of love that she got from him for months. When he said it, icy prickles shot down her spine. She wanted to ask him what made him say it, what was going on, but she bit her tongue. In her usual way, she thought, *Take this at face value. He is saying that he loves you. Everything is okay.*

But, of course, it wasn't. He didn't try to make love to her later, and when he left for Manhattan early the next morning, she didn't wake up and he didn't wake her. The alarm went off at seven a.m., and she sat up with a start, immediately looking at his empty side of the bed and feeling an overwhelming sadness. She had no idea that it would be the last time he would be by her side, that she would never see him again.

She remembered to ask Sandra why she thought Jack had had a premonition that he would die. Sandra said that it wasn't anything specific, just that he kept making references to not having regrets, to doing things you wanted to do because it was all over so soon.

Pam wondered if that was one of the reasons he had been unfaithful. He didn't want to regret not doing it. But that didn't make any sense. She supposed she would never really know what he was thinking. She would just chalk it up to what Sandra said—bad judgment. She said they were getting bored with it, and she suspected that he was thinking of ending it.

When she pulled up to the house, the lights were on, and it shown like a jewel in the dusk. Other cars were blocking the garage, so she parked in the driveway. She could hear the waves hitting the beach when she got out of the car. She loved this house, this area. Her love for it transcended her pain and grief. It was a dichotomy she couldn't explain—how the tragic death of her husband could be made tolerable by the love she had for her life. It was not something she would share with another.

Tonight she would have to socialize. Her sisters—Marie and Sharon and Susan—were all there. The flurry of activity in the house went right over her head. Everyone was talking all at once; there was nothing solemn, no respect for the dead. There was a board game out on the kitchen table that wasn't finished, so dinner would be served in the dining room. Pam couldn't remember the last time they used it. She tried to squelch her concern about the Battenberg tablecloth. Now was not the time to be miserly. She put herself in neutral and allowed everyone else to make the decisions.

Earlier in the day, Sandra had helped her regain some feeling. Instead of the on again–off again emotional roller coaster she had been on, she was able to express her grief and stay in that mode for several hours. When Sandra left the second time, they had both cried for the man whom they had loved and who loved them. Now, back in her house, Pam was thinking a little numbness would be helpful. She wasn't in sync with the jovial atmosphere in the house, yet didn't want to be the one to stop it. And she was getting a headache.

She put her handbag down and went into the kitchen. Anne was tossing a salad and Nelda was there, slicing corned beef on a platter. She looked at her daughter.

"Dear, how are you holding up?" Nelda asked.

"I'm okay, Mother, just tired I guess." She walked over to her and kissed her on the cheek. "I think I'll go right to bed after dinner if you think you can get along without me."

Anne looked at Pam's face.

"Pam, if you want to eat alone, I'll fix you a tray and you can take it to your room." She nodded toward the den. "Things got a little out of hand today. It's all the children, I think."

"I would love to eat in my room, but I doubt if I can get away with it." She took a loaf of rye bread and a platter of sliced vegetables and walked toward the dining room. "I wish there was a little more recognition that someone in this house has died," she said loudly, surprising even her. If the parents couldn't control their children, she would make sure they knew she didn't approve. She heard shushing sounds, and the TV was turned off. Sharon came into the dining room, followed by Susan.

"Pam, we didn't hear you come in. I am so sorry about the noise. Forgive me?" Susan leaned over and gave her sister a peak on the cheek.

"Hi, Suz," Pam said, acknowledging her sister. "How was your trip?"

They exchanged pleasantries, avoiding the obvious, until Susan said, "I'm so sorry about Jack! I just can't believe it." Then Susan hugged Pam.

Pam gave up. She succumbed to Susan's hug, to her outpouring of sympathy. In front of her family, for the first time, she began to cry. She pulled out a chair from the table in her formal dining room, moving the plate aside so she could put her head down and have a good cry.

It provoked silence. The men turned away, and the children gathered closer, wanting to see their Aunt Pam for themselves. Too young to understand, they wondered what it meant when someone you loved had died. The smallest child, Ava, just three, Sharon's youngest, put her arms around Pam's waist. The touching act of kindness brought a smile to Pam's face. She lifted the child up on her lap. Nelda came in then and told everyone to sit down.

She went and got Bernice and Marie and called Lisa and
Brent to join the rest of the family.

Sixteen people squeezed in around Pam's table
meant for twelve, but it was okay. They made corned-beef
sandwiches and had potato salad, coleslaw, beet salad, and
chocolate cake, thanks to Marie who went on a baking
binge that day.

"Can we talk later?" Marie whispered to her.

"Sure, but can it wait? I'm beat." Pam could only
imagine what Marie had to say.

"Later," Marie said.

That evening after dinner, everyone went his or her
separate ways. Pam's sisters and their families, except for
Marie, went to the bed-and-breakfast with Bill and Anne.
Nelda and Bernice stayed at the house. Lisa and Brent got
into bed with their mother and watched TV while she
dozed, until the news came on at eleven p.m. They kissed
her good-night and went to their own rooms.

Pam stood in the window, looking at the surf as it hit
the beach, the moonlight exaggerating the foam on the
white caps, the stars brilliant in the inky black sky. *Tomorrow will be a day to be gotten through*, she thought.

She heard a tap on her door. Thinking it was one of
the children, she said to come in. But it was Marie.

"Come out and I'll make tea,' she said.

11

They sat in peace, not talking for few minutes, and then something came over Marie, and she had to purge herself, had to be honest with Pam. The wedge between them all weekend had been the secret Marie was keeping from her. She had to tell her but needed to be careful not to divulge what she had read into it and just stick to the facts.

"Pam, I have to tell you something. It is bugging the crap out of me."

Pam looked at her. "Okay, go ahead," she said.

Hesitating, but needing to get it off her chest, Marie said, "I saw Jack with Sandra Benson on Saturday morning." She looked at Pam.

"And?" Pam asked.

"And...I saw them is all. If this hadn't all happened, I don't know that I would have ever told you. But since... well, everything, I needed to let you know, to be honest with you."

Pam took a sip of tea. She wondered if there wasn't an ulterior motive here.

"I'm not sure what I am supposed to say. It's over, so don't worry about it anymore." Pam didn't know where this was going, but she wanted to give Marie a chance to express herself. She wanted her to hurry though, to get it over with so she could go back to her room.

"I'm not worried about it, Pam. It was bothering me because I saw them together; I knew what they looked like together. You seem to find something disarming about Sandra Benson, and I think she is a snake."

Marie was going where she didn't want to go, but it was too late.

"This is really about Sandra, then. Am I correct?" Pam fought the urge to get up and refill her tea cup with hot water. She knew that would appear to be an aggressive move.

"Are you more concerned about my befriending her now than what she meant to Jack?" Pam knew that if she weren't careful, she would get swept up into a passionate confrontation with her sister. It had been building over the past days, and she recognized it, yet continued to ignore it.

"Are you befriending her? Did you go into the city to see her? Or did you go to the apartment?" Marie's voice was starting to shake.

"Both. I think it is understandable that I wanted to talk to the woman who was in love with my husband by myself." Then she did stand up. "Jack was my husband. It was my marriage. It is my business. If that seems harsh, so be it. This is not exactly the easiest situation to be in." She turned her back for a minute to refill her cup. When she turned around, Marie was obviously fighting back tears. Pam was tired of her interloping. She would do what she wanted, as far as Sandra Benson was concerned. Marie could go back to the city if need be. "Look, Marie, you might as well accept the fact that Sandra will be here tomorrow. Even if I had never found out about the two of them, she would still be here because she worked with him. Now, what I would be interested in knowing is if I hadn't found any of this out, would you have been able to keep your secret? Or would you have found it irresistible to hurt me?" Pam knew she was challenging her sister, but she wanted it out there. *What was this all about?* She began to think that perhaps this idyllic relationship Marie had with Pam's family was really a smoke screen. *Could Marie have been jealous of her all along?*

Marie sat at the table open mouthed. Marie wondered if she was jealous of her sister. She wanted to react, to lash out, but was able to control herself for the sake of the family.

"I guess we had to have this conversation. It was inevitable. I am not going to start the 'I did this for you' conversation. It is what it is. Our relationship is what it is. I hardly know what to do now." She sat there, finally spent, regretful of having brought up the subject of Sandra fucking Benson. It was amazing what Jack stooped to for a piece of ass.

"Let's just get through tomorrow, okay? Life will return to normal on Wednesday. You'll go back to work, the kids will go back to their summery pursuits, Mom will hopefully go home, and Bernice back to Columbus Circle. Right now, I need things to stay peaceful for just another day. I can get through the funeral if everyone will just stay calm and not expect too much. Can we do that?" She looked directly at Marie.

Marie, looking through her, nodded yes. At that moment, Pam had the realization that something deeper was going on, something that she didn't have the strength to deal with right then, but that it would have to be dealt with later, after the funeral, after they had gotten back to normal.

Marie tried to pull it together, tried to move past the last half hour. She would go through the motions instead of being so self-seeking, so selfish, and let her sister have her way. That was the adult thing to do.

12

Tuesday morning came. It was overcast, but dry. Pam stood in her black silk suit wanting to fade into the wall, but knowing she was about to be on display for the hundreds of people who would come from all over, from Massachusetts to Washington, D.C., to pay their respects to Jack.

Poor Jack, he would have loved this! He loved people. She could hear him now, *For Christ's sake, where the hell were all these people when I needed a loan?* The focus had not been on Jack these last three days, but on his behavior, his final deed. Of course, no one knew about it but Marie and Pam. Pam believed the kids thought their father was a sainted knight who just had a lapse in stamina.

She had not heard from Sandra Benson and didn't attempt to contact her. She would be there that morning, or not. Pam would stay back and let Sandra make the decision about how much involvement she wanted in the festivities. If she wanted to be up front with the family, she would be. If she wanted to stay back, out of sight, that was okay, too. Pam wouldn't watch the reactions of Jack's colleagues. Surely, they knew of the liaison between Jack and Sandra and would be watching for any interaction between the wife and the mistress.

Marie, on the other hand, was on edge and would be looking for the slightest reaction. She had tossed and turned in her bed until just after three a.m. Now, trying to get up and get ready at eight a.m., she felt like her eyelids were gritty sandpaper. She had a headache, too. She was worried that she would explode at the slightest provocation. For the kids' sake, especially Lisa's, she had to maintain control.

She dragged herself to the closet. She was wearing pants and a shirt. It was supposed to go up to eighty degrees; no way was she layering a suit. She put lipstick on and brushed her hair straight back, securing it with a barrette. This was the way Jack liked her hair. "No nonsense," he called it. "You are my no-nonsense girl, and Pam is my high-maintenance girl," he would say. "Don't wear makeup," he'd tell her. "I like seeing how clear your skin is. You don't have one blemish!" Pam would say, "She's a teenager, too! It's because she knows how to take care of herself!"

She walked to the bed and sat on the side of it, shoulders slumped, and put her head in her hands. *Oh Jack, what I am going to do now?*

By eight, everyone was up and dressed. They were eating the last of the gifted food, fruit salad, homemade muffins, and bakery sweet rolls. Pam hadn't come out of her room yet, so Brent went to see if she was up and ready.

Knocking, he whispered to the crack in the door, "Mom, you up?"

She opened the door, remembering her purse and then turning to get it. He followed her in, closing the door behind him.

"Mom, Marie is being really strange. I'm not sure how to handle her."

Pam looked at him.

"Give her some time, okay, Son? She is sad, too. Dad was her one and only for a long, long time. Not sure what she's going to do." She turned around and looked at him. "Is she bothering you now?"

"Sort of. She came into my room last night and got into my bed. She was crying and mumbling something. Bubby came and got her and took her back to bed." Looking down at his petite mother, he noticed the fine lines around her eyes and mouth for the first time and wondered when his parents had gotten old.

"Okay, well lock your door tonight. She might be going back to the city, and then we won't have to worry. Let's just get through today. I feel like that is all I keep asking people—let's get through today. What will my excuse be tomorrow?"

"Jesus, Mom, give yourself a break, okay?" He went up to her and put his arm around her shoulder, steering her toward the door. "Come on, I want to leave. We should be there to see him before anyone else gets there."

They walked out of her room together, a unified force, looking for Bernice and Lisa. Pam wanted the four of them to go together, his family and his mother. Everyone else could figure out whom they would go with.

Brent drove the Lexus with Bernice in the front seat and his mother and sister in the back. He was the man of the family now.

13

Bernice was despondent. She looked lovely in a dark-blue silk shirtwaist dress, her silver hair swept up in a chignon. She wore the pearls that Harold had given her the day she had Bill. She couldn't speak without weeping, so she kept her mouth shut. She had grasped the hands of her grandchildren before they got into the car, just shaking her head back and forth. She clasped an ironed cotton handkerchief in her hand, but had a whole box of Kleenex in her purse, just in case.

They waited in the parked Lexus on the street while everyone else got into their cars. When the last door shut, the procession began, traveling slowly down the streets of Babylon. The neighbors who were home that week were either preparing to go to the funeral or, if not, standing solemnly, waving at the family as they passed.

The same men who waited on Saturday afternoon were there waiting again. They opened the doors of the car, offering their arms to the ladies to assist them out of the car. Brent hurried around and took his grandmother's elbow, while Lisa stood by her mother. The next car to pull in belonged to Bill and Anne. Pam wanted to wait for Jack's brother to join them as they viewed the body for the first time.

They walked into the funeral home, Pam averting her eyes from the bust of George Washington. When they entered the room set aside especially for Jack, Pam gasped at the abundance of floral arrangements.

"Oh my goodness! All of this for Jack?"

Everyone exclaimed in agreement, "All for Jack!" There were at least twenty-five huge arrangements, reaching from one end of the room, lining up behind the casket, to the other end. There was also an overflow of arrangements in the hallway, which Pam failed to notice, thanks to George Washington.

"All but these three bouquets here have cards," the director said. "We're attempting to find out who they are from." Pam thought of all the thank-you cards they would have to write.

"Make sure they go to the nursing home when this is over," Pam stated. The smell was heady, intoxicating. When Marie walked in, it made her headache worse. They should have put a no-flower request in the obituary, but it was too late now. She remembered her grandmother's perfume, Cashmere Bouquet. The smell of it was so dry it brought tears to her eyes. The funeral flowers were doing the same thing to her.

Pam and Bernice, flanked by Lisa and Brent, walked up to the casket and looked in. Bernice brought her hankie to her face. The children began to weep.

Pam grew stony. *He looked fabulous. How could that be possible? How does someone who looks so good, so healthy, so life-like, be dead?*

"He doesn't even look dead," she said out loud. Everyone turned to look at her, but said nothing.

Then the comments began. "Wow, look at how good he looks! They did a great job! Jack was always so handsome."

Pam muttered under her breath to those immediately around her, "He wouldn't dare look bad on his funeral day." They all agreed that it was so Jack. *So far, so good.* But it was inevitable that it was bound to get more difficult.

When Marie came in, she took one look at the casket and began to wail, "Oh Jack! Oh Jack!"

Pam looked around the room for her mother. "Come on, Sis, sit over here." She dragged Marie over to the chairs. "I have to greet people," Pam said.

She walked back to the casket and stood between her mother-in-law and her kids. Guests began to line up to view Jack's body.

People took her hand and expressed their condolences, "What a wonderful guy...It was so sudden...We feel awful..." *Blah, blah, blah.*

Pam did notice that eventually the Manhattan contingency arrived, including Sandra Benson. She came with the others from the office, as a "smoke screen," she had called it, explaining that it would look too obvious if she refused and came alone. But when she reached Pam in the receiving line, she bent down and embraced her, taking her hands and telling her how terribly sorry she was, and Pam felt it was genuine. It was clear Sandra actually felt worse for Pam's loss than she did for her own.

What was in reality only an hour seemed like an all-day ordeal as Pam greeted all of his golf buddies, some of them crying, and his coworkers and colleagues, including many, many young women who said they worked with him. *Hmmm*, Pam thought, *in what capacity?* But said nothing. She would have to investigate this further, at another time.

At the funeral, Pam spoke first, thanking everyone for coming to Jack's final send-off. Bill gave the eulogy, a lovely, funny memoir that did not hide the raucous nature of Jack. Several times, inappropriate though it might have been, the audience broke out in laughter. *Oh, he was a comic all right.*

The rest of the day went by in a fog for Pam and the rest of the family. She vaguely remembered hearing her nieces and nephews crying or fighting or whining. *What a bunch of brats they were. Thank God it was almost over,* she thought to herself. Marie held it together, keeping away from Sandra Benson. Nelda kept her close, supporting her. At the graveside, just the immediate family attended. Sandra did not come.

Because of the delay between going to the cemetery and lunch back at the house, just a handful of mourners came to eat. Pam spent most of the time saying good-bye to her loved ones. Bill and Anne were taking Bernice back to the city, Marie was leaving and taking Nelda with her, and Sharon and her family were leaving before traffic got too bad on the turnpike. With each good-bye, Pam became more exhausted. She wished everyone would just leave for their homes and let life get back to normal!

Finally, by six p.m., it was just her children. Lisa was going to stay until Thursday; Brent had to get back tomorrow. Pam changed into sweatpants and got out the biggest trash bags she could find; everything left from the past three days—every roll, every piece of cake, bowls of unwrapped candy, fruit and pasta salads—was swept away into the trash.

The kids got into it as well. Brent went to each bedroom and stripped the sheets off the mattresses, took every towel and washcloth that looked used, and stuffed them into a series of plastic laundry baskets in the laundry room. He decided he wouldn't wait for the cleaning lady to come; he started the washer right then. Later, he told his mother it felt so good that he actually looked forward to doing his own laundry after that. There was something about cleaning up, washing everything, that spoke of new beginnings. Lisa helped her mother rid the kitchen of any leftovers. Several bouquets of flowers were tossed, and all the sympathy cards were packed away.

They scurried around, cleaning and straightening, with the music on the radio turned up loud until nine p.m. Then they got into the Lexus and went to Shore Pizza and ordered a large pie, two-dozen hot wings, a greek salad, and a pitcher of Bud Light for Brent and Pam and a Diet Pepsi for Lisa. They talked and ate until eleven p.m.

When they got home, Brent dragged the twin mattress from one of the guest bedrooms and placed it on Pam's bedroom floor. They needed to be together tonight. It would be the last time the three of them, what was left of their family, would be under the same roof for a long time. No one mentioned it, but they also wanted to be close to what was left of their father, his clothing and personal belongings all right there in the bedroom closet.

In the morning, Pam got up and made breakfast for her two children. She and Lisa would drive Brent to JFK later in the afternoon. She could hardly stand the thought of it. While they ate, they tried to stay off the topic of Jack, but he kept popping up, and when he did, someone was bound to cry. Pam kept the coffee coming. Rather than reminiscing, this time around they spoke of the things their father would miss—college graduations, marriages, and grandchildren. It was this sadness of unmet expectations that would haunt them for the rest of their lives.

Finally, it was time for Brent to leave. He had to be at the airport by two. There wasn't much left to say, so they turned up the radio and sang along, laughing at made-up lyrics. It was just the sort of thing their father would have done. They arrived on time, not parking and walking in with him, but dropping him off and keeping it brief. Pam didn't think she could take a prolonged good-bye.

Getting Lisa to Newark was harder. Pam wanted to take her, but six hours round-trip on a good day might be too much for her. She decided to take her back to JFK and hire a limousine. By Thursday afternoon, Pam was alone.

When she returned to the house, she parked the Lexus back in the garage. The mail had come, and there was a paper on the porch. She wanted all loose ends tied up. She didn't want to think about having one single thing to do. She locked the front door behind her and put her purse and the mail down on the kitchen counter. Then she proceeded to go through the house the shutting every shade or curtain that faced the front or could be looked upon. She wanted privacy. She needed peace. She shut the shades in the unused rooms and the children's rooms and closed the doors.

If there were anything of Jack left in the house, besides the bedroom closet and the garage, it was the den.

She couldn't deal with that yet. *Let it be.* But she closed the shades and door to that room as well.

The house was secure, and it was relatively neat. She went into her room, pulled the shades in there too, got into bed, and stayed there for the rest of the week.

14

Marie gave her mother, Nelda, an ear full on the way home from Pam's house. She was livid about the way she had been ignored at the funeral, like a nonentity, not given the opportunity to speak, and then afterward, tossed aside like a chauffeur, not invited to stay with the rest of the family as she had all of her life. She hated being there anyway. It was obvious to her that Jack had left years prior to his death; there was nothing of him in the house now, nor had there been for years.

Her mother was mortified. It was clear to her some jealous streak that lay dormant for years was rearing its head in death. *Why now?* Why it took Jack's death to make her daughter react to it was a mystery. Nelda had always thought Marie's involvement with Pam and her family a huge mistake. She and her husband, Frank, had fought over it. Then the truth was revealed. He thought that Jack would pay for Marie's college, and he was right. Nelda never forgave Frank for basically giving Marie up for servitude, the price of a college education.

But now she was frightened that some of that animosity was going to be directed at her. *Was Marie going to go down memory lane as part of her coming to terms with wasting her life in return for being a full-time, live-in servant for her sister?* Nelda didn't think she was up for that sort of restitution. Marie would demand it—a lot of it.

When they got to her flat in Brooklyn, Nelda didn't invite her in. The tirade was not over yet, but she had had enough. She insisted on managing her own bags, saying, "The meter is running. You better go!" She kissed her youngest child on the cheek and went up the steps.

Marie didn't seem to notice that she was being dismissed. But as the cab pulled away from the curb, she realized there was no one else who would listen to her, no one else who cared. Her mother and Pam and Jack were the only people on earth who knew all the players, who understood the dynamics of the family. She had not yet recognized her role in Pam's family for what it truly was, a diversion for Jack and a buffer for everyone else. Since Pam didn't care for nightlife, she wasn't used as a babysitter much. Although the day would come when she would begin to resent where that path had taken her, to nowhere, with no family of her own, right now, the only deficit she felt was being excluded from the grief of the intimate family circle. *The kids even withdrew and clung to their mother! What was that all about?* Marie wondered.

She went home with a head full of rebuttals to everything that was said to her during the funeral. Someone actually said, "You must be strong for Pam." *What the hell did that mean? What about being strong for myself? I loved Jack like a brother—like a brother!* Although her counter-ego said, *Really? Like a brother?*

Sandra drove in with a group of people from the office. Afterward, after the farce, they were going to a diner in Brooklyn, but she couldn't stand the thought of sitting and making small talk, rehashing the funeral, or worse, talking about Jack, so she had them drop her off at the entrance to the subway.

It was hot and smelly in the train car. She drew her dress close around her legs and sat back, closing her eyes. She took deep, slow breathes of the stinky air, forcing her shoulders and back to relax. Pictures went through her head: moments in time, fleeting glimpses of Pam, Jack's children, Jack lying in the casket. Pam standing like a statue, barely moving her facial muscles, hands clenched at her sides. When approached by a guest, Sandra watched her go through the exact same motions for each one. She raised her hands, grasped the forearms of the well-wisher, and forced a modicum of a smile onto her face. Sandra could almost read her lips from across the room, "Thank you so much for coming; it would have meant so much to Jack." When it had been her turn to go through the receiving line, Pam grabbed her like an old friend, tears coming to her eyes. "Oh, thank you so much. Thank you so much. It's so sad, so sad." She could smell Pam's perfume, a light, floral scent. Sandra could hardly control her grief at that point and didn't look down at Jack; it would have been too difficult to stay calm.

Now she regretted not looking at him. The last time she had seen him was in the hospital. The others had remarked how good he looked. No one included her in the conversation, a fact she would be grateful for. No one mentioned anything about them being together or acted like they knew. Perhaps that secret had been maintained after all.

She had to change trains. The last stop for her was Broadway, about ten blocks from her apartment. There was no way she was walking in those shoes, so she got a cab. It took forever to get to Eighty-second.

The cool air of her apartment was welcoming. She was not going back out for the rest of the day, and she wasn't going back to the office for possibly the rest of the week. She didn't care if she got fired; she needed to be alone.

She got out of her dress and promptly threw it in the trash, knowing she would not wear it again, ever. She found soft pajama bottoms and a T-shirt to put on. Her skin felt like it couldn't tolerate anything else. She thought she might be coming down with something, having woken up queasy and feeling a little queasy now. She went to the kitchen and poured herself a glass of water. She no sooner turned to walk back through the living room when she began projectile vomiting, a stream of regurgitated water, which hit the opposing wall with a splash. It shocked her. But a little voice deep in her brain said, *Oh...oh....*

15

On Sunday morning, Pam woke up to rain and a renewed energy. She would get back to living. The past four days had been spent in despair. She didn't answer the phone, unless it was her kids, ate only junk, and watched reruns of *The Twilight Zone* and *Law and Order*.

Every morning she got up and went through the motions of living, just in case she would return to her life. She took a shower, carefully applied makeup, and did her hair. She found a stylish, but comfortable outfit to wear. If anyone saw her, they would think she had made a full recovery, that her grief had been swift and complete, in less than a week.

She made herself a dozen chocolate-chip muffins, and every morning she ate two with a pot of coffee. She sat on the veranda, shaded from the neighbors by high stone walls, mosquito netting, and pampas grass. When the sugar from the muffins hit her, she returned to her bedroom and crawled back into bed, flicking the TV on with the remote. There she stayed until hunger beckoned her out of bed again.

But she was slowly coming back to life. After her morning beauty ritual, she made her standard pot of coffee and went from room to room opening the curtains. She left a message on her cleaning lady's phone to please return to work as soon as possible. Then she grabbed her purse and her own car keys and left for the gym.

She worked herself without mercy after a week furlough. No one asked her where she had been, and if they knew about Jack, reading something in the *Times* or the local paper, they didn't acknowledge it. She enjoyed her anonymity. How she had maintained that after living in the same house for as long as she did said something to her about the busyness of life. You were either born into an area or remained a stranger forever.

After her workout, she freshened her lipstick in the car and drove to her favorite grocery store. It was part gourmet delicatessen, part carry-out restaurant. There, she would buy enough food to stock her refrigerator for a week and not have to cook a thing. She was only thinking up until Friday. She would have to deal with those painful issues of Jack not coming home from the city then, and not before.

This week, she would get the death certificate, go to Social Security for the kids, see their lawyer, go to the insurance company, and into the city again to clean out the refrigerator in the apartment, once and for all. She hadn't thought about what to do with the apartment much, but the idea crossed her mind to rent it out. She would think on that for a while.

The groceries needed to be put away, so she went straight home. The rain was letting up, and some blue sky peaked through. She wanted to walk on the beach, a good, long walk. But first, she would go to the library and choose some books to read. *Okay, I have exercise, reading, walking on the beach, and eating. When those things are done, what is left?* She began to get frightened. She was alone.

16

Marie let herself into her apartment, violently jiggling the key in the lock, pushing the door with her fist, and then slamming it shut. She stomped around the place, throwing her bags on the floor of the closet and pulling the curtains open with such force that they swung back and forth for a full minute.

Finally, she plopped down on her couch and put her head in her hands and began to sob, wondering what she was going to do now. There wasn't one single thing to look forward to. She hated her job, only going through the motions to make Jack proud, since he had gotten it for her. No one who worked in her office cared if she showed up or not, and she felt the same way about all of them. Pam used to say, "You have to pretend sometimes, and then the feelings will grow to be genuine." Marie thought that was the tritest rationalization she had heard. *No way!* Most of the people she worked with commuted from New Jersey anyway. *What good would friendships with those people do?*

The one single thing that gave her life meaning was leaving on Saturday and driving to Long Island to see her sister and Jack. After the kids left for college, she thought it would change, but if anything, it became more focused on Jack and, therefore, more fun for Marie.

He taught her to golf when she was just fourteen, and now she lived for her golf outings with him. He had gotten her a set of specially made clubs. She devoured the golf clothing catalogues and had an impressive wardrobe of golf wear. It gave her something to talk about with other men. Her scores were impressive as well.

Now what would become of it? Pam didn't golf and had no interest. They had a membership at an expensive country club. Marie wondered if she could interest Pam. *Why bother?* She didn't want to golf with Pam; she wanted to golf with Jack. But he was dead! "Fuck!" she screamed loudly, not caring if the entire building heard her.

She sat on the couch looking out the huge picture window with its view of the Hudson River just beyond Javitz Center. She really was a spoiled brat. Here she had this great apartment, she could walk to work, she was close to transportation, and she could go just about anywhere she wanted by walking two blocks, and yet she was miserable.

She'd get ready for work for the rest of the week. That would give her purpose; it would make her feel like she was accomplishing something. She'd call her mother and offer to take her somewhere over the weekend. It would give them both something to look forward to. She would even swallow her pride and call Pam to ask if she wanted some company. Those decisions made, she got up, wiped her face off with a tissue, and began living again.

17

Sandra felt better the next morning and got ready to go to work. Still just a little queasy, she decided it was due to stress. She left her apartment and began walking south on Broadway. She tried not to think about how the past four days had changed her life, that the day before she had attended the funeral of her lover incognito. The ideal situation would be if she never had to cross the threshold of that goddamned office again. She wondered what the mood would be.

The train was hot, and she loathed the ride that day even more than usual. Probably knowing that there was no one to greet her, no cocky grin, no graying temples, no hunk waiting for her. She would eat lunch alone, go home to her empty apartment and, having no one to go to dinner with, maybe even skip the meal. She imagined her hips getting slimmer, her breasts disappearing, clothes hanging on her. It had happened in the past; it could happen now.

She needn't have worried about the office. There was a meeting for Jack's department, probably going over his clients and the projects he was immersed in, which they would divide up among the others. She was guaranteed a peaceful morning.

What she hadn't counted on was what she found hanging over her credenza—the vibrant painting of Riverside Gardens. He had called right after their breakfast together, bought the painting, and had it delivered and hung there. She closed her eyes, imagining him talking on his cell phone, extracting promises of anonymity, and then hanging up and falling over with a heart attack.

She walked to her door and shut it, closing the blinds on the sidelights. She couldn't help herself, but the tears came yet again. *Will I ever be over it?* How much he had impacted her life was directly proportional to how much she felt it being destroyed. She would no longer be able to eat at Chantal's, listen to Sting, look at certain art, or read mystery novels. This job, not a high point in her life, now had the potential to be intolerable. She didn't even know if she could stay in the city.

Walking around to her desk, she sat down and looked at the phone. There was only one other person on this earth she could think of at that moment who knew what she was going through, who could imagine her frustration and nonacceptance of Jack's death, and that person was his wife.

Sandra picked up the phone and dialed Pam's number. It rang for seven rings, and the answering machine picked up. It was a homogenized male voice instructing her to leave her name and number, which she did. When she was finished, she put her head down on her desk and had a good cry.

18

Marie went back to work on Wednesday, although she honestly thought she deserved to have the rest of the week off after what she had been through. She tried calling her sister, but got the answering machine. Softening, she thought maybe Pam was just lying low, allowing herself time to get caught up with her feelings.

Going to work turned out to be helpful after all. She had a lot to do. None of it was emotion based, and her brain had to really work to sort things out. No one at work knew Jack, so the comments were limited to "Sorry about your brother-in-law," and that was that. It was as if it hadn't happened. He was still alive, at work two subway stops down, and all she had to do was send him a text message: "Meet me at the hot dog stand on the corner of Exchange and Wall." He'd be there like clockwork, standing with a dog and a soda, all ready for her. They'd walk down the street and lean up against a granite wall and eat, easily talking, sharing intimacies that no one else would hear, or so she thought. He never, ever breathed a word about Sandra Benson. *Was he, in essence, cheating on me as well?*

She sat at her desk. The loneliness was palpable. She needed Pam now like never before. She left another message, then a third.

On Friday evening, walking home from the office, she imagined that it was going to be like any other weekend. She would go home and pack a bag, get her car gassed up, and the next day, Saturday, if she didn't have anything to do in the morning, would be spent going to Long Island. She would usually stop at a farmers' market on the way to the house and pick up whatever caught her eye; it was the least she could do.

She had her own room at Pam's. It was in a separate wing from the master and guest suites, shared by Lisa and Brent when they were children and now when they returned home from school. When they were away, Marie missed them terribly, although then she had her own bath as well. There was something about knowing that all she had to do was knock on one of their doors, and she would have ready companionship.

In retrospect, she wondered if her niece and nephew minded her presence. She had always been there, but the family still treated her like an honored guest. When Lisa fought with her mother over permission to date an older boy, Jack spoke up and said, "I'm sure Marie doesn't want to listen to this squabbling." Lisa and Pam turned and looked at her with impatience. "If she is going to be here every weekend, she'll hear more than this!" Pam looked at her sister. Marie would have packed up right then and never come back, but Jack leaped to her rescue. "She's keeping us civilized! Let's go hit a basket of golf balls," he said to no one in particular, but Brent and Marie headed out the door with him. It was that sort of interaction that kept her coming back. She is sure now that if Pam had minded, she would have said, "Don't come this weekend. It is too much." The rare weekend she had other plans, one of the kids would be on the phone asking her if she was coming, and then she would either feel welcome there or guilty for not going.

It was too late. She had spent her life there as either an interloper or a welcome guest. It was too late to change anything; she couldn't remake history.

She let herself into her apartment. She was hungry, but didn't feel like cooking, so she got out a loaf of bread and the peanut butter jar and made a sandwich. She poured herself a glass of wine and went and sat on the couch overlooking the river. She picked up her phone to thumb through the caller ID and one name jumped out at her; Sandra Benson. She put the phone down. What the hell did she want? She picked up the phone again and continued searching through the caller ID numbers and saw that Pam had called earlier as well as her mother. She picked a glob of peanut butter off her tooth.

She sat her sandwich down on the coffee table, without a plate under it. She called her mother first. She didn't have anything to say about Pam, except she hoped she was okay, as she wasn't answering her phone yet. She returned Pam's call next. The phone rang for five rings and was answered with a soft hello.

"Did you call?" Marie asked.

"I did. Sorry I didn't leave a message. I wanted to tell you that Sandra Benson called, and she really needed someone to talk to. I was hoping you would meet with her, be a sounding board, if you are able. It is the least we can do. She loved Jack, Marie, she really did." Pam was silent then for a few minutes. "I just can't talk to anyone yet. Do you understand? I have to sort through my own feelings about his death before I can help you and the kids and Sandra sort through your feelings. I am okay with his affair. I don't hold that against her. It was of my own making."

"She called here. I saw her number on the caller ID," Marie said.

"I tried calling her back and left your number on her answering machine. I am truly sorry if that was not okay with you, Marie." Pam took a deep breath and then sighed. "I can't talk anymore. I'll call you in couple of days, okay?"

They said good-bye then, Marie feeling empathy for her sister, but still a little icy, still a little jealous. She could not rationalize her feelings.

She tried to understand what it would take to have made her feel better about everything, when she realized that she didn't feel like part of the family now, and probably never would again. It was Jack who made her feel welcome, who seemed to want her there. *Was he just being polite?* She would never know.

She pushed some papers off the couch and lay down sideways on it. She watched the sun go down in the western sky and the lights go on around her and across the river in New Jersey. She didn't turn the lights on in her apartment and eventually fell asleep.

Sometime in the night, Marie woke up and went to her bed to sleep. Sandra Benson kept popping into her head, but she just couldn't make contact with her, not yet anyway. She wanted to see her sister, too. In the still of the night, she missed Pam, missed her cordial, if not cool, demeanor, the way she never allowed her own discomfort to stand in the way of the comfort of others. Case in point: Sandra Benson. *Why, oh why did Pam care whether or not Sandra was happy? Or sad?* Marie tossed and turned for a while, and finally fell back asleep.

19

Saturday was hell for Sandra Benson. *How did a week pass already since Jack's death?* She was beginning to feel the four walls of her apartment closing in on her. She was going to have to get out this weekend and visit friends or go shopping.

The other problem, if it was a problem and not just a figment of her imagination, was not going away. She was still a little queasy, a little tired. Her period was due that day, Saturday. She kept running to the bathroom every time she felt the slightest moisture. Nothing. She took the pill, albeit not without some forgetfulness. *Today was the day*, she thought. It was never late; because of the pill, it was always like clockwork. But she had forgotten to take it two days in a row at the beginning of the month when she went on business to Philadelphia and stayed overnight.

By noon, she had had enough and left to walk to the drug store to get a pregnancy test. There, she had said it, or thought it. *Pregnancy test. Pregnant. Baby. Jack's baby.* She walked quickly down Broadway. The drugstore was crowded. She prayed that no one she knew would come in while she was waiting in line.

She read the labels on the different brands of test. They were all similar. One had a pink plus sign if the test was positive. Another had a smiley face, a yellow, round circle with a black smiling face on it if you were, in fact, pregnant. *Were they kidding? Where was the skull and cross bones if it dared to be positive?* She didn't want cutesy; she didn't want plus signs and balloons. She wanted negative. A giant NO printed in black.

She chose the test that was the quickest and also guaranteed to be accurate even before your missed period. She put it in her handbasket and walked over to the candy aisle, grabbing bags of M&M's and mini Almond Joys, knowing she would end up eating every piece of candy. She couldn't wait to tear into the bags and pop little candy bars into her mouth or handfuls of M&M's. She put the obvious out of her mind and thought of a recipe her late mother used to bake, cupcakes that had a piece of Almond Joy in the center of it. She would find that recipe in the box of cookbooks she had that had belonged to her mom and bake them tonight.

She paid for the test and her candy and hurried out of the drugstore before she ran into someone she knew. Getting home couldn't happen fast enough. Throwing the candy bags on the chair in the sitting room, she dug the test out of the bag and read the directions again. She took the plastic stick out of the box and took it into the bathroom with her. She placed it on the edge of the sink and unbuttoned her jeans, pulling them down to her ankles. The stick was short so she had to contort to get the thing close enough to her crotch to pee on without taking her jeans off.

If it turned green, she was pregnant; blue, she wasn't. She peed on it and waited. The she looked at her watch and waited some more. After a minute, she looked, and it was green. The stick turned green. She thought, *Great! What the hell am I going to do now?*

She threw the stick in the trash and washed her hands, pulling her jeans up and buttoning and zipping them. The box of cookbooks that had belonged to her mom was in a closet downstairs. She ran down and dug it out, ripping the packing tape off and lifting the books out. She thought it was in a self-published, church fundraiser book and picked several of them out to thumb through. Taking the stack of books upstairs, she turned the teakettle on. A cup of tea, a muffin, and looking through cook books—a good diversion.

Sunday came. Marie spent Saturday going through the chain of events of the previous Saturday, remembering each thing and trying to imagine what she could have done that would have altered the outcome. If she had made her presence known when she saw Sandra and Jack on the street, he wouldn't have gotten on the train, possibly having his heart attack in a place where help could've come sooner. She could've taken him back to her apartment and made him a drink so he would've relaxed, possibly not even having a heart attack. He would be alive. She would have been on her way to Pam's then, expecting to spend the next three days on the beach; eating hot dogs and burgers off the grill, Mom's potato salad, and cake and desserts from Heavenly Cake; playing Uno with Lisa; and sneaking a smoke from Bill's pack.

Instead, she had the worst week of her life, and her beloved Jack was dead! *What the hell am I going to do with my life now?*

Sandra slept like a dead person on Saturday night. Having eaten three cupcakes with Almond Joys stuck in the center of them had no effect on her. They were hot and gooey, the candy bar melted and delicious.

Sunday morning came, and she was so depressed. Getting out of bed was a struggle. *What am I going to do today? Would another two thousand calories of candy help get me through the day?* She couldn't force herself to bathe or dress. She stuck a cup of tea made the day before into the microwave and sat at the table looking at her brick wall and drinking the stale tea. She suddenly felt so alone, so empty.

Pam couldn't concentrate on the book. She made herself a huge iced tea, arranged cheese and crackers on a plate, got a sweater out in case it was chilly out on the veranda, and then picked up her book and went out there to sit. She made the effort, but just couldn't get into the book. She read the flyleaf, the last page, the back of the book. Maybe it wasn't going to be a good fit.

She stood up and looked out at the water. Her footprints from earlier in the day were visible halfway down the beach and then mysteriously disappeared, as though she had picked herself up and flown away. The water had lost its allure so early in the season. She had no one to walk the beach with now, no one waiting for her at the house, no one inquiring if she found any of her favorite beach glass. There was a large, clear glass ginger jar on the kitchen counter filled with small pieces of blue and green glass and the rare red. Marie came into her mind. She walked to the phone and picked it up, keying in her number. She answered on the second ring, a breathless, questioning hello.

"It's Pam, Marie. I was thinking of you. How are you?" *Inane. How did she think she was?*

"I'm surviving. How about you?" Marie really wanted to know. She felt tender feelings for her sister, hidden by her jealousy.

"The same, I guess. I am worried about Friday. What will the weekend bring if he doesn't come home? Well, he's not going to, so I guess I better get over it!" she said. "This week was a blur. How about for you?"

"I worked." Marie said, and then asked, "What'd you do?"

"I stayed in bed Friday and Saturday, watching reruns, eating forbidden foods. And then today I managed to go to the gym. Oh, that was fun! And I walked on the beach. But I thought of something. You don't have to answer now. But think about coming out for the weekend, why don't you?" She didn't say anything else.

"Okay, I'll think about it, Pam. And Pam? Thanks for the invite."

They spoke briefly about their mother. Before they said their good-byes, Marie mentioned Sandra Benson.

"I'm not ready to call her yet. I know you think it would help her, but I am not so sure."

"Whatever you think. It was just an idea," Pam said, and then they said good-bye.

Pam didn't want to get ahead of herself. She fully intended on calling Sandra and inviting her for the following weekend. She would tell Marie if and when she got a positive response. She didn't fully understand what was compelling her to bring these two together. Sandra was closer to Lisa and Brent's ages than Marie's.

But Sandra had loved Jack, as she was sure Marie loved Jack. They could offer some support to each other. Right now, all Pam felt was numbness. It was so strange. She had crying jags and those two days of relative inertia, but other than that, she wasn't dwelling on his absence—yet. By Friday, when there was no chance of his weekly homecoming, she would be able to evaluate her mental status more realistically.

She picked up the phone again and keyed in Sandra's phone number. She, too, picked up with a breathless and questioning hello.

"Sandra, its Pam Smith, again. I am sorry to bother you on a Sunday. Your name keeps popping into my head, so I thought I would call you. Is this a bad time?"

"God, yes! I have a house full of important guests. The servants are all busy serving. I barely have a minute to myself." Sandra sat down again, her head hanging down, despondent. "No, I'm not busy, Pam."

Pam giggled nervously, not sure what to say next. Sandra was immediately regretful. Here was the woman whose husband had died. She needed to show some respect.

"How have you been, Pam? Has it been difficult for you?" Sandra asked.

"I guess I am doing as well as can be expected. How are you holding up?" She really wanted to know.

Sandra thought of the unspoken, the unmentionable, the not-yet-revealed.

"I'm okay. The office was strange." Sandra thought it might be helpful for Pam to know how lost everyone was without Jack, but maybe not.

"I'd like to hear what happened. No one called. I thought maybe Pete would call, but nothing. Jack's partner not even acknowledging his death? They are probably worried I will ask for money." Pam laughed, thinking how inappropriate that comment was. *Oh well, to hell with them.*

"Good point! You should ask for money! I would if I could. All day Wednesday was spent in meetings, dividing up Jack's projects. I hid in my office. No one knows or suspects anything about the other, you know. So there was no reason to treat me in any special way." She stood up and started pacing. Measuring her words was nerve-wracking. "Not that I would have wanted that anyway." She stopped yammering. *Oh, this was so hard!*

"Did they make any announcement? I still think it is slightly amusing that Pete never called me! He barely said anything to me at the funeral. Oh well, let the attorneys handle it."

"Yes, well he is a strange one. I got in late, and they were already in a meeting. I think if anything would have been announced it would have been at that time. You know better than I do what Pete is like. He could hardly make eye contact when times were good."

There was a brief pause. Pam remembered the real reason for her call.

"I'd like to have you here next weekend. It's supposed to be beautiful out; we are on the ocean, so it would be like having a mini vacation. You can spend the night if you are comfortable with that, or just stay for the day. My sister,

Marie, is thinking about coming, too. What do you say? I'd love to have you." She was sincerely hoping the answer would be yes. *How strange was this?*

Sandra was speechless. She thought the idea of spending the night in Jack's house, with his wife in the next room, was totally wrong. She didn't know what to say, but the silence was awkward enough.

"I'll think about it and call you later?" It wasn't an unreasonable response, considering the circumstances.

"Absolutely!" Pam replied. "I'll look forward to hearing from you then."

They said their good-byes, and Pam hung up, feeling better than she had all week. She put the phone down and walked back out on the veranda. It needed sweeping, so she went into the utility closet off of the mudroom and got a broom. *Maybe some good old-fashioned housekeeping was in order. The cleaning ladies would be here in the morning, but that was no reason to leave this mess for them.* She swept away, making a little pile of sand and pushing it off the stones into the sandy garden.

She continued sweeping down the pathway of boardwalk Jack had built for his mother when she broke her ankle. They could push her in a wheelchair to the end of the property, almost to the beach. She was content to sit there in the circle of wood, watching the sea gulls swooping and her grandchildren playing volleyball. Her son, always doting, brought her glasses of lemonade sweetened with aspartame, just the way she liked it. "Mother," he would say, "How can you drink this crap? Why not let me make you some Kool-Aid instead?" She laughed at her son, amused at his concern for her. "Just give it to me, will you?" She would grab at his hand for the glass.

Pam thought about Bernice. Jack would take the subway up to her house and take her to lunch at least once a week. She liked a little café on Amsterdam, where she ordered the same lunch every time—a veggie burger with red onion and avocado on a whole wheat bun and sweet-potato fries. He said the same thing to her every week.

"How can such a demure little old lady eat red onion and then go out in public and breathe on people all afternoon?" She would make a point of breathing her onion breath in his face, and exaggerating her vowels, she'd say, "It's not so bad, is it? You wouldn't deny me this small joy, now would you?" They'd laugh about it each time. Or he'd look around furtively and, lifting one hip, let out a small amount of gas, just enough that only his mother would hear. She'd make a fuss, acting appalled, all the while the two of them hysterical at their bathroom-humor jokes. The waitresses were usually tolerant, but happy to see them go. Jack was a big tipper.

Pam hadn't noticed, but it was so obvious now that those frequent mother-son reunions ended right around this same time last year. *Had he found out that Harold wasn't his father? Did he confront Bernice at that time?* She would never know, having decided to not ask her mother-in-law. She had been through enough without having that thrown in her face.

The day passed, Pam killing time, hoping for the night to come quickly and then be gone. She wanted Monday to come. Something about Monday was always so comforting to her—a clean slate to start the week, a week that would end alone. She saw her life stretch before her, empty, without purpose. *What was the point of it?*

Marie decided she was going to take a walk. She needed some food in the apartment and was doing nothing but pacing back and forth all day anyway. She pulled on a pair of jeans and a clean shirt, combed her hair and pulled it into a ponytail, and walked out into the street. There wasn't a chance in hell of getting a cab in this dead neighborhood, so she walked the few blocks to the subway. She'd run up to Zabar's; there was nothing open closer to home.

The subway stop was the one at Broadway where she had last seen Jack a week before. She got off the train and stood aside to let the few other passengers pass her. She wanted to take her time there, to see if she could feel him. She walked up the steps to the street, trying to remember where it was that she saw him stop and turn around to look back up at Sandra. She thought she found the step and stood there for a moment with her hand on the railing. He had held the railing there, first his left hand, and then when he turned around, his right. She looked around to see if anyone was watching her, and when she saw that she was alone, she did the maneuver. Pretending she was walking down into the station, she paused, turned changing hands, and looked up. Someone was coming down then so she went ahead and went up the rest of the way. "Jack's last move," is how she would think of it. *He was so gorgeous. It was impossible that he was fifty-five years old. He looked more like he was forty-five.* She wouldn't allow herself to think of more than that.

She contemplated what groceries to get. It was too expensive to buy a lot, but a few necessities, coffee and butter and something to eat for lunch the next day, would do, just enough to get through the week until she could do a big shopping next weekend when she went to visit her sister—if she went.

Marie walked up Broadway, imagining she saw Jack and Sandra walking hand and hand toward her. She crossed the street to rid herself of that vision. Another vision popped into her mind, one she didn't allow too often now, as it was too painful, too humiliating, but on the street it would be safe, it wouldn't lead to anything she would later regret. She remembered his hands around her waist. She was bending over at the beach house, pulling beach grass up out of Pam's stupid flowerbeds, and she could see him coming toward her, upside down. He put his hands around her waist and pushed her down into a squat.

"It's not good for your back to bend at the waist like that, my dear child." She turned her head to look up at him, squinting into the sun overhead. "Someday, you'll thank me for it. Bend at the knees." He stood there looking down at her, an obvious erection tugging at his madras shorts. She wasn't sure if he was purposely trying to show her he was hard, his crotch at eye level, or if he was hiding it from his wife who was just across the veranda. She fought the urge to take any jaunts down memory lane. She knew that it was just a matter of time before all of those incidents with Jack would rise to the surface to be dealt with, one way or another. It was entirely up to her how it would play out.

Eighty-second Street was coming up. Marie stood there, acknowledging to herself, for the first time, that her real reason for a late-afternoon stroll to Zabar's was because she wanted to see Sandra Benson. She didn't hesitate at the corner, but turned left to go down Eighy-second toward the river. She came to Sandra's building and went right to the door. She found the buzzer and pressed it. The speaker came on, and Marie could hear Sandra's voice.

There must have been a camera someplace because the door clicked, and Sandra said, "I'm at the end of the hallway, Marie. Come in."

The door opened, and standing there, looking like hell, was the hated Sandra Benson. *She doesn't seem so threatening now. She looks sick.* Sandra stepped aside for Marie.

"Please, come in," she said.

Marie stepped through the door and looked around. It was a nice place, she had to admit. She found herself wondering if Jack had paid for it.

"Nice apartment," Marie said.

Sandra thanked her, telling her that she loved being there, and as long as her rent didn't go up too much, she hoped to stay there forever.

"I've been here for four years now. It feels like home. And I love the neighborhood." She pointed to a table and chairs situated by a window. "Do you want something to drink?" she said.

Marie, looking out the window at the alley and the tree with the birdhouse, said okay. Sandra went to the refrigerator and pulled out a pitcher of water. She filled the teapot and set it on the stove, turning the stove on. She seemed to measure each task, each movement, with purpose. Marie thought she might be feeling self-conscious. She noticed Sandra was painfully thin. Her legs, encased in skintight spandex shorts, were like sticks. Her arms were sticking out of her T-shirt like tree branches. When she bent over, Marie could see the bones in her hips. Suddenly overcome with compassion, she stood up and went into the little kitchen.

"Can I help you? You seem a tad tired." Marie hoped her words sounded okay and not too critical. She wanted to take the kettle out of her hands and force her to sit down.

"I guess I am sort of tired. Can't believe tomorrow is Monday already." Sandra arranged cut lemon wedges on a little plate and put a sugar bowl, creamer, and tea bags on a tray. She brought the tray to the table and went back to get the mugs and teakettle. She debated putting the leftovers of her baking binge out, but wasn't sure of the purpose of this visit. She thought it might be wise to keep the refreshments brief.

Marie put a tea bag in her mug, and Sandra poured the hot water in.

"What brings you uptown?" Sandra asked.

"I need some groceries, and there is nothing in my neighborhood," Marie replied.

"This is a long way to come for food," Sandra said. "I don't tell everyone this, but I go into New Jersey once in a while to stock up." She laughed.

"I imagined I was walking in your footsteps along Broadway," Marie said suddenly. Sandra looked at her, questioning. "You know, the path you took with Jack on that Saturday."

"I don't understand," Sandra said. *What the hell was she talking about?* And then she remembered. Marie had told her at the hospital that she saw Jack and her together on the street. She shook her head yes. "Oh, right." She felt so tired. *What did Marie want?*

"I guess I didn't realize that when you said you saw me that it meant you followed me."

Marie ignored that.

"When I came up the subway steps, I imagined I was Jack. I saw him turn around and look at you before he went down. It was the last time you saw him before the hospital, wasn't it." She stated it as a fact. She stood up and went to the window again. "I was so angry at him I kept thinking, 'How am I going to face Pam?' I would make him tell her himself, I decided. Then, of course, he died. If only I had stopped him on the street that day. He wouldn't have been on the train. I could tell from across the street that he was in love with you. I never saw him look at anyone with that intensity." She lowered her head, tears starting to roll down her cheeks. "I don't know what I am going to do with myself now." Marie stood up and walked to the window, weeping.

Sandra couldn't move from her chair. *Why did this have to happen now?* She couldn't find it in her to say anything comforting. There was a tone in Marie's voice, an accusatory undercurrent. She was probably imagining it.

Marie was losing it, she knew it, but was unable to control herself.

"Pam wanted me to contact you to make sure you were okay. I kept telling myself, 'Fuck Sandra!' I knew there was something wrong with Jack, I was just too stupid to know it was another woman."

Sandra was getting tired of this conversation.

"I'm sorry," was all she could think of to say.

Marie looked at her, frowning.

"You are so young," Marie said. "You don't realize the impact his infidelity will have on the whole family."

Sandra put her hand on her belly under the table, thinking, *Oh, I think I do.*

"Are you going to the beach next weekend?" Marie asked, changing the subject. Sandra was confused again, but then realized she was talking about Jack's house on Long Island. "I know Pam is thinking of asking you, if she hasn't already."

"Would it be a problem for you if I go?" Sandra asked. "I'm not sure what good it would do for me to go regardless. If you would rather I not go, please don't hold back."

"I don't want you to go. But it doesn't make any difference what I want. Jack wasn't my husband. Pam wants you there. For some reason, you make her feel better. She feels close to you, did you know that?" Marie wasn't giving her time to respond, and Sandra didn't know what to say anyway. "All I can picture is you fucking my brother-in-law." She started crying again. "Oh God! Oh God! Jack!" She slumped into her chair.

Sandra was starting to become concerned. Marie hated her, and now she was losing control. She worried that she wasn't safe in her own apartment. She stood up and went into the bathroom to get a washcloth, squeezing cold water through it.

She went back into the kitchen and approached Marie, saying, "Here's a cold washcloth; let me put it on your neck."

Marie complied, leaning forward slightly in her chair and pulling her ponytail around to the front. Sandra, who was not nurturing in the least, folded the cloth in half and placed it across the back of the crying woman's neck. Its effect was immediate, Marie taking a deep breath and saying, "That feels good. I'm sorry I am giving you such a hard time."

Sandra didn't reply, but stood at the side of the chair. She had not touched Marie's neck with her hand, nor did she place a comforting hand on her shoulder or arm. She was really confused. Jack had never even mentioned a sister-in-law in all the months they were a couple, yet this woman was talking as though he was integral to her life, to her overall well-being. Suddenly, Sandra had an epiphany. *Had Jack been intimate with his wife's younger sister?* Smiling behind Marie's back, she put a serious expression on her face.

"You seem to have been really close to Jack," she said. She was not beyond baiting someone to get the information she wanted, not beyond lying, if need be. And then she added, almost whispering, "He spoke of you often."

Marie straightened up and turned in her chair to face Sandra.

"He did?" she asked in a small voice.

Sandra was thinking fast. The point here was to get Marie to spill her guts, not to fabricate a bunch of lies that might make her life more difficult.

"He didn't go into much detail about you, but I got the feeling that he was dependent on you, that he relied on you." She thought that could probably be said about anyone in his family. Marie was silent. Sandra thought she would take it a step further.

"Jack did say that he would be lost without you." That seemed to do the trick.

Marie smiled a large, toothy smile, but it transformed her plain face into one that was almost beautiful.

"He did need me, that much I know. Pam didn't like a lot of the things Jack and I liked. Going to the theater, golf, swimming. Jack loved to put his suit on, grab a towel, and run down to the water. We played together in the surf like a couple of kids." She hugged herself, eyes closed, smiling. "Last year we took boogie boards so far out that the guards whistled for us to come back in. It is so shallow way out there—shallow and warm."

She thought for a while, staring out the window.

"Pam saw us and got angry at Jack, telling him that he was acting like an ass. She didn't get jealous of the time we spent together. But she didn't like to see us having fun, either. 'You should be doing those things with your children,' she said to him." Marie picked up her teacup and took a sip. It had gotten cold, but she drank it anyway. "My favorite time was late at night, after Pam went to bed. Jack and I would stay up all night playing Scrabble, with the dictionary, or poker. The kids were with us during the summer, but eventually they went away to school. The weekends were so wonderful."

Marie was becoming totally animated now, almost bouncing up and down in her seat.

"Pam looked forward to Jack coming home all week, and then when he did, she would take a book out on the veranda and read all weekend. Don't get me wrong, my sister loved Jack. She made his home peaceful, comfortable, and relaxing. She is a superb chef. He used to say that he ate like a king. When the doctor told him to lose weight last year, she was so relieved. She worried about his weight. She is in excellent shape for a middle-aged woman. She would go to the farmers' market for fresh vegetables every day when he was home, get her eggs from the guy on the corner, and all local, organic meats. She was picky about everything. And then when he went back to the city, she would eat a lettuce leaf and a can of tuna. God only knows what he ate when he wasn't home."

Sandra thought of the cheese omelet and bacon he had for his last breakfast.

"No, it wasn't that she didn't take good care of him. It was just that Pam is boring. She doesn't like to do anything but go to the gym, walk on the beach, and putter around her house—a total dud. After they moved out there, out to Long Island, she hated coming back into the city. So I started going to the theater with Jack. If he had any social obligations that required a companion, he would call me and say, 'Do you have an appropriate dress for such and such?' We went out at least once, usually twice, a week. Until a few months ago, we had lunch together almost every day. Now I know it was because of you that he stopped calling me midday. I was out there, out at the beach house, every weekend."

Her voice had gotten progressively higher and higher, faster and faster.

"I knew what I would do both Saturday and Sunday, every weekend, month after month. When the kids needed to go to visit colleges, I went with either Jack or Pam. If Pam wanted to go antiquing or to a craft show and Jack couldn't bear the thought, I would go with her. Now, nothing! There is nothing! I have to start all over again!" She lowered her head for the third time that afternoon and started crying.

Sandra understood more about Marie's relationship with the Smiths, but not about the specific intimate relationship between Jack and Marie alone. But she was almost certain there was something more than met the eye. But, for now, she had had enough. She had to find a way to get Marie out of her apartment.

She got up out of her chair and came around to Marie's, yet again. Placing a reluctant hand on her shaking shoulder, Sandra said in a soft voice, "You've had a lot today, Marie. Maybe you would benefit from a nice nap. Let me get you a cab, okay? You can be home in no time and get some rest."

Marie didn't resist, didn't argue. She stood up and straightened her shirt, then bent over to pick up her purse off the floor. Sandra walked toward the door, willing her guest to follow. They left the apartment together and walked out to the sidewalk.

"Let's walk toward Broadway, okay? It won't take long on a Sunday afternoon."

They didn't need to walk far. A cab rounded the corner, Sandra stuck her hand out, and it zoomed to the curb. She opened the door, and Marie slid in, looking straight ahead. Sandra said good-bye and shut the door for her, Marie seemingly in a trance. The cab took off.

Sandra stood there for a moment, relieved. *What the hell was that all about?* Now she most definitely was not going to Pam Smith's next weekend. She would call her and tell her tomorrow. She turned around and walked back to her apartment. Feeling drained and, if possible, worse than before, she decided she was going to take a couple of sick days. She had weeks of them available, and although she needed to save as many as possible for future use, right now she knew she couldn't go on like this much longer.

Back at her apartment, she took all the evidence of Marie to the kitchen sink and squirted dish soap and hot water all over it. She felt at loose ends. She tried to remember what she was going to do that day, and nothing presented itself. *Maybe taking days off from work wasn't a good idea after all.*

Feeling hungry, she decided to walk to Big Nick's and get a burger. She would get fries, too. She went to her closet and took a long-sleeved blue denim shirt that a long forgotten date had left behind and pulled it on over her sleeveless shirt and spandex. She felt disheveled. It was evidence of her being at the end of herself that she would go out in public with her hair pulled back in a ponytail, no makeup, and spandex and denim. She went to her jewelry box and pulled a wide, colorful enameled bracelet out and shoved it above her elbow. She slipped low-heeled mules on and checked herself out in the mirrored closet door, confirming she looked okay. She put on a small brimmed straw hat and dark glasses, grabbed her wallet and keys, and went out the door.

The sun was just starting to bend over the river. She walked up Eighty-second toward Broadway, looking at the houses along the block, the bright sun, the blue sky, the beautiful brownstones, and the old church on the corner. *God, I love this neighborhood.* She thought for a moment what raising a child would be like here in the Upper West Side. It was fate that she moved there four years ago, just out of college. It was fate that she lived on a street that had the best day care in the city at the local Methodist church. It was fate that she had a two-bedroom apartment. She slowed her walk, humbled at these facts that her life seemed to have been preparing for just this moment in time. For the first time, she realized how absolutely lucky she had been to be transferred from the Bronx to Wall Street. Without that, she would have never met Jack. Suddenly, she realized that she loved her baby. She loved the little tadpole, or whatever it was, the two cells that had joined and were rapidly dividing and expanding and were now big enough to have caused her body to respond to its presence. She stopped and looked up at the sky.

Without hesitating, she said, "Thank you, God."

20

Bernice Smith was riding in a car, having spent the week at her son Bill's house in the Village. She never got tired of looking at the buildings as they passed. The montage of the buildings, the people, and the angle of the sun was never the same. She especially loved driving through the Village. The old storefronts, in the summer some with planters overflowing with colorful annuals, and in the winter, Christmas lights decorating the windows, people sitting at tables, drinking wine, talking, and laughing.

As the cab approached Columbus Avenue and her neighborhood in the Upper West Side, she no longer looked out the window. It was where she had lived for the past sixty years, where she had raised her boys. Now her only surviving son, Bill, had done what he could this past week from hell to keep her sane. He insisted that she stay with him and his wife, Anne, and their two boys for as long as she was comfortable. She knew when she got up that morning that she wanted to try going home. Monday was a new day. Like Pam, she liked starting out the week on Monday—a clean slate, ready to be filled with activities and with friends and family.

Since Harold died the year before, she no longer took the same comfort in being in her home, in her beloved neighborhood. Places that she had loved previously now caused her pain. She couldn't look at the buildings on Broadway near her house on Eighty-ninth. She no longer went into her favorite coffee shop since Harold died, less that he was not there to go with her, but because it was a place that she and Jack had loved together, had dined at weekly, until that horrible, painful discovery. And now, even he was gone. There was no chance for restitution, for penance. She would go to her grave soon (she hoped) with an unresolved heartache, the knowledge that she had hurt her son and destroyed what had been a full and enviable relationship by an omission. Its purpose was open to examination if only he would have. The opportunity never presented itself because he refused to hear her out.

Her objective this week, one that she was determined to complete, was to gather what items she had of her son's and make a shrine for him. She was not a particularly religious person, but she was spiritual, and she must have some method of being close to him. She would do what she could to garner his forgiveness, albeit late. If only she had known she would have tried harder to engage him, shown up at his office, or hounded his wife for more invitations to the beach. Whatever it would have taken, she should have done it. She should have forced it.

She was at the light at Broadway and Eighty-second Street when she saw a young, glamorous woman rounding the corner, walking south. She looked so familiar; she had just seen her. And then she remembered—at Jack's funeral. Although she was dressed in a suit that day, her hair and dark glasses gave her away. She suddenly felt she must speak to the young woman right that minute. She must have been a colleague of his; she sat with Pete at the funeral. She could tell her about Jack at work. What he must have been like around the office. She knocked on the glass, and the driver reached over and pressed a button to open it.

"Let me out here, please." He pulled over while Bernice kept her eye on the young woman. She opened the door herself, getting out on the street side and leaving the door open for the driver to get.

Traffic was light, and she didn't have to wait long until she could safely cross the street. She walked quickly; she was in good shape for a seventy-seven-year-old woman. When she reached the other side, she continued south on Broadway, keeping her eye on the woman, who stopped and turned into a storefront. Bernice could smell onions frying the closer she got, and looking up, she saw the sign, Big Nick's. *Oh well, my clothes can be cleaned*, she thought.

She entered the restaurant, noticing right away that she was not the usual customer, but she did not care. They wouldn't refuse her service because she was overdressed. The grill was right at the front of the place, the window greasy. She saw the young woman seated at a table in the back. Bernice slowly walked toward the woman, who had taken her dark glasses off but left her straw hat on. She was reading the menu, not seeing who was around her. Bernice approached her slowly and paused at the table, waiting until the woman, girl, really, looked up from her menu. When she did, she looked slightly frightened, with recognition on her face.

Bernice smiled warmly at her. "Forgive me, please, for interrupting you. My name is Bernice Smith. I believe we met on Tuesday." She waited, smiling, patient. Sandra, shocked beyond speech, tried to stand up, but Bernice touched her shoulder. "Please, don't get up. I saw you from the car window and needed to talk to you, if that is okay. I hoped we could talk about Jack, what he was like at work." She continued to smile down at Sandra, who finally found her voice.

"Please sit down. Join me for dinner, won't you?" She realized that a burger at Big Nick's might not be Mrs. Smith's idea of a meal. "We don't have to stay here," she said.

"Nonsense," Bernice said. "I feel like eating some-thing different from my usual Sunday-night can of soup." She picked up the menu and saw that salads were abun-dant on it. When the waitress arrived, Sandra ordered a burger, fries, and a chocolate milk shake, and Bernice got a garden salad.

"What can I tell you about Jack?" Sandra couldn't help staring at Bernice Smith. She was stunning, at least five feet ten inches. She was straight as an arrow, not hunched over at all. *Must be from exercise*, Sandra thought. She had her hair cut since the funeral; it was very short, no more than an inch at the most, and stood out like feathers on top and combed smooth on the sides. Her makeup was perfect. Her skin was taut and smooth, and Sandra didn't see evidence of any plastic surgery, but she must have had some.

"What was he like at work? You know, I have never been to his office, at least since they moved it downtown. When the only branch was in the Bronx, I used to go up every week and have lunch with my son. It was the high-light of my week." She stopped then, thinking of the final betrayal, the final straw. "I did something to hurt him, unintentionally, and now he is gone. I can never make it up to him." Out of character, she lowered her head and started to weep, right there in Big Nick's.

Sandra couldn't take it. She reached across the table and grabbed Bernice's hand.

"He loved you so much, Mrs. Smith, he really did. Whatever it was that happened between the two of you, he never mentioned a word."

Bernice looked at her curiously. Sandra had revealed too much. She began to feel awful that his involvement with her took time away from the people who loved and needed him the most—his mother and Marie. Both used to lunching with him, seeing him for dinner when he was in the city all week, blamed themselves for his abrupt exodus from their routine, when, in fact she thought it probabl had nothing at all to do with them.

The waiter approached with their food, and Bernice patted the area under her eyes with a hankie, blotting away the tears and keeping her makeup intact. Jack had been surrounded by a bevy of vain women. She picked at her salad, the confessional proving to be an appetite depressant.

Sandra couldn't look at her food. She sipped the milk shake, fighting the sudden urge to confess everything to this stranger, hoping the tale of infidelity would give the needed excuse for his behavior without tainting his mother's opinion of him. She would think about it.

"Where do you live? Here? Close by?" Bernice asked. "You know I am just a few blocks from here, don't you? Our place is on Columbus and Ninety-fourth."

"Actually, I'm just up Broadway on Eighty-second. Jack told me that his mother was close by." She may have revealed more than she bargained for by confessing that. *Why would Jack have talked about his mother to an employee?* It was too late.

Bernice finished with her salad, pushed the plate to the edge of the table.

"This may sound strange, but could we exchange phone numbers? I feel like we need to stay in touch. Maybe because of Jack, I am not sure. It feels so strange, actually." Bernice chuckled. "Maybe I am getting old after all."

Sandra couldn't take anymore. That comment, yet another swipe meant to take blame for something she had nothing to do with, made the decision for Sandra. She would reveal her relationship with Jack to his mother. She would need to know in nine months anyway.

"Are you finished eating? I would like to talk to you, but this isn't the place." Sandra pushed her untouched plate away and reached for the check.

"I'll get that," Bernice said. "Do you want to come up to my house?" she asked.

"I hate to impose." Sandra didn't know if either of their homes was the right place to lay this out. It might be the worst possible thing to do. She hesitated. *It was so early. What if the pregnancy didn't take?* Sandra decided she wanted an ally, a witness to the tiny cells growing in her, part of this woman's son.

"My car is right across the street. Come home with me. I'll make tea, and we can talk there. Now you have my curiosity! An old woman doesn't get many chances to hear interesting news!"

Sandra thought, *What an understatement.*

They left the restaurant. When she said she had a car, Sandra thought a regular car, not a limo. But there it was, the driver leaning against the side, waiting. When he saw Bernice, he put his finger up and got into the car.

"He will pull around. God forbid we have to walk across the street!" she said, smiling.

The car pulled out, and the man maneuvered it in a perfect U-turn. He hopped out and opened the door for the two women, ignoring Sandra. They got up to her house in record time. Sandra tried not to gawk. It was a huge five-story brownstone. There was a deep front yard enclosed in grand wrought iron. *Its price would be, well, without price!* She couldn't imagine living there. *Why would Jack have that bland apartment when there was this fabulous place right at his disposal?* She would never know.

"Oh my God! This house!" Sandra exclaimed.

Bernice laughed out loud.

"Isn't it wonderful? We raised our boys here. It belonged to Harold's family first, so it is full of family treasures. We updated everything, although you would never know it. Harold was a stickler about historical accuracy and all of that baloney."

She led the way up the walk, opening the gate and shutting it behind her. The car pulled into a driveway, which was also gated with a long, double gate that opened automatically. *The car would disappear around the back of the house, to what? Garages? Who had this kind of money anymore?* By the time they got to the front door, a beautiful, deep-oak double door, a uniformed maid opened it, greeting the women with a big smile.

"Welcome back, madam!" she said.

Madam? Sandra felt totally underdressed in her spandex and denim. This might have been a big mistake.

The maid stepped aside, taking Bernice's purse, and closing the door behind them.

"Tea and sandwiches in the den, okay, Mildred?" Bernice gave the order, and the maid smiled and walked to the rear of the house. *Who else worked here?* "You didn't eat a thing, and that garden salad was just for show. We will have a real meal now."

Sandra followed her, Bernice walking backward when she spoke, stretching her arm to point out portraits of the boys in their youth and Jack's tennis racket encased in a shadow box with awards surrounding it—things of interest only to the family in residence. It was a real home.

Calling the room a den was an understatement. It was at least a thousand square feet. At one end, there was a huge walk-in fireplace surrounded by beautiful leather furniture, wingback chairs, and solid tables and flanked by fifteen-foot-high bookcases. On the other side of the room was a flat-screen TV that took up half the wall.

Bernice saw her looking at it.

"It's a three-D. There are blackout curtains on the windows. We have a theater in the basement, but I don't like subterranean rooms."

In the center of the room, there was a pool table with legs that were covered with carvings, and there were three game tables—a room that a family would play in. Along the walls stood eight pinball machines. *It was an arcade!* She imagined the grandchildren loved coming here.

Bernice led her to the fireplace end of the room. Somehow, she had managed to make this area feel intimate and cozy, in spite of being surrounded by fun and games.

How did she do it?

There were two wingback chairs on either side of a high round table, a tea table. Bernice pointed to one of the chairs and told Sandra to make herself comfortable. She excused herself to change out of her suit, promising it wouldn't take but a minute, and asked her to, please, not wait, to start eating without her.

She was gone less than a minute when Mildred returned with a tray covered with a white linen cloth. Another worker followed, pushing a cart with the tea items, including a large silver tea service. Efficiently and quickly, they set everything up on the table. Mildred poured tea into a cup and offered it to Sandra, pointing out the sugar and cream as well as the honey and lemon. The linen-covered tray was uncovered, revealing a delicious-looking selection of sandwiches, pastries, cookies, and petit fours. Mildred, forcing her to eat, handed her a plate and presented her with the tray. She balanced the tray on her forearm and placed little cakes and what looked like a cream-cheese sandwich on her plate.

"Take more," she said.

Sandra laughed out loud. "I just ate!"

"Hogwash!" Bernice was back, looking youthful and comfortable in a black cotton outfit with drawstring pants and a short-sleeved shirt. She took a plate and piled on sandwiches.

Sandra took a cream-cheese sandwich first; it was a sweet rye bread and had smoked turkey with horseradish. Bernice pointed out nut bread with a gorgonzola cream cheese spread and half a fresh pear sliced on it. They were so delicious that Sandra forgot that she was in this stately mansion and ate like a starving boy. There was butter lettuce with a ham spread on white bread and a small hard roll with butter and some kind of anchovy paste on it, with a slice of cherry tomato. It was meant to be popped into your mouth.

"Is anyone joining us? Or is this all for us?" Sandra asked, smiling.

Bernice told her it was just for them.

She drank more tea and then started in on the desserts. The petit fours were filled with almond paste or milk-chocolate cream or vanilla custard. She ate one of each kind. When she couldn't eat another mouthful, Bernice instructed Mildred to package up the leftovers for Sandra to take home. She would have delicious lunches this week, at the very least.

They sat in their chairs then, looking out the bank of french doors, which lead out to a courtyard. Mildred had opened one of the doors, and Sandra could hear the water fountain, meant to block the noise from Broadway. She didn't care about that. She knew they were only a block from Central Park. She loved the city so much.

Bernice grasped her shoulder.

"Oh my God! I am so sorry!" Sandra sat up abruptly, having fallen asleep. *What the hell is wrong with me?* She looked up at Bernice, who was looking down at her with motherly concern.

"I would have let you go on sleeping, but you cried out. I was afraid you were having a bad dream," she said.

"How long was I out?"

"Not long at all, about twenty minutes. You must be exhausted." Bernice pulled up an ottoman and sat in front of Sandra.

"It was probably the anchovy paste and the chocolate cream." Sandra said, embarrassed. "I should probably get going. I've infringed on your hospitality long enough."

"Don't go yet," Bernice said. "I have the feeling you were on the verge of telling me something about my son." She looked at Sandra with a penetrating gaze. The trays of food had been removed when Sandra was in nod land. She needed to empty her bladder.

"Can I use the ladies' room?" she asked. Bernice showed her the way.

The bathroom was as elegant and exquisite as the rest of the house. The tile was a work of art; the stained-glass windows, she assumed, were Tiffany; and the fabulous vessel sink of a cobalt-blue glass was hand blown, with a gorgeous goose-neck faucet.

People really did live this way.

When she came out, Bernice had gone back to the den. She stood when Sandra came into the room, pointing toward the courtyard.

"Let's sit outside, shall we? The bugs aren't bad yet, and the traffic has died down. Sunday evening is the best out here." She started to walk out. "It is surprising how rarely I do sit out here. When the boys were young, they loved this part of the house, and you could always find them here. Harold built them a tree house in that ancient oak. We thought the neighbors would sue us for harming it, but the house wasn't really nailed to the tree. They are really such asses. We had a portable pool, not really portable, because it was inground, but just a vinyl thing that Harold sunk into the ground, knowing that when they grew up, they would no longer use it. It was small, but they loved it." She turned to look at Sandra then. They were sitting at a round glass table, what you would expect in the courtyard of a mansion in the middle of New York City. "What did you want to tell me, dear?"

Sandra decided that she would not be apologetic. She would state the facts, as she knew them.

"I was having an affair with Jack. That is why he no longer spent as much time with you, not because he was angry or disappointed about anything. It was because he was with me." There, she had said it. But there was more. She would get it out now, rather than later. Give her time to mash it through. "And I just found out today that I am pregnant. Not far, just a few weeks. But I knew right away that my life has been preparing for this moment for years. And you finding me in Big Nick's in the middle of Manhattan, that was no coincidence." She stopped, sat back, and took a deep breath. She was afraid to look over at Bernice. Of course, Bernice would be loyal to Pam. She was her daughter-in-law and Jack's wife. But the truth, although not easy to hear, would be better in the long run. Her baby deserved that much.

"Let me think for a moment" was all Bernice said. She was staring off into the night. While all of this was happening, the sun went down, and it was evening. She moved her hand under the table and must have pressed a hidden button because Mildred appeared with yet another tray, this time with a pot of coffee, cream and sugar, and two cups.

"It's decaf" was all she said. Mildred left it and Bernice poured.

"Want a cup?" she asked, distracted. Sandra was a little worried that Bernice may be angry. She waited, picking up the cup and saucer, grateful for the distraction. Finally, Bernice looked at her. "There is more to this that needs to be discussed. You have no idea the parallels in our lives. None. You couldn't know. But I think we have had enough for one evening. You, young woman, have work tomorrow. Jack may have told you that I am a stickler about work. Easy for me, right, who has never punched a timecard?" She laughed out loud. "But that is neither here nor there. If it were Saturday, I would beg you to spend the night. But you must get home and get ready for tomorrow. You are carrying my grandchild; you must get rest and take care of yourself." She stood up, wringing her hands. "I just thought of poor, silly Pam. What will she make of all of this?"

Reeling from the insult to Pam, Sandra simply stated, "She knows about me, but not the baby."

Bernice led her out of the den. She was not so much dismissing her, as trying to do what was best for her. Mildred appeared with a large brown kraft paper bag with Whole Foods printed on it in green ink. It was filled to the brim with foil-wrapped food and plastic containers of who knows what. She would have plenty to eat this week.

"Ben will take you home. I must think about everything. You understand?"

Sandra was taken aback. *Loving kindness must run in this family.* Silly or not, Pam was the most understanding woman she had ever met, and now Jack's mother, showing such graciousness in the face of her son's sexual misconduct with a girl young enough to be his daughter.

"Thank you for this afternoon; it was really lovely. I am grateful for your kindness," Sandra said.

Bernice walked her to the car, the driver standing there with the door open, and Bernice kissed her cheek before she got in.

"Good-bye, my dear. Please call me tomorrow, okay? Promise!"

Sandra replied, "Yes, of course. Good-bye, Bernice."

The car sped out of the driveway. The driver seemed to know right where to go, wasting no time. She was at her door in five minutes. She said good-bye to him and ran to her door. He watched her until she was safely inside.

When her apartment door closed, she was flooded with relief. The stress of the meeting would be apparent later in the night, when she couldn't sleep. *Would Bernice be on the phone with Pam, this very minute, telling her the news that her husband would be a father again?* The derision of Pam by those who were supposed to love her was difficult to bear. Sandra fell on the couch in a stupor, with her head thrown back and legs sprawled apart. She wondered why she hadn't stayed in that afternoon. She sat up and put her head in her hands. Then she looked up at the ceiling. *Was this yet another part of the plan for her life?*

Running into Jack's mother like that...*It wasn't even running into her! She had sought me out on the street. How did she even remember me from the funeral? Did she have a premonition about me when she saw me that day? Why would she cross Broadway, risking her life, and chase me down in Big Nick's?* Sandra would never forget that first glance as she looked up from her menu and saw the elegant woman standing there, so completely out of place in that greasy restaurant, dressed in a beige silk suit, perfectly groomed. Sandra shuddered to think what she must have thought of her own getup—spandex, denim, and a straw hat, for God's sake. *Oh well, what a hell of a day.*

21

The cab pulled up in the front of Marie's building. She wasn't sure where she was. Sandra must have paid the driver because he didn't say anything to her but "Here you are." *Had she even told him where she lived?*

She opened the door and got out of the cab. Slowly, she made her way up to the door of her apartment building, barely having the strength to open it. She got into the elevator and pushed her floor button, feeling like she was under water. Even the sound of the elevator motor was distant, muted. She wondered if she was having a nervous breakdown. Stumbling into her apartment, she was suddenly stricken with a stomachache so ferocious that it could only mean she must get to the bathroom immediately.

When she was finished, she was so glad she had made it home, because if that had come across her in the cab, she would have shit all over the place. She wondered what the hell was wrong. Then she remembered that she never got any food when she went out. Here she was, ill, both physically and mentally, in an apartment in Midtown with no food. There was literally nothing to eat. She would call in a favor. God knew she was always available to anyone who needed her, and now, she was in need. She picked up her phone and keyed in her mother's number first. Nelda answered on the first ring.

"Mom, I'm sick. I need you to get on a bus and come here." She tried not to sound whiney.

"What's wrong with you?" Her mother was a bundle of sympathy. "It's going to be dark soon. What could I do to make you feel better?"

"Mom, I just need you to come here. I'm lightheaded, I have diarrhea, and there is nothing to eat here. I was out, trying to shop and had to take a cab home." No point in telling her the truth, and it was almost true.

"Just drink water and go to bed. For heaven's sake, Marie! Why do you let yourself run out of food anyway?"

It was clear Nelda was not going to budge from Brooklyn.

"Thank you, Mother. I knew I could count on you." She hung up without saying good-bye. But she did feel better already.

Goddamn it, there has to be something to eat in this house! She went into the kitchen and started opening cupboards. She had a box of spaghetti. She would make that with some butter. It would help her stomach. She got a pan out of the cupboard next to the stove and filled it with water, putting it on the burner.

While Marie was fixing her meager dinner, uptown, Sandra was putting away the contents of the bag of goodies Bernice Smith had insisted she take with her.

There were foil packages of sandwiches and little cakes, several baggies of homemade cookies, plastic containers of Jell-O salad with fruit, and what looked like sandwich filling. There was also a foil-wrapped loaf of homemade bread. She decided to assemble a lunch for herself tomorrow. In the morning, it might seem like too much trouble. She took the already-made sandwiches and baggie of cookies and put them in a brown paper sack and stuck it back in the fridge. Then she put the teakettle on. *One more cup before bedtime*, she thought. She was exhausted, but it was a ritual she wasn't about to skip. She needed all the comfort she could right now. Jack didn't drink tea, and now she was glad. It wasn't something that would have one bit of association with him.

She picked up the phone and saw that Pam had called her. Jack's family was starting to get on her nerves. She decided to delay the return call until the next day. She would call her from work; it would give her a chance to hang up if things got dicey.

She went into her room while the kettle heated up and got out her clothes for work. She took a navy-blue suit out of the closet. Still covered in a cleaner's bag, there were warnings printed all over it to keep it away from children, as it was a suffocation danger. She shuddered. There would be all kinds of new dangers heretofore unheeded.

She thought about her own well-being. She would be more careful from now on about eating and not skipping meals. She had a hot flash of fear, wondering how many glasses of wine she drank in the past several weeks. She sat down and started counting. *Oh God, please*, she thought, *don't let anything be wrong with the baby*. She decided to call her gynecologist first thing in the morning and make an appointment. It might be early, but she wasn't taking any chances.

The teakettle started whistling. She had her lunch ready, her clothes were laid out, and her tea was made. She could sit up in bed and write in her journal, for God knew she had enough for several entries. She wanted to document all the coincidences that had happened that "brought her to this place." That phrase was her mantra. She would try not to complain about anything from this day forward; it was all part of the plan.

22

Bernice closed the door after she saw Sandra off. Mildred was in the den cleaning up after the coffee. She went in and told her she was going up to bed. The stairs seemed so steep that night. Her age was creeping up on her. She promised herself she would work extra hard at the gym the next day. There was no room for decrepitude now. A new grandchild would be coming in nine months. She wanted to be available to care for him or her in every way.

She giggled. *What was dear Pam going to say when the news of the baby came to her ears?* Bernice couldn't think of a nicer person to have this happen to. She thought of her daughter-in-law, mistaking her shyness with snobbery, even after all of these years, not knowing her character at all. *It would serve her right.*

Once in her room, she closed the door behind her. Framed pictures of her men adorned the fireplace mantel. She picked up Jack's picture and took it with her to her chair. She sat down with it in her lap, running her hand across the glass, tracing his face with her fingertip. She held it up to look at it, and in a clear, soft voice, she said to the image of her dead son, "Touché."

23

Monday morning, day of new beginnings. Pam was already sick of that trite phrase and did her best to banish it from her thoughts and her speech. She felt horrible when she got up. Going through her routine early, before the sun was fully up, she realized how much she had underestimated her capacity for grief. She was able to go through the motions of life, taking care of her physical needs, but there it stopped. She forced herself through her day.

The most important act that day would be the reading of the will. She knew what it looked like superficially. Jack's mother and brother had no need for his money. He would leave the bulk of what they had to her, keep the trusts for the kids intact, and give something to Marie to take the pinch off working, but not eliminate the need for it altogether. *She should work for a living.* Other than that, the only real snare left to untangle would be the company. Jack owned half of it, and Peter owned the other half. They had never spoken about what it would mean if he died. There must be something in the corporation papers that would be revealed when necessary.

She needed to be at the lawyers by nine-thirty a.m., so she went to the gym first. She wanted to be out of the house when the cleaning lady and her entourage showed up. At least her morning would be occupied.

Across the world, what was left of her family was starting their day as well. Her mother was puttering around her kitchen, preparing her coffee and breakfast, avoiding the phone, which had started ringing at daybreak. She knew Marie was angry that her mother had ignored her cry for help, and it would be a tough day trying to get out of talking to her. She didn't put it past her daughter to make a surprise visit to Brooklyn to harass her.

Nelda was tired. She raised four daughters, and three of them married—well, now two of them, as Pammy was a widow at such a young age. Susan and Sharon were happily married and had lovely husbands and children. And then there was Marie. She should have never had her. One more child about did her in. From the get go, Marie was a clingy, needy kid. Fortunately, Pam, her eldest, loved her like her own from the beginning. Nelda was able to easily resume her life with all the assistance Pam gave her with the new baby.

When Marie needed a parent, after a fall or something happening at school, friends would ask, "Does it bother you that the child goes to her sister instead of you?" And she could frankly say no. When Pam met Jack, everyone knew they would get married right away. *They were so young!* And Marie was furious, crying, clinging to Pam. She was inconsolable at the wedding shower, refusing to participate in the games, whining and yelling if anyone came near her. And, of course, rather than spanking her ass as the other girls would have had done to them, her father and sister caved, promising her she could go see the newlyweds every weekend.

Nelda could never understand how Pam could tolerate that intrusion of privacy. Nelda fought with her husband passionately about it, but nothing changed. Once Pam got married, Marie practically moved in with her and Jack. During the week, when she was at home, the only leverage Nelda had was the threat that if Marie didn't behave, there would be no trip into the city for the weekend. And she used it to her best advantage. That kid had the neatest room, the highest grades, and the most perfect behavior. But when Friday came, she was history. Either Jack or Pam would pick Marie up after school and take her back into town. They would always stop in and see Nelda first, which was lovely. Then there would be peace and quiet for the weekend.

But, occasionally, Nelda would want Marie to stay home for a family outing. The repercussions would be horrible. Again, the only leverage would be the threat that if she didn't cooperate and be on her best behavior with a smile on her face, she wouldn't go back to Pam's for a very long time.

Nelda could see the error of that now. There was something not totally right about the whole Pam-Jack-Marie thing, but as yet, nothing had come to light. Her daughter was trying her best to manipulate her mother, but it would never happen. Nelda was too strong for that. If any nighttime forays would take place, they would be to Long Island to help out Pam. It would be interesting to see how the dynamic would change now that Jack was gone. *Would Marie still cling to Pam? Or had it been only Jack who was the attraction?* Time would soon tell.

Marie struggled to get to work on Monday. It was never easy, but Mondays were awful. Usually, she would be coming in from Long Island with Jack. He would drop her off at the Fulton Street Station, and she would take the train up one stop, get off, and get the crosstown bus to her office. The entire trip took two hours, and by the time she lugged her suitcase up the steps of the building, she was ready to call it a day and go home. In spite of the fact that she had only a few blocks to walk on this particular Monday, she was still exhausted. The night before had been horrible as she tossed and turned, the slights of the day running through her head. The retorts she didn't give at the time haunted her for the rest of the night.

Her encounter with Sandra was especially troubling. *Why did I treat the woman so poorly?* Sandra never reacted, never got defensive. All the while, Marie insulted her and cursed at her. It was unbelievable that she had sunk to such a low. She would have to make some kind of restitution. If Sandra ever spoke of it to Pam, there would be hell to pay in the family. Pam. She questioned why she cared what Pam thought. But the truth was, she did care, terribly. Pam was her light, her strength. She paved the way to love, to life for her. Without Pam, there would have been no Jack, no Lisa and Brent, no purpose to living. Old childhood patterns reemerged; she would work hard all week, be kind to her associates, apologize to Sandra, and go to Pam's on Saturday as she had for most of her life. She was hopeful she would find Jack there again.

Sandra was straightening her desk when the call came through. Her assistant buzzed, "Bernice Smith on line two." Sandra thought she might hear from Jack's mother that day, but not first thing. She hadn't had time to rehearse what she would say to her. *Oh well.* She picked up the phone.

"Sandra Benson," she answered.

"Sandra, it's Bernice Smith. How are you this morning?" They exchanged pleasantries, and then Bernice got right to the point. "I thought about your...um...condition all night. First of all, let me tell you how thrilled I am!"

That caught Sandra off guard. *Happy, accepting, resigned, but thrilled?* She wasn't sure about this.

"I've been thinking," she continued. "I need to talk to you. There are some parallels here that are fascinating that I would like to share with you. But that aside, I have a suggestion, a request, really." She paused, seeming to be collecting her thoughts. "I don't think you should tell the others—not yet. I am going to come right out and say this, with the knowledge that you may be offended, but we have to have the truth between us at all times. Is that a deal?"

Sandra agreed, wishing the woman would get it out and over with.

"I'm afraid they would try to pressure you into having an abortion. Of course, you would refuse, but that seems like such an ugly way to great our newest member into the world. I tried to imagine what Jack would think, what he would advise. I know he would say, 'It's no one's goddamned business.'"

Sandra sat down. She didn't like the idea of keeping Pam out of the loop. It seemed like one more cruelty to someone already betrayed.

"Bernice, can I think about this? I appreciate your concern, I really do. I also feel as though I want everything to be straight-up between us. I just need to think a bit more before making a decision."

They agreed and then said their good-byes.

Sandra pushed the buzzer on the phone. When it was answered, she said, "No more calls for an hour, okay?" It seemed like Jack's family traveled in multiples. She was sure there would be more calls from them to follow Bernice's, and she didn't think she could handle anymore.

24

Pam struggled at the gym. Each exercise was more brutal than the last. She couldn't have imagined working with the trainer that day. When she was finished, no amount of lipstick reapplication was going to help her. She went back home and started over again, getting in the shower, washing her hair, reapplying her makeup, and blow-drying her hair. She was ten minutes early to the attorney's office, a feat considering her morning thus far. He was running behind, and his secretary offered to get her a cup of coffee. She was tempted to ask how old it was, and thought, *I pay him a fortune for his services, and I deserve fresh coffee.* So she asked. The secretary said she had just made it. So, yes, Pam would have some coffee.

It was good, too, strong and bitter. Pam sat in the comfortable office and drank her coffee, getting out her calendar and checking the week. She had two more important dates—her meeting with Peter in the city and Social Security. Bernice thought it was quite amusing that Pam was going to file for Jack's Social Security benefits for the children. Pam became rather annoyed at that, pointing out that Bernice didn't think it was amusing when she started collecting at age sixty-five. They were rich as Roosevelt, yet that check arrived each month.

And, of course, if Sandra agreed, she would have company for the weekend. She thought it was a contradiction that, last week, she couldn't wait for everyone to leave, and now, this week, she couldn't wait for them to come back. It was the tyranny of urgent, she decided. On one hand, her emotions were so flat at the moment that she was concerned for herself, yet on the other hand, she willed every person she encountered not to say anything that would cause her to lose control. She would have to find the middle ground somewhere. She could hear Brent's voice, *Give yourself a break, Mother!* She would try.

The attorney finally came into the room and greeted her, offering his hand to her. She took it, stood up, and followed him back to his private office. It was a beautiful place. Everything was clean and new, his carpeting obviously custom, with the initials of the firm in a petite-point weave. It was almost gauche; it spoke of wealth, and more specifically, the wealth of his clients. Pam found herself annoyed at the blatant display of money. She would consider changing attorneys if everything didn't go perfectly, preferring to give her money to someone struggling. He put a folder down in front of her and took one up for himself.

"How was the last week for you?" he asked. "I can't imagine what you are going through."

She was grateful for that last comment. Someone at the funeral had said to her, "I know how hard this must be." Pam, always gracious, couldn't stop herself from saying, "Do you? I thought your husband was still alive." Lisa, overhearing, rushed over to lead her mother away.

"Let's read this together, okay?" The lawyer continued. " First of all, Jack revised his will two months ago, without your knowledge. I realize that the information is going to come as a shock to you, Pam, but he didn't change the terms of the will as far and you and the children are concerned. He simply added a codicil to it, which instructs the disbursement of the business." Thumbing through the sheath of papers, he continued, "Control of his share of Lane, Smith and Romney to Miss Sandra Elizabeth Benson. You, Lisa, and Brent will continue to receive the same amount of income from his share. Miss Benson will pick up a portion of Jack's draw. If she decides to sell it, you will have first refusal." He stopped at that point, looking at her to see if she understood.

Pam had always thought the business would go to Brent. She was confused now. Maybe this was how she would find the anger she needed to vent against her wayward husband.

"I gather Miss Benson is not news to you," he said.

She looked at him, shaking her head.

"No, it's not news. But this is. I rather thought he would take Brent on as a partner someday. Why would he give such a huge gift to Sandra? It doesn't make sense. Why not just give her money?"

"We will probably never know what he had in mind. I got the feeling that he knew he was going to die soon." He was watching her to see how she absorbed this news.

"You are the second person to have said that. Where was I while he was planning his demise? Honestly, I must have been in a daze." She could feel herself beginning to lose her self-control. It mustn't happen here, in this office. "Are we almost done?" she asked. "I need to take this in alone, at home." She stood up.

He reached for her hand and walked around his desk, preparing to lead her out.

"The insurance company has been contacted with the death certificate. You should be receiving a check from them soon. All of the bank accounts will be transferred to your name. Are you okay for cash in the meantime? I don't think you'll have any problems cashing checks, but just in case, take this." He reached into his wallet and produced a plastic gift card. "It's a few hundred dollars, just in case."

She took it from him, knowing it came from Jack's money. They kept thousands in a safe in the house, but she wasn't going to reveal that to him. She thanked him and scurried out of the office before they could remember she had to sign something or the secretary said anything more to her. She had enough of that place.

She got into her car and slammed the door. It was hot, but the heat felt good. She grasped the top of the steering wheel and put her head down on her forearms. *What did this all mean? Why would Jack give his business to Sandra? If Pam and the children continued to get their share of the profits from it, how would that benefit Sandra?* Jack may have been losing it himself at that point. She would never know. She did know that Brent had no interest in his father's business, and that was the only consolation she had. Her mother and sisters would never hear this revelation from her. It was sort of disrespectful of him—worse than sleeping with Sandra, than loving Sandra. She wanted a relationship with Sandra based on their mutual respect for each other, not because she was beholden to Sandra for her livelihood.

She started the car and pulled out of the parking space. There was no one she could talk to, no one who knew all the players, the details. Bernice would be a good person to bounce all of it off of if she knew the story of Sandra and Jack, but that wasn't happening, at least not if she had anything to say about it.

That afternoon, Jack's lawyer called Sandra and asked her if they could get together, as there were some things in Jack's will that pertained to her and he needed to get her signature on a couple of things as soon as possible. Sandra hung up the phone thinking, *What next? What could Jack have possibly said or done in his will that would involve me?* She imagined him leaving her a thousand dollars. *But that amount would hardly require a signature, would it?* He'd stick a check in the mail with a note, "Jack's legacy to you."

They made plans to meet at a coffee shop by the Brooklyn Bridge. He didn't have a Manhattan office anymore but needed to come into the city to give his daughter, a student at Barnard, her birthday present. He'd run his errand and then meet Sandra after work. She didn't mind going out of her way for what could end up being half her rent. As it turned out, it was a whole lot more.

They met and each ordered coffee. Sandra was too nervous to eat anything and wanted to get it over with. Folders were produced, and the lawyer began to read from a thick wad of papers attached by a giant clip. The essence of the will was that Jack was giving his half of the business to Sandra. She would collect a draw each year, enough to live comfortably and without worry. *And,* she added silently, *enough to support our baby, give her or him a good, secure life,*

173

and have a savings, a future. The profits from the business would continue to go to Pam and to the trust set up for his two children. The year before, it had made well over two million dollars in profits, split with Peter. If Sandra wished to sell her half, Pam had first right of refusal, followed by Peter.

She was dumbfounded. She sat with her mouth partly open, staring at him. She didn't know where to begin. *In the first place, what was Peter going to say?* According to the lawyer, he already knew. Jack had clued him two months ago, and although he probably thought, at the time, that there was no chance in hell of his partner dying, he did. He died, just like that. And Sandra was Peter's partner.

This was simply the preliminary meeting; there would be a meeting of the partners and corporate attorneys in a week. In the meantime, if she didn't already have a lawyer, she needed to get one. He could recommend someone in town who would watch over her and protect her rights from the dreaded Peter.

She was in shock. *And what was Pam going to say?* The lawyer told her that Pam was confused. That was all he would say. She would call Pam as soon as she got home that night. She stood up and shook the man's hand and left the coffee shop. City Hall was across the street. She walked toward the subway entrance, still numb. The crowds were thick at this time of the evening, but she didn't feel or much care about the jostling she was getting, pushed on the train and packed in like a sardine. She stood up, holding on to a filthy pole until she reached her stop.

Getting off the train in a throng of people, with the fresh air coming down the steps of the station and hitting her in the face, she felt her gorge rising. She rushed up the stairs to get some fresh air. She hailed a cab, anxious to get the few short blocks home without getting sick.

Her apartment was cool. She let herself in and went right to the bathroom, running the water and washing her face in the cold stream, brushing her teeth, and letting the cold water flow over her hands. She turned the water off and grabbed a towel, drying her face and looking in the mirror. The gaunt, pale stranger who stared back at her was a scary apparition. *So this is what you get when you commit adultery*, she thought. The guilt she was feeling was making her sick. She had to purge it soon, that night if possible, by talking to Pam. Whatever Pam wanted, she would do. If Pam was angry about the business, and she had every right to be, she could have it.

She changed into her beloved spandex and T-shirt and went to the kitchen to put on her teakettle. She picked up the phone and saw that Pam had called, as had her sister, Bernice, Peter, and a number she didn't recognize. The urge to flee or hide was strong. She made her tea, got a pen and paper, and sat at the table, looking out at her tree and birdhouse in the lowering light. She picked up the phone and dialed Pam's number.

25

Pam drove the car through town, trying to decide if she should just go home or if she should try to stay out a little longer. There was nothing she needed at the food store, and she didn't feel like mall shopping. She passed a small framing shop, an art gallery, and a gift shop. Pulling into a space in front, she got out of the car and walked up to the gift shop. It was full of china knick-knacks.

She was determined to buy something. *What did I need?* She thought of Jack. She wanted to make something, a memento of sorts that would hold some of his treasures, the little odds and ends he saved. She browsed the store, looking at what was hanging on the walls, not seeing anything suitable. The shop owner suggested she try the frame shop next door. There, she found the perfect solution—an oak shadow box with tiny cubicles and shelves in it, which would hold all his keepsakes. She wasn't a creative person, but this box would make it possible for her to put together a tribute to her husband. She paid for it and took the wrapped package back to her car.

She sat in the car again, trembling. *Tribute.* That word opened the floodgates. *My tribute to you Jack!* She started laughing through her tears. *And your tribute to me? Thank you, Jack! Thank you for that wonderful surprise today!* She couldn't stay there, crying and yelling, so she started up the car and pulled out, heading toward home.

"No wonder he didn't want to fuck me anymore!" she yelled out loud. "He was too guilty giving his business away, the business that we sacrificed for, that I did without for, that I worked for."

She made it home without killing anyone. The key was not going in the door, and she struggled with it, growing in anger and frustration. When the door finally gave way, she dropped her purse in the hallway and slammed the door behind her. She marched into the kitchen and picked up the coffee cup she drank from that morning, and although it had already been washed, she squirted dish detergent into it and scrubbed it with a vengeance. The cleaning ladies had been there, and the house was sparkling; there was nothing for her to do. She was growing in frustration, anger, and confusion. *How did this happen? Where was I when my husband was losing his mind? Giving his business away? Changing our life forever?*

She didn't fully comprehend why leaving the business to his girlfriend made her angrier than having the girlfriend in the first place. She wished she could go back to the gym and run on the treadmill until she fainted. She didn't want to think about this anymore.

"Okay," she said to herself, "pull yourself together. What can you do, right now, right this second, to feel better?" She thought for a minute and then said out loud, "Have a cup of coffee."

There, it was something she could do. She pulled the coffee can out of the pantry, grabbed a filter, and walked to the coffee pot. She measured the coffee with a measuring spoon, leveling off exactly the spoonfuls of coffee and dumping them into the filter. She poured the water into the pot and turned it on. She took a deep breath, feeling the tension across her shoulders and neck. When the coffee was finished, she poured a cup. Pam confronted her pain in its entirety. Her life was empty, useless. She didn't do anything for anybody else. Day after day, she took care of only herself. Jack was a weekend diversion to her week of empty self-serving. After the kids left for college, she should have moved into the city during the week with her husband, taken a class, or looked for a job.

The regrets were overwhelming her. Desperation was building. She stood in the middle of the kitchen, wringing her hands, wondering what she could do to make herself feel better. Finally, the thought entered her head. *If only I could just die.* Killing herself would be too gruesome for her. *Why did Jack have to die? Why couldn't I have died instead?*

Still standing in the center of her beautiful home, Pam lowered her head and, with a heaving chest, began to sob. Then the phone rang. She turned to look at it, walking to its cradle and picking it up to read the caller ID. It was Sandra Benson. Unbelievably, Pam wanted to talk to her, needed to talk to her. She pressed the talk button.

"Hello." She couldn't control the tremor in her voice.

Sandra could hear the despair. *Oh, oh,* she thought. She steeled herself.

"Pam. Pam, I spoke with the lawyer today. I had no idea Jack was planning this. And the truth is, I am shocked. If you want the business, and I told this to the attorney, it's yours. Okay? I know that doesn't make the fact that Jack did it any better." Sandra stopped, giving Pam a chance to say something.

"I can't make any decisions right now, Sandra. But I do appreciate the offer." Not trusting herself to say anymore, but not wanting to be rude, she asked Sandra how she was doing.

"I'm okay. I am doing pretty well. But I do want to see you, Pam. I know you had planned on having me to the beach this weekend, but I want to see you before that. Do you think you could come into the city tomorrow?"

This was probably just exactly what Pam needed. Jumping at the chance to have something to do, she didn't question the motive or reason, or what the outcome would be.

"I would love to come to the city! What time can you meet? I can come to you so we will have more time for lunch!"

Sandra told her she would be available all day and then asked her if she was okay.

"I am feeling pretty aimless right now. What to do? I have been to the gym, my house is clean, and I've been shopping. What's left?" *The tiniest bit of self-pity?*

"Your husband just died, Pam. Give yourself a break!" Sandra said, feeling her way along unfamiliar territory. "And I don't want to trivialize what you are going through. Jack used to say that you loved reading on your veranda. He said the views were breathtaking and that he was never happier than when he was sitting out there with you, he with his laptop and you with a good book." She was out of breath, hoping that she hadn't overstepped her boundaries.

"I do have a stack of novels I got out of the library last week. I tried reading one, but I couldn't get into it. I'll try another! Thank you, Sandra!"

They said their good-byes, Pam cheerful now, her old self. *Maybe I am a simpleton*, she thought. Former sadness forgotten, the change in her demeanor was sudden and swift. Pam went from being despondent to having excited expectation over a day in the city with a friend. However, she didn't know what was awaiting her. So while Pam sat in her comfortable chair on her beautiful veranda, looking out upon a spectacular ocean and trying in vain to forget her anger and disappointment by reading a book, Sandra prepared to unload a fresh bucket of heartache upon her.

26

The baby was becoming, in the few short days its existence was known, a purpose for living. Sandra still felt sad that Jack was no longer alive, that he would miss this wonderful part of their life together, but she wasn't lost, as she had been, as Pam was. Jack's death was the end of something bigger than she had known. Pam and Jack and their two children were a beautiful, vital miracle. She was responsible for tainting the loveliness of it, and she had a feeling that if karma were real, she would be making restitution in some way, that her dues had not yet been paid. That realization petrified her. She would pray, *Please, God, don't make the baby suffer on account of my sins.* "Do not be deceived, God will not be mocked, a man reaps what he sows," she remembered from Sunday School.

But first, she had one more painful revelation to convey. She must tell Pam that Jack was going to be a father again, that Lisa and Brent would be having a baby brother or sister, that she, Pam, would become a stepparent. Sandra needed Pam now, as Pam had seemed to need her. She was her connection to Jack. Together, the two of them and the three children would be responsible for the continuation of Jack.

A few miles south, Marie was walking home from work. She had worked late. The project was there, available for the taking, and God knew she needed the distraction. The good intentions she had a day ago went by the wayside the night before. She was so angry at Pam, at Sandra, at Jack. They had either betrayed her, or dismissed her, or a combination of the two. This journey she was forced to take would be one of stops and starts, two steps forward, one step back, over and over and over.

Coming to terms with what much of her adult relationship with Jack had been was a painful, embarrassing experience. She alone was responsible, she alone in control. If Pam had ever had an inkling of what was going on in her own house, between her sister and her husband, she would have been shocked and furious.

When she was just fifteen, Marie started flirting with Jack. Up to that point, for the ten years she had known him, she spent every weekend, holiday, and summer in his presence. He was her big brother, her beloved brother-in-law. She was spending more and more time with him, doing the things with him that Pam didn't want to do through lack of interest, or probably because she was exhausted from having two babies close together.

It was innocent enough at first. Marie remembered the first time she had that feeling that she wanted something from Jack that was more intimate, something that was just for her. They were playing tennis, and she was beating him. Game after game they played, he was having an off day, or she was having a fabulous day. But, in the last game, she blew it, and he won. He was so glad that he was like a small boy, running around the court, jumping up and down, and yelling. She didn't care that she didn't win and was amazed at his childish behavior, shaking her head and smiling at him.

Then he hopped over the net and picked her up in his arms, swinging her around, yelling, "Did you let me win? I won that for real, right?" Nuzzling her neck, and then putting her down, still laughing and out of breath, he kissed her right smack on the lips. He put his arm around her shoulder as they walked across the park, and Marie noticed people looking at them, the handsome, fit young man and his younger partner, both in gleaming tennis clothes, rackets swung over their shoulders, looking like the elegante of the Upper West Side.

If they had been a real couple, they would have gone back to their apartment, taken a shower together, and made love. In the real world, however, the apartment was inhabited by a mother and her two children, who were all napping. Jack changed his clothes and went into their tiny den, turning on the TV to watch the news. Marie took a shower, and when she was done, instead of getting dressed, she put on a robe and went into the den where Jack sat. She walked in front of him and opened her robe. He, totally taken by surprise, looked up at her face first, shocked, and then he looked over his shoulder, to make sure they were alone, and then, starting at her breasts, he looked, down, down, and when he came to her privates, he reached forward and touched her there. She became a little weak in the knees and opened her legs slightly, but he had come to his senses.

"Honey, you better get dressed before your sister wakes up," he said and, not until a second later, withdrew his hand.

Suzanne Jenkins

She was trembling, frightened at the intensity of her physical response, but followed orders and closed her robe. He got up, clearly excited by the straining of his erection in his sweatpants, and went into the kitchen to get something to drink.

She went back to her room and got dressed. When she returned to the kitchen, he asked her what she wanted for dinner, smiling at her as though nothing had happened, because nothing really had. They decided to make Mexican food to surprise Pam when she and the kids woke up from their nap.

It was a fun dinner. Pam and Jack drank wine, and they were more animated than usual, Pam following Jack's lead as she always did. Once again, she would benefit from the presence of her little sister.

That night, their lovemaking woke Marie up. She could hear Jack's voice murmuring and the squeaking of the bed. She got up and tiptoed out of her room and down the hall, kneeling down on the floor to peek through the keyhole of their ancient bedroom door. She could see clearly; they had a bedside light on. Pam's legs were spread wide, and Jack was lying over the edge of the bed with his head right "there."

Not yet familiar with oral sex, Marie had no idea what was going on, until Pam came. She started moaning, and Jack grabbed her hips with his hands. Marie could see his head bobbing around. It didn't take much imagination to figure out what was going on. Next, he got up on his knees, with his legs spread, the teenager able to see his scrotum hanging down and see him grab his own penis and put it into his wife. Pam's legs were wrapped around

Jack's waist. Marie was fascinated. They started rocking together, and before long, Jack grunted and that was that. He must have been done, because he got off her and stood up at the side of the bed.

Marie realized that he was going to come out of the bedroom to use the bathroom, so she vaulted, on tiptoe, back to her room. It took a moment for her to assimilate everything she had just seen, and when she did, the laughing started. She buried her head in her pillow, screaming laughing. She heard Jack at her door, peeking in to see if she was sleeping and closing the door. She heard him going back to his room. She was laughing so hard tears were rolling down her check. She had to blow her nose. Sex was so funny. *What was God thinking when he made that?* There was nothing beautiful about it at all. It was in the same league as going to the bathroom.

She debated whether or not she would say anything to him and decided not to because she wanted to watch again, and if he knew, he might block the view. She couldn't recall knowing they were doing it before that night.

Marie got to her apartment. She switched on a light and picked up her mail. There were mostly bills, a few ads, and a few cards—people, friends sending sympathy. It was already late, she wanted to get a few things done before bedtime, so she took her shower and put her pajamas on. *What to have for dinner tonight?* Food was a constant problem for Marie. She loathed eating alone. If anyone asked her to go to lunch during the week, she jumped at the chance. She would eat heartily, and then if dinner were meager, or skipped altogether, she wouldn't be starving

Suzanne Jenkins

to death. It looked like the best she could do was some cheese and crackers, some crudités, and a can of diet soda. She put everything on a big dinner plate, and picking up a book and the sympathy cards, she went into her bedroom and switched on the bedside lamp. She would sit up in bed and read and eat.

She popped open her can of soda and picked up the first card. It was a trite, religious card, the front printed with a dove and the words, "He knows your pain." On the inside, the writer said, "I know Jack will always be in your heart." She put it down and put her head back on the headboard. Closing her eyes, she thought about another day at the park, about two weeks after the tennis match.

Pam didn't want to go, so Jack and Marie and the two kids took a blanket and a picnic basket and walked to the playground. After they ate, they pushed the kids on the swings, ran after them, pushed them on the merry-go-round, played Frisbee, and then, both of them, exhausted, fell asleep on the blanket. Jack was reading a book for school; Marie was lying on her back, her eyes closed, and hands across her stomach.

She felt Jack spread a blanket across her, and then he moved in close to her, lying on his side, eyes closed. He slipped his hand under the blanket and onto her knee. His hand slipped up her leg, moving to the inside of her shorts. She ever so slightly moved her legs apart, one eye on the sleeping children.

"Don't worry," he said, "no one is around." He pushed her legs a little farther apart. His fingers slipped under the

188

elastic of her underpants. She forgot her earlier derision of sex. He snickered. "You like that?" he asked.

It took her about ten seconds to reach the conclusion that she had just been molested by her twenty-five–year-old brother-in-law and that the ramifications of it could have devastating consequences for him—*if* she told, that is. He didn't seem to get that, never asked her to keep it a secret, and acted like it was his duty to take care of her since she flashed him the day of the tennis match.

She threw the blanket off of her and sat up. They weren't exactly alone, but she didn't think anyone noticed them messing around under the cover.

"Let's wake these kids up."

She got up and straightened her clothing and started getting things packed away so they could go home. Jack put his arm around her shoulder as they walked home, she pushing the double stroller, he carrying the picnic basket. Even at that young age, even at fifteen, she thought of the futility of their relationship. It would never be anything more than game-playing.

When they got back to the apartment, Pam was sitting in a chair with her feet up, reading. She looked so happy and refreshed.

"So, here's my family!" She bent over to take the kids out of the stroller. "Did my babies have fun?" she asked. "I certainly did! Thank you, both of you! It was a wonderful, relaxing afternoon. Did you two have a good time? Or was it awful?"

"No, it was fine," Jack said. "After we played a while, I read my book, and the kids got a little nap in."

The rest of the afternoon was spent in preparation for dinner and a night of movie-watching. Marie felt slightly miffed at Jack, though. It was a scene that would replay itself over and over again in their life together. Jack would use her in some way and then act beatific, as though he were serving some noble purpose for mankind.

Seeing Pam and Jack interacting, recognizing the afternoon for what it was, a step over an invisible boundary of trust and unforgivable behavior, Marie lost it.

"I don't feel good," she announced before dinner. "I want to go home."

Pam rushed to her, patting her and hugging her, while Jack made a display of concern.

"Here, sit down, Marie, you are probably dehydrated." Pam reached for a pitcher of water.

"No, I really want to go home." This was a first. Pam was really concerned and began to get suspicious.

"Did something happen at the park?" Pam looked right at Jack.

Jack lied through his teeth, he was so smooth.

"Not that I know of. What's wrong, Marie?"

She couldn't answer. After that day, she often thought that if she had made a stand, insisting that they take her home or that her parents came to get her, that her life would have been vastly different. Jack had his hand on her arm and was applying pressure, not squeezing it, but just enough weight so she would know to keep her mouth shut. She felt a tear behind her eye but controlled it. If she started crying now, it would all come spilling out—the spying, seeing them making love, Jack fondling her. All hell would break loose. Instead, she clammed up and stayed with them after all. Later that night, Jack made love to his wife, thinking about Marie, and Marie watched them through the keyhole.

Eventually, he would come to her bed at night, and she allowed it, initiated it, and encouraged it, night after night, year after year, losing herself in the process.

Cheese and crackers finished, Marie opened the drawer in her night table and pulled out a Milky Way. She ate the chocolate off the top and then nibbled the candy bar, savoring it until the last bite. It was wonderful. There were so few pleasures in life, so few delights.

27

The next morning, after spending a comfortable evening at home, which included reading through a compelling mystery and having a glass of wine on her veranda before bed, Pam woke up refreshed and rested. She was excited about spending the day in the city. As she dressed, it occurred to her that she should pack a bag and spend a few days. She could have lunch with Sandra, dinner with Marie and Bernice, go to the library, the museums, she could be a real tourist. That settled it.

Bags packed, she had enough clothing, underwear, and accessories for a month in Paris. She was as happy as she could remember being in a long while.

Looking around her house to make sure everything was in place before she left for her overnighter, she took one last look at the beach. It would be there when she got home the next day. She poured herself a cup of coffee in her travel mug and picked up her purse. Coming back to drag her bags out and lock up, she glanced at Jack's Lexus in the garage as she closed the trunk of her car. It dawned on her that for the years she and Jack lived apart during the week, she never went into the city to see him with the excitement she felt now. That made her sad. She wondered if it had bothered him that she never visited.

Getting into the car, she opened the sunroof and turned the radio on. She felt like listening to familiar music from her youth. The idea that her comfortable little life, and that is what it seemed to her now, a little life, would soon be over grew as she got closer to the city. Sandra would make it impossible for her to "stick her head in the sand" anymore. Pam hated that phrase. Marie used it all the time. "Get your head out of the sand, Pam," she would say. Jack would come to her defense. "You're fine, Pam. Shut up, Marie."

There was some truth to it, however hated it was. Pam had her head in the sand. Her husband had an affair right under her nose. He had changed his will without telling her. The information about Harold not being his father was never shared with her. She wondered what else would she discover before it was over.

As she drove, she remembered what living in the city had been like. As a child growing up in Brooklyn, getting to the city was a goal to be reached. No one wanted to stay in Brooklyn in her crowd. And then she met Jack at school. He was from a wealthy family who lived right by the park in a mansion. She found she could fit in if she just looked good, kept her mouth shut, and didn't share her opinions.

By the time she and Jack got married, she no longer had any opinions. They would live in the city because that was always what he had done. He went to school there and started his successful business there. But secretly, she hated it. She hated the crowds, the expectations, the playacting of the day-trippers, the women in their look-a-like suits and briefcases, the men trying to look like Ralph Lauren models—it was all too much. All she really wanted to do was quit her job and start a family.

Not working brought with it a whole package of unwanted activities. She was expected to join the Junior League, volunteer for charity events, and raise money for only God knew what needy proposition. Having Bernice for a mother-in-law would further lower Pam's self-confidence. Nothing she did was ever correct or enough. The first years of her marriage were spent trying in vain to please her. Bernice was a perfectionist of the obsessive-compulsive variety. She employed a staff of cleaning ladies who were continuously cleaning and polishing her huge, empty house. When they were finished there, she sent them to her sons' homes. Pam would have to spend the morning hiding anything she didn't want thrown away or touched while an army of people she didn't know scrubbed through her apartment. The humiliation and intrusion just had to be dealt with because she was also expected to entertain almost continuously. At least having a clean house was one less thing she had to worry about.

Pam stopped taking birth control pills the day Jack finished his master's thesis. She wanted a baby so badly. Jack did his best to impregnate her, coming home mid-day to have sex, never passing up a chance for lovemaking. "We were like a couple of rabbits," he once said, teasing her.

Jack loved Pam. She was completely unlike his mother, who was a strong, foreboding woman with high, uncompromising expectations for her sons. He loved his mother, too, though. And although Jack was a success at whatever he attempted, she loved him, conditionally, he thought, although she denied it. Her relationship with Jack was different than that of Bill's. Bill was more his father's son. He followed Harold into the family business, taking over when Harold retired, although he still made armchair decisions, something Jack never would had tolerated.

Jack protected Pam. Bernice was informed as soon as he knew that Pam was the woman he wanted to spend his life with that she better embrace her and respect her. So although it was difficult, Bernice was gentle with Pam, or perhaps gentler than she was with most. Bernice let Pam know when something was inappropriate or improper. She critiqued her cooking, took her shopping for clothes and insisted that she dress a certain way, made suggestions for decorating their apartment, and then put them into play. Jack told her that if she really hated what Bernice was doing, he would put a stop to it. But he assured Pam that having his mother take over the unimportant things in their life would allow her to spend the time doing what she really loved—working out, reading, trying to get pregnant. He said that with his hand on her breast.

Jack got Pam a membership to the expensive New York Athletic Club right after they got married. While she was there, she was her own person. Bernice didn't exist; infertility wasn't an issue. Belonging to the club made living in the city tolerable. Jack took pride in his wife's fit physique and attractive face. Anything she wanted for herself, he made sure she got. Facials, manicure, and spa treatments filled her week.

When she finally got pregnant with Brent, Bernice took over. She doted on Pam, sending the cook over to prepare their meals, making sure she ate properly. She wasn't allowed to walk anywhere; their driver became her personal chauffeur. She was showered with gifts; parties and baby showers were given in her honor until there was no room left for the baby. Whatever torture Bernice had previously bestowed on her daughter-in-law was forgiven immediately. And Pam actually began to like Bernice.

As soon as she got settled into the apartment, she would call Bernice and see how she was doing. *What a hell of year she had had.* Pam felt genuine love and respect for Bernice. She hoped they would continue to be friends even though Jack was gone. Having heard of families in which all the bonds were broken after a death made Pam determined to make sure it never happened to her family. Her kids needed both grandmothers.

Traffic was backed up on the parkway right before she got into the city, so the hour trip became two hours. Pam was okay with the delay. She sang along with her favorite old songs, relaxing from the hectic drive into town. There wasn't much that could get Pam down that day, least of all crappy city traffic.

Sandra was waiting nervously for Pam's arrival. She got ready that morning, dressing with care, fixing her hair and makeup. She needed confidence for this. She was going to simply tell Pam the truth, without apology. There was nothing left to apologize for, nothing to rationalize. She was sorry everything had happened, but couldn't take it back. Her actions had been brutal and selfish, but they were finished. Jack was dead. Now, Pam could acknowledge this pregnancy or not. It was entirely up to her. But Sandra fully intended on telling Pam she needed her. She was the last link to Jack. Pam had said as much about her. The baby only strengthened that link.

She made herself tea and toast, sitting in the window and gazing out at the tree. The birds she fed throughout the winter were bringing their babies back to the feeder. Sandra felt as though they wanted her to see their children. She would sit on her patio at dusk and watch silently as the mothers and their little birds came for dinner. It emphasized the life she was making for herself here; the birds depended on her for food, and she was diligent about providing it. This task was just a little thing, but one of several seemingly unrelated activities that helped define who she was—city dweller, reader, worker, bird caretaker, girlfriend, and soon, mother. She avoided using any negatives—mistress, betrayer, liar. Others would provide those terms. She wondered what was keeping Pam and considered calling the apartment, but decided that God's timing would be perfect, as trite as it sounded. *So far, it had been right on target.*

Pam pulled into the parking garage on Madison Avenue. She hauled her heavy suitcase out of the trunk, pulling the handle up so all she had to do was pull it along behind her. *Whoever had invented the rolling suitcase was a genius.* She did her best to keep it rolling smoothly to the elevator. The fifteen floors up went quickly. She was getting ahead of herself, thinking of buying some groceries and staying more than a day. She decided to allow herself the freedom to leave when she had had enough. She'd order a few things to be delivered, coffee in particular if Jack didn't have any. There were plenty of places to shop in the neighborhood.

She decided to unpack, rather than rushing out. She needed the few minutes of peaceful organization to gather her thoughts. She hadn't allowed herself to fanaticize about what Sandra wanted to talk to her about. It probably involved the business. She had already come to terms with it. As long as she had enough money to live and support herself and the children, she really didn't care about it. It was the idea that pissed her off—the idea that Jack could think so little of her and she didn't realize it.

She spent the next ten or fifteen minutes putting her clothes away and organizing her beauty products in the bathroom. She knew she was stalling. Going into the living room, she picked up the phone and keyed in Sandra's number. She answered on the first ring. They made plans for Pam to go to her apartment. Then, if they felt like it, they could go to lunch later.

Sandra added to herself, *If they could eat after what would be revealed.*

Pam left Jack's apartment at noon. She got a cab without a problem and was at Sandra's in fifteen minutes. She was waiting for Pam at the door of the building so she wouldn't have to buzz. When the cab stopped, Sandra walked out and met Pam on the sidewalk. They embraced like old friends. Conversation was easy between the two of them, like mother and daughter. Pam asked how the week was going at work, and Sandra told her about Pete and how he wouldn't come out of his office the day of the will reading. They walked down the hall together to Sandra's door. Pam walked through first and was truly awed by the apartment.

"Oh my goodness! It's so bright! I love what you have done with it." She looked at Sandra, smiling. "You have a real knack, my dear!"

They went to the small table and sat down, continuing to chat. Sandra got up and put the kettle on. She remembered Pam liked coffee, getting some instant crystals from Zabar's. She set the kettle on to boil, took the mugs out of the cupboard, and gathered up the cream and sugar. She was starting to get nervous, wondering when was she going to do it. She imagined she would just speak it out the moment Pam walked through the door. But she hadn't counted on the immediate connection they would have. They hadn't seen each other in a week. She had missed her. The reading of the will had taken place, and if that didn't alienate Pam, this next revelation may.

She decided she had to preface her news with a little speech. She had to build up to it. Pam needed some preparation. Sandra was tempted to let Pam ask what the meeting was about. Her nerves led to fright. *What if I lose it?* Carrying the tray into the dining room, she decided to just say it.

"Thank you for coming all the way into the city today, Pam. I know this isn't your favorite place in the world!" She put the tray down and started pouring.

"I brought an overnight bag! When you called, it pulled me up out of such a state of self-pity. Thank you!" Pam reached over and hugged her. She continued to praise Sandra for her ability to inspire Pam that afternoon.

Sandra put the teapot down. She sat back down with her head hanging.

"Please don't, Pam. Please don't." She shook her head back and forth. Pam reached out for her, concerned.

"What's wrong, dear? What did I do?"

"I'm pregnant." There, it was out. "I took a test, and it was positive. I'm very early."

Pam was frowning, looking at Sandra. The color had drained from her face.

"I don't understand. I mean, I hear what you said, but I thought you said he was going to break up with you? Did you plan this?" Her voice was shaking, almost uncontrollably.

"I'm sure he would have broken up with me eventually. It was not planned. Pam, I'm sorry I hurt you! But, please, can I just say something and then you can let me have it?"

"Go ahead. I'm not going to let you have it! I'm just shocked! I mean, Jesus Christ! What next?" Pam had her head in her hands and was looking up at Sandra through her splayed fingers. Pam, always so poised, was suddenly full of doubt and uncertainty. *What is happening to me? Am I a complete ass?*

"I am sorry, Pam. I'm sorry I hurt you. Because of me, your husband betrayed you. You didn't deserve that. But the baby," she started to weep now, "the baby means so much to me. The minute I realized I was pregnant, I felt like all of this has happened for a reason. I felt like I needed you so desperately to be in my life and the baby's life. Maybe because you were so kind to me, so forgiving, I've stayed on that continuum of us being a family. Now we will be related." She stopped then. Looking at Pam, seeing the hurt in her eyes was the final straw. With her head hanging down, she just let it out. "Everything will be horrible without you. I can't imagine having this baby and raising it without you."

Pam was speechless. So it wasn't bad enough that her husband betrayed her with this woman who was young enough to be his daughter, walked around town with her so that Marie, her own sister, knew of the betrayal, but now she would have to explain Jack's infidelity to her children. The evidence would be in the living, breathing baby for the world to see. *Was there anything to privacy anymore? Did the entire world have to know that her marriage was a sham?*

"I ran into Bernice yesterday, and she said I shouldn't tell you about the baby yet, that you might pressure me into having an abortion. I couldn't keep it from you, though. I want to build a friendship with you, Pam."

Pam took her hands from her face; she was livid, eyes wide open.

"My mother-in-law knows?" She was struggling to keep her voice low, to stay in control. "Why on earth did you tell my mother-in-law? What earthly purpose would that serve? How do you even know her?" Pam stood up now and was pacing. She was on the fence between caring that Sandra's feelings didn't get hurt and wishing her dead, along with her late husband.

Sandra began relating the story of Bernice, Big Nick's, and the trip back to the mansion, when Pam abruptly put her hand up.

"Stop!" She shouted. "I don't want to hear another word. Do you have any idea how destructive you are being? This is my life you are fooling with! It's not enough that you sleep with my husband and don't protect yourself against a pregnancy, but you tell my mother-in-law?" She gathered up her purse and started walking toward the door. "Good-bye, Sandra. I think it is better if we don't talk to each other for a while." She opened the door and walked out of the apartment, slamming it behind her.

The warm air of the June afternoon enveloped her as she stepped out of the building. It was humid out, and the damp air clung to her bare arms and gave her a chill. It reminded her of having menstrual cramps when she was a girl, and the hot, humid weather would make her feel like she was hot and cold at the same time. Comparing what she had just gone through with cramps brought a smile to her face. She took some deep breaths and started walking toward Broadway. For the second time in their life together, Pam could hear Sandra calling her name. Pam stopped walking and turned around to see Sandra running up the street, tears flying. When she reached Pam, she began begging her for forgiveness.

"Please, Pam, please give me another chance." She stood with her head bowed and her hands folded in front of her, in a praying stance. *Please, God, let this woman forgive me my sins.*

Pam was already calming down. But she was sincerely tired of the whole Jack-Sandra drama. She wanted to grieve the loss of her husband. She was tired of grieving the charade of her marriage.

"I will give you another chance, if you give me some time. I hope I don't sound like a mother here, Sandra, but you are very young, and although I think you are wise, you don't know what I am going through. I need some time to sort out what I am going to tell my children, who worship their father, or worshiped him when he was alive, and now will find that not only did he cheat on their mother, but will have a child that will be their stepbrother or stepsister." She felt strange discussing this on the street, Sandra standing there sobbing. She was not going back to Sandra's apartment and wanted to give her some resolution before she left the city, because she was getting out. There was no way she could stay in Jack's apartment tonight. "Go back home, dear, I want to get back and get on the road before traffic gets too bad." She patted her arm and turned to walk up the street.

Pam got her cab. She was glad she hadn't called Marie or, for God's sake, Bernice, because she would have had to cancel any plans she made with them. Repacking everything, she couldn't wait to get out of that place and back in her car and head toward the ocean.

She felt slightly guilty about the scene back at Sandra's. It would have been so "Pam" if she had said, "Oh, that's perfectly wonderful! You are having my husband's baby! You discussed it with my mother-in-law who loathes me and probably thinks I deserve it. Here, let me give you my children's cell phone numbers; call them and let them know about their new stepsibling!" But she would never do that, because she thought of others more highly than she thought of herself.

As she maneuvered her car through the afternoon traffic toward the bridge, she began to relax. She would allow herself the luxury of not thinking about what she must do until she was safe at home. The ride would be spent listening to music and trying not to get killed. *What had I been thinking when I drove in this morning?* From now on, if anyone needed to see her, they could meet her in Babylon.

28

Three women, joined by their love for a dead man, moved forward through the week with their eyes on the weekend. If all went well, they would meet at the man's beautiful house on the Atlantic Ocean. They would spend time eating delicious food, watching breathtaking sunrises, walking on the beach, and if the mood was right, accepting this latest challenging news.

Pam wanted to do what was right. If she could, if she only had herself to think of, she would deny Sandra's baby's birthright. She would threaten her with bodily harm if she revealed the embarrassing truth of Jack's betrayal to their friends and family. She fantasized about packing up and driving through Canada to Alaska and hiding there. If she only had her own life to worry about, she would do that.

That wasn't going to happen, however, because of Lisa and Brent. This had become about what was right for them. She had to include the unborn baby in the equation. So fantasies about getting revenge aside, she would, from this moment forward, only consider what was best for the baby. That would mean having a united front of the adults. It would mean Pam would have to deal with Bernice, whatever her deal was seeking out Sandra. It would mean telling Marie and suffering her wrath.

By Friday, Pam was used to the idea of a baby. It disgusted her how simple she was. It was probably why she was so easily walked over all of her life. But that was that. She spent the week shopping for just the right food, lots of healthy drinks for Sandra, and wine for Marie and herself. She got steaks for Friday, salmon for Saturday, and if the women stayed until Sunday evening, the ingredients for shrimp scampi. She hadn't cooked in over a week, and it felt good to stroll down the aisles of the big organic food store, thinking always in terms of what would be best for the baby.

She hadn't spoken to either woman, but on Tuesday, she sent cards, cute friendship cards, with the same words written in each one: "Don't forget this weekend at the beach! See you Friday night." And both women had called and left messages that they would leave for Long Island right after work on Friday. Pam thought it was probably a good thing that they weren't traveling together. She didn't know how Sandra was going to get there, probably the train. She was a big girl; she would figure it out. Marie would drive over; that was the way she always did it. She liked to have the freedom to leave late at night and not worry about walking back to her apartment. Cabs were a rare commodity in that part of the city.

Pam discovered a positive consequence of the weekend plan. She barely thought of Jack all week, odd, considering he had only been dead two weeks. Her anger was palpable. Her disgust at how he had discounted his children in his will and basically disregarded them all by his behavior served to force her to look outside of her grief. Possibly, it could pop up again down the road, but for now, she didn't care. She wanted that control, that total all-encompassing smugness that being pissed at her husband gave her. She had never really gotten mad at him. *It was possible that was a symptom of a tragically empty marriage.*

She thought of the last time they made love. He had pumped away on top of her, and when he was finished, he got off of her and went into the bathroom. She started laughing when she thought of the expression on his face. It was one that said, "I'm so good!" He was such an egoist. To his credit, he always made sure she was satisfied first. The problem with that was she was finished before he got started and really didn't care if it was over quickly. Now, of course, she understood. He was a middle-aged man having sexual intercourse with two women. She didn't know if he used drugs to enhance his performance, but she doubted it. She shook her head to rid herself of those thoughts. All they did was make her sad all over again. And she had managed to stay happy most of the week.

Having an entire week by herself was sobering. She realized how friendless she was. Prior to Jack's death, she didn't need other women. She had her sister for companionship, her mother to bounce ideas off of, Bernice to make sure she was involved in senseless activities, and Jack to take care of. His clothes alone were a part time job. She went to the cleaners on Monday to drop off what he brought home from the city and again on Friday to pick it up. He always had shoes or belts that needed repairs and watches to go to the jeweler. His car was in the shop more than it was out for upgrades or repairs—satellite radio, new tires, detailing, and oil changes. His golf clubs always needed some attention. She took his tennis racket to be restrung. Shopping for their food for the weekend was exciting for her. During the summer, they grilled every night, especially when he started to watch his weight. She would go to the farmers' market on Friday and Saturday and to the fish market and the bakery. Everything was fresh and delicious.

Of course, that was the past. Now she had nothing, no friends, no husband, and no memories that were real. It was a sham, her whole life. And she was proud of herself for having let go of so much so quickly. She was a good woman. She could see what was needed to make others safe, to make others happy. This self–pep talk was just what Pam needed.

She took fresh flowers out on the veranda and arranged them on the dining table. Hosting—now that was something she could do with pizzazz. Pam put a box of Marie's favorite chocolates on her nightstand. She had fresh sheets on the bed and flowers on the dresser. She debated where to have Sandra sleep. They had several guest rooms on the upper level, but they were far away. She didn't want her guest to feel lonely, but the only other bedrooms were the kids. She decided she would ask Sandra where she would be more comfortable. The upper guest rooms looked out upon the ocean, and later that night, with the full moon and stars and the ships at sea, the light would be beautiful.

At seven p.m., she heard a car pull up in front. It was Marie. Pam hadn't seen her sister for over a week. She went to the door and opened it, waiting for her to get her bags out of the trunk. Pam was shocked. Marie had obviously stopped eating, a problem they dealt with once when she was sixteen and again when she was thirty. It had escalated to the point where she had to be hospitalized twice, once for six months and once for almost a year. She would starve herself until her body was unable to sustain her. At five feet eight inches, she was thin at her normal one hundred and fifteen pounds. She had clearly lost at least ten pounds. Pam did her best to hide her concern. Past history taught her that the best thing to do was to say nothing. She put a smile on her face and rushed out to embrace her sister.

Marie put herself into neutral in order to get through the week. She didn't allow any more walks down memory lane. No more entertaining jealous thoughts of Sandra. But the worst battle was with her guilt over the betrayal of her sister. It was a roller coaster. She hated not being able to express her love for Jack and her grief over his death and was enraged that all the sympathy was going Pam's way. Then she would be despondent that she could be so selfish and not be there for her sister. Seeing Pam scurrying toward her filled her with anxiety.

"Marie, I am so glad you are here. We will have a good visit this weekend. I have your room already for you," she said as she lifted her suitcase out of the trunk. They walked together toward the house, chattering about work, their mother, Brent and Lisa. "I was even thinking that you might like to golf tomorrow." If Marie didn't take advantage of the country club, there was no earthly reason to keep their membership current. "It is a shame that it is going to waste," she added, hoping that would spur her sister into going.

"It would be so boring out there without Jack" was all she said.

Pam had to agree.

"It would be boring with him, in my opinion."

They both laughed. Going into Marie's room and putting the bags down, Pam could see the tension in her sister's face start to melt. Marie was surprised at how comforting it was to be back in Jack's house. She was dreading it in theory, but in actuality, it was familiar, and it was home. She wondered if the weekend would kill her peace; seeing Sandra again and knowing what she meant to Jack might do it. So much of what was important to her lived in the house. She loved the kids. Staying in touch with them while they were away at school, writing weekly, texting constantly, sending gifts from street vendors was on the continuum of life. When they both decided to spend six weeks of their summer vacation away, she was beside herself, and the fact that the plan wasn't cancelled after the events of the past month really had her baffled. She wondered what would she do that summer, who would play on the beach with her, go for ice cream or pizza, and hang out in town on a hot summer Saturday night. If all went well this weekend, she was going to approach Pam about getting them home. They should be here.

"Brent golfs. If he were home now, it wouldn't go to waste" was all she said.

Pam didn't respond. She knew that the best thing for her children was to be away from this mess. Their peace would be shattered soon enough, and then she doubted they would ever want to come back. However, she was not going to discuss it with Marie. Those two fabulous beings were Pam's children, not Marie's. That was one source of contention she wanted to keep out of this weekend.

Pam was debating whether or not to tell Marie herself that Sandra was pregnant, thinking it may take some of the heat off of Sandra. If she did so now, Marie would probably leave. *Then, she thought, why did Marie really have to know right away? It was so early, and so much could happen. Maybe Bernice was right, that any negative vibes directed at the baby should be avoided.*

Pam felt that part of her metamorphous into an adult, finally at age fifty-five, was the realization that she couldn't control everything, that her advice wasn't wanted, and that people should be left to their own devices most of the time. It certainly made life easier. She had enough on her plate right now. How people would react to her once the word was out that Jack was going to be father again and Marie's reaction to learning that Jack had left his business, of all things, to his mistress, all of the fallout from those two issues alone, boggled the mind.

It was Sandra's baby, so if she wanted to tell Marie over the weekend, that was up to her alone. She, Pam, was not going to do it.

"Sandra should be here any minute," Pam said. "Would you like something to drink? We can sit outside while we wait for her. Give us a chance to catch up."

She went into the kitchen, Marie following her. Pulling the cheese tray out of the refrigerator and piling grapes on it, she secretly hoped her sister would dig in. Marie went to the pantry to get crackers, renewing their old routine of working in tandem on the weekends—two women who had lived together for a long, long, time and knew what was expected of one another.

"I'll take this out if you want to get that bottle there," Pam said, pointing to the wine and two glasses. She omitted, "Sandra won't need a glass."

They walked out onto the veranda. The sun was just getting ready to set behind the house, casting a warm, gold glow over the water. Couples walking hand in hand, a boy running with his dog, a group of teenage girls laughing and conspiring; the beach was a vital part of life here in this house. You didn't need to participate, just observe from the safety of the veranda. Pam was content to do so, while Marie not so much. She wanted to be part of the action, to walk hand in hand with Jack, run with her niece and nephew chasing a Frisbee, beachcombing for glass and shells. Pam was a solitary woman; Marie needed others around her to breathe life into her.

Pam had stopped walking on the beach each afternoon. She had the sensation that when she was out there, her house kept getting farther and farther away, as though an undertow in the sand was working to remove her as well. It was an empty shell, with no husband, no children, and no life. After the fiasco early in the week with Sandra, she had an urgency to get home when she had to go out. Taking books back to the library, working out, and picking up groceries were accomplished without wasted steps. She wanted to get her chores done and get back home. She had taken to closing the drapes again against the outside world. Her house was her cocoon. She nestled in, and there was nothing better.

"What did you do this week?" Marie asked her as she poured her a glass of wine. "I thought about you, but decided to leave you alone. I know I have been kind of needy lately."

Pam watched from the corner of her eye as her sister picked up a cracker and spread Rondele on it. She tried not to breathe a sigh of relief.

"What did I do? Not much. I had a couple of things to do outside of the house that occupied some time." She thought of her flight into the city, short lived, but didn't mention it. Marie wanted to hear more of what she was dealing with emotionally. "I am angry at Jack right now. It's gut-wrenching." Pam didn't need to tell Marie the real reason for that anger; she knew enough without knowing the entire story. "But it's nothing that I won't get over with time."

Marie thought, *I hope you are right*, thinking that she was not going to add to her sister's burden of shame.

"The timing just isn't right," Pam went on to explain. "I feel as though I should be doing something beneficial, but I don't know what that is yet. I'm not even sure what that means." She realized she lead a selfish life, but wasn't ready to confess that to anyone, especially her sister.

Marie was shaking her head in understanding while she picked up another cracker.

"I know what you mean, Sis. What have I done with my life? At least you have the kids." And then, treading lightly, she said, "I sort of wasted my life playing with Jack."

Pam looked at her, embarrassed.

"I'm sorry for my part in that, Marie. You did fill in for me when I wasn't able or didn't want to participate in whatever shenanigans he was up to. In retrospect, maybe that was why he played around. Who knows if Sandra was the first?"

Marie, squirming in her chair, took a big slug of wine. At that moment in time, she knew that her sister was doing some important work toward self-realization, something she would need if she were going to have a happy life. It might mean exposure; it might mean shame for Marie if her relationship with Jack came to light. She wanted a real life. Already, two weeks of his absence made Marie see that her relationship with her brother-in-law was abuse. He used her, not caring whether or not she left them, but while she was there, he would take what he wanted of her. It was a cheap and easy way to get thrills without responsibility. And now, of course, he was dead and off the hook. *Forty-five years old and never had a date, it was sick! Did Pam think so?* She decided to be brave and ask, not worrying if the question would make Pam think more deeply about her sister's relationship with her dead husband.

"Pam, can I ask you a question?" Marie was red-faced and scared, but determined, the wine providing the courage.

"Of course! What?" Pam was sitting with her feet up on a chair, looking out over the golden ocean and azure sky mixed with purple, pink, and scarlet. Turning her head, she looked at her sister.

"Did you ever think it was weird that I didn't date?" Marie was leaning forward in expectation.

Pam looked at her, then through her, thinking.

"Yes, I thought it was weird—but only for a short time. Truthfully, I thought you might be a lesbian, but afraid to come out. Jack and I discussed you never dating, and he suggested that for a reason."

Marie sat, immobile, with her mouth hanging open.

"Jack thought I was a lesbian? That's what he told you?" Marie spoke in a clipped, strained voice. Pam nodded yes. "When did this conversation take place, if I may ask?"

Pam looked out over the ocean.

"About twenty years ago" was all she said.

Marie was not ready to give this up.

"What would prompt him to say something like that about me? What was the conversation? Come on, Pam, you can't say something like that without some background!" She was trying to lighten up, to pretend it didn't matter that her lover used a word like "lesbian" to describe her.

"I was angry because you and he had spent the day at the park together. I saw the two of you walking along with his arm around your shoulder. I was in the apartment all day with the two kids; I think Brent may have been around two, Lisa an infant. It was so long ago. I think I accused him of being in love with you. He denied it, of course. I asked why it was that you never dated, but spent every weekend here, hanging on his every word. He said he thought you might prefer women. It was as simple as that." She turned to look at her sister, who was white as a ghost, and asked, "Was he correct?"

Marie was ready to explode, but determined to be the bigger person, not to upset the apple cart when Miss Perfect was due any second, she just shook her head no.

"No, Pam, I'm not a lesbian, have never been one, never even thought of it. I am a little shocked that you were jealous of me. Why didn't you ever say anything? I mean, I could have stayed home and gotten a life! I thought you wanted me with you!" She laughed and shook her head. "Unbelievable."

The doorbell rang at that moment.

"Saved by the bell!" Pam exclaimed.

She got up to let Sandra in, Marie following. She was not going to miss out on one second of the next forty-eight hours. Pam opened the door to a perfectly coiffed, made-up, sundress-wearing goddess. She was surrounded by her suitcases and accompanied by a sweating, panting cab driver who had hauled all of her things to the porch. When she saw the door was going to be answered and she wasn't stranded out there, she turned and gave the driver a stack of bills.

Then, turning to Pam and Marie, she said, "Over the river and through the woods! My God, what a trip!"

Pam ushered her in, and the three women chattered like magpies, dragging bags up the stairs to the proposed room.

"If you don't want to be up here alone, you can have Lisa's room. I am letting you decide," Pam said.

But Sandra was easy. "Up here is great. Then, if I get insomnia, I won't disturb you when I am up walking around." She looked around the room Pam had picked out for her. "Lovely. Thank you."

They placed the bags on the floor and turned to walk back downstairs, continuing to talk about the trip from the city for both women, what the weather was supposed to be like, and how hungry everyone was.

Pam got Sandra a glass of lemonade, and they returned to the veranda. When Marie and Sandra were seated, Pam said she wanted to start dinner. It was simple—steaks on the grill, salad, roasted asparagus in season, garlic bread and flan, all store bought. She went and got the meat and vegetables to grill, while Sandra and Marie talked. They were speaking so softly Pam couldn't hear them.

"I am sorry about the other day," Marie said. "I think I was having a nervous breakdown."

"How are you feeling now?" Sandra asked, expressionless.

Marie was a little taken aback; there was no acceptance of her forgiveness, no "oh that's okay" speech.

"I'm fine. Why do you ask?" Marie wondered what Sandra was referring to.

"No special reason." Sandra sipped her drink. "Pam," she called, "can I help you with anything?"

Pam walked out with a tray of food.

"You both just relax. This is the easiest meal ever." She put the tray down on the granite counter. Lighting the gas grill, she turned around to her guests while it heated up. "We are supposed to have fabulous weather all weekend. I thought tomorrow we could have a leisurely morning and then hit the antique trail before lunch. There are supposed to be several flea markets around the area."

Sandra smiled at her, but said nothing. The last thing she wanted to do was run around Long Island spending money. Marie wasn't so tactful.

"Ugh, no thank you. I'm not moving from this chair if I can help it."

Pam started laughing. "Okay, well that is fine, too. I thought we could have a choice in case boredom set in."

"Boredom would be welcome at this point in my life," Sandra said.

Pam grilled the food while trying to keep the conversation going. But the moment she turned her back to attend to the food, it died. She decided to stop working so hard and let things take their natural course. If Marie and Sandra had nothing to say to each other, it might be for the best.

When the steaks were done, Pam dished up food for each woman and placed the plates on the table. She put extra veggies on a serving platter and placed it in the middle of the table. A large salad and the breadbasket and they were good to go. *It was just the kind of meal Jack used to love,* she thought. She sat down and looked at her guests, some of Jack's favorite people. She raised her glass.

"I'd like to propose a toast to my late husband, Jack, who would have been thrilled to eat a meal with the three of us."

They raised their glasses in honor of Jack. "Cheers," they said, and drank.

Marie had it on the tip of her tongue to say, "Maybe if one of us wasn't alive, he would be," but thought better of it. She cut her meat and speared a piece, popping it into her mouth. It was tender, the edges crisp and caramelized. There was just enough fat to make it moist and give it flavor.

"Delicious, Sis," she said. Keep it positive; keep it bland. That would be her modus operandi this weekend. "This used to be Jack's favorite meal," Pam said innocently. Sandra was mildly surprised. Jack never ate anything richer than a piece of fish with a salad when they went out for dinner; breakfast was another matter. She remembered stacks of pancakes, dripping in syrup.

"In August, when corn and tomatoes ripened, we had the steak with boiled corn and tomato salad every night. I never got sick of it," Marie said. "The first thing I thought of when I got off the parkway was which farm stand I would stop at to get the corn."

The three women ate in silence. Pam yawned, surprised at herself. It was probably the strain of jockeying what was said in front of whom. She got up and cleared the plates when everyone was finished, intending to bring the dessert out.

"Before you leave, Pam, I wanted to say something, if I could." Sandra looked up at Pam, who set the plates back down and pulled out her chair. *Oh God, what was it now?*

"Okay, go ahead," she said hesitantly.

"Thank you both for your graciousness. I am humbled over and over again by your acceptance of me. That is all I had to say—for now." She looked at Pam and then at Marie.

Marie was forcing herself to keep quiet. She didn't feel gracious at all. It was a minute-by-minute surrender trying to keep her mouth shut.

Pam smiled and got up again. "My pleasure!" was all she could get out. If Sandra felt accepted, then more power to her. Piling the dishes up again, she took them out to the kitchen and put them in the sink. There was plenty of time later to scrape and rinse. She heard voices coming from the outside and decided to give them some privacy. Maybe she'd do those dishes now.

Marie couldn't help herself any longer. After Sandra's little speech, she had her say.

"My sister is the gracious one, Sandra. Its Pam you've hurt—at least in the public eye. I wonder how different things would be if Jack were still alive. I fully intended on making him confess to Pam that weekend." She sat looking at Sandra, her lips set in a thin line.

"What do you mean in the public eye?" Sandra was on shaky ground here. Once the pregnancy was out, the world would know Jack had been screwing around on Pam. But since Marie didn't know about the baby, she wasn't sure what she meant. She wanted to know.

"Just what it sounds like! You think she is the only one who loved my brother-in-law? Of course, the public simply looks at Pam and sees the widow! All of their sympathy goes out to her. The rest of us who loved him get nothing, no recognition. That's what I mean!"

Sandra was quick, and it took just a few seconds to figure out. She smiled a slow, sly smile.

"So are you saying you loved Jack? I mean loved him like a lover, not a brother-in law?" That explained the decomposition in her apartment last Sunday. She had been in love with him, too. *What a mess.*

Marie stood up, face contorted, and shoved the chair under the table with force.

"Doesn't take you long, does it? My sister lived with it right under her nose for almost thirty years." Suddenly, she pulled the chair out and sat down on it, lowered her head, and started sobbing. This time, her voice was loud enough that Pam heard and came running out from the kitchen.

"What is going on?" She thought Sandra might have sprung the baby news.

Sandra mouthed "no" to Pam, and Pam looked at Marie again.

"Marie, what is going on? What's wrong?"

Sandra repeated, "Yes, Marie, tell Pam why you are crying." There was no way she was going to drop this bomb; let Marie do the dirty work.

Marie was out of control now, head down on her folded arms on the table. Over and over again, she said, "Jack, Jack, Jack."

Pam was getting frightened. She came around to the side of the table next to Marie, putting her arms around her.

"Oh, Marie, I know you miss him! We all do!" She patted her head and said "shhh" to her sister.

Sandra was at an impasse here. *Should I sit and be quiet, or should all the cards be put out on the table?* She was fairly sure Marie and Jack had been lovers. No forty-five–year-old woman responded to the death of someone like this unless they had been intimate, of that she was certain. She decided to speak up.

"I think it was more than that" was all she said.

Pam stood up, looking at her.

"What's that supposed to mean?" She was pissed. What was Sandra implying?

223

Once again, Sandra smiled her sly, slow smile and shook her head in disbelief.

"Marie, what does Sandra mean?"

Pam was thinking, *No, this can't be,* because in her innocence, she knew all along that her husband had an unnatural relationship with her baby sister and she chose to look the other way. Now, it would be out there; it would have to be dealt with.

"Marie, stop that sniveling and talk to me!" Pam yelled.

Marie lifted her head. Pam gave her a napkin, and she wiped her face with it. She blew her nose into it. Sandra had her head resting on her hand, a silent observer. *So this was the man I had an affair with! He was not only a philanderer, but he was a child abuser. Marie had said thirty years, had she not? That would have made her just fifteen years old—a child.*

"Marie, tell me what is upsetting you. Please." Pam pulled out a chair next to her sister. She sat down, facing Marie. She needed to hear the story, no matter how awful. No one would ever recover from this if the entire thing weren't exposed right then. "Marie, did Jack touch you?" It didn't sound right since she was an adult, but Pam was at a loss.

Marie shook her head yes.

"When?" Pam whispered. "When did it start?" she asked, knowing the answer even before she spoke.

"Remember the day in the park when I was fifteen and I wanted to go home?"

Pam did remember. She stood up. Both of her kids had been with them that day. *Where had they been while he was molesting his sister-in-law?* But she didn't say anything or ask any more questions. Marie had opened the flood-gates, and as sometimes happens, she couldn't stop once her mouth was open.

"He fondled me under a blanket that day. The next night, he came to my room, and we did it. Every weekend after that, we either did it while you were out or he came to my room at night. Last year, I knew something was wrong because he stopped coming to me. Now I know it was because of Sandra. He was making love to her instead of to me." She put her head down onto her arms and start-ing crying again.

Pam was looking out over the ocean. *Fucking Jack. What a royal jerk! A felon, for Christ's sake!* She turned around. *What can I say to my sister that would matter? What can I say that would matter to anyone?*

"Marie, I am sorry. I should have known. I should have put a stop to it. I'm sure the reason it continued was that he was controlling you. I don't blame you." She walked around the table and put her arm back around her sister. She probably needed some therapy—big time. *What an awful relationship!* It would paralyze a person, that kind of perversity. No wonder she had an eating disorder. She looked over at Sandra who didn't seem fazed by any of this. "Can you believe this?" Pam asked of her.

"What else can happen to you?" was all she could say.

Pam had to think quickly. Certainly, the weekend could not progress as planned. And it was too late to think about either woman leaving for Manhattan until Saturday. *What to do?* She could let things take their course, go on as planned, serve dessert, keep talking. Her head was buzzing. Another slap in the face.

She wanted to be alone to think about each time she feared there might be abuse being committed under her roof. *How was I able to convince myself otherwise?* She confronted Jack again and again: "What is going on when the two of you are out? I don't like the touching, the hugging," she would tell him. He laughed her off. "You are imagining it," he would say.

Year after year, he was abusing her sister, with intercourse, not just fondling. *Didn't Marie say herself that he came to her bed?* Pam closed her eyes for a moment. They made love almost every weekend. *Was he leaving the marriage bed to go to his teenage sister-in-law for sex?* And then she wondered something that had bothered her for years, something she never gave voice to then and wouldn't now. But she said out loud in her mind, *He always satisfied her*, and then would proceed, *Did he actually come?* She was so naïve. *Was it possible he wasn't finishing?* She detested this type of mind play. He was a filthy pig. *Why rationalize it? What difference did it make now?* But her flesh wanted details—the how, when, and where of deceit.

Marie was pulling herself together. She sat quietly at the table, aware that it was over; there was no need to hide anymore. Finally, her side of the story was out. And Pam believed her. *Pam, sweet, gentle Pam.*

Sandra sat silent, taking it all in. *What was this family?* she thought to herself. *What a horrible, perverse mess.* She put her hand over her belly, thinking, *Thank God he was dead. He wouldn't put a finger on this baby.* Finally, after two weeks of grief, she felt vindicated. He was dead because he was too sick to be alive. Marie would have never disclosed her secrets otherwise. She said he had stopped sleeping with her when Sandra came along. *How could I know for sure?*

"I think we need to be honest about everything now. Pam? Are you behind me in this?" Sandra asked.

"Now is probably the worst time!" She was incredulous that Sandra would bring that up in front of Marie.

Marie was alert now, smelling out more intrigue. What could be worse than what she just revealed?

"What? What? I want to know, for God's sake! Was he molesting his own kids?" she yelled.

"No! Jesus Christ, Marie, stop it! Of course not!" She had no way of knowing if this was true, but she wasn't about to open that can of worms. "I'm pregnant!" Sandra said, sitting up ramrod straight, defying anyone to stop her from stating the truth. "I'm about four weeks along."

Marie was staring at her, her mouth open and eyes wide. "You're lying," she said.

Sandra laughed. "I'm sorry, Marie, but it's true. You are going to be an aunt again. I hope you'll agree to be in the baby's life!"

Pam and Marie continued to stare at Sandra. *She had to be nuts!*

"You have got to be kidding me! You're going to have it? How fucking selfish can one human being be? I told you she was a snake!" Marie said to Pam.

At that point, Pam stepped in, placing her hand on Marie's arm.

"That's not our business, Marie. We have to allow Sandra to do what she needs and support her."

Marie shook her off. "No, I disagree. You want another shocker? I had two abortions—Jack's babies. He wouldn't hear of it. Once when I was in college, at twenty, and the other four years ago, right after Christmas. When I told him I was pregnant, he went into a rage. 'You did it on purpose!' he screamed at me. I was afraid everyone in my apartment would hear him. 'There is no way you are having a baby, do you hear me? Get rid of it!' When I started to cry, he put his hand over my mouth, like he wanted to strangle me. I couldn't breathe. 'Stop crying!' he shouted over and over. And he wouldn't even allow me to recover. He came to my apartment after I had it done, after the abortion, and rammed into me. When he was done, he got up and left. I didn't hear from him for the rest of the week. That weekend, he took off golfing in Las Vegas with Brent. I stayed in the city. I think I told you I wanted to do some Christmas shopping. Mother came and took care of me. I was so frightened; this time I got an infection. No one tells you how common that is. They make it sound like you just go in and zip zip, it's over, baby gone. I blamed Jack for it; he practically raped me.

"Things got better after that; he was at least cordial to me. But he was still rough at night, like he was pissed off at me. I tried to get him to stop coming to me, but he would fly into a rage if I even brought it up, accuse me of being ungrateful, of using him. I got so confused that I believed him. We did more physical stuff together—golfing, tennis, swimming. He seemed okay about everything, not so angry.

"Finally, last year, he stopped coming to my apartment during the week, and on the weekends, he never came to my room. It may have been because we almost got caught; Lisa walked into my room just as Jack was leaving. He told her he was in the kitchen and heard me crying and thought I was having a bad dream. I'm not sure she believed him. The smell of sex hung in the air. It was pretty intense for the rest of the weekend. I thought she would go to you and tell you. Now I think he stopped because he was sleeping with Sandra, and there was no chance of anyone catching them doing it." She finally stopped.

Pam was frozen. Sandra, white as a ghost, was disgusted. No one dared to say a word.

"Why in hell should you have his baby? Do you think he would want it? Do you think it is fair to have everyone knowing whose baby it is? Lisa? Brent? No!"

She was speaking Pam's thoughts. But now, in the face of this latest travesty, the baby was the last thing on Pam's mind. *Was Marie insane? Did those things really happen to her? How could she prove it?* She had to believe her husband was a moral, if not faithful, man. That he wouldn't risk the well-being of his own children by having sexual intercourse with their aunt right next to their bedrooms. The Jack who forced Marie to have an abortion, then came to her apartment, raped her, almost choking her to death—that was not a man she knew. Sandra was looking at her with a questioning gaze. Pam shook her head no. She didn't believe it.

Pam looked at Marie. "I don't believe you" was all she said.

Marie smirked. "What don't you believe? The child abuse? The abortion? The rape? The choking? It's true, I tell you. I have the bills from the clinic, with Jack as the responsible party. You can ask Mom. She was there for me the second time. If we can find my roommate from college, ask her! She saw Jack there, saw me hysterical. And she was there when he brought me home afterward."

"The bills mean nothing." Pam was shaking her head no. "He could have been helping you out of a pregnancy from someone else. And I can't believe you would tell Nelda! She hated Jack! No wonder!"

"It's true! Why would I lie about something like that?" Marie was near tears again.

"No!" screamed Pam. "No! I don't believe it! I choose to believe you are lying, that you would rather make me feel like shit about my husband because he was my husband! Not yours! If you slept with him as an adult, that was your choice! You should have run from him! You should have told me then what was going on! Not wait and then, when he dies and can't defend himself, pile all of this crap on me. No!"

Sandra had crept back into the house sometime. Pam and Marie were alone out there in the dark, no candles having been lit, the sun down.

"If my husband molested you when you were a child, I truly apologize for that, for sticking my head in the sand. If you became pregnant by him and had an abortion, that must have been awful for you. But I will not have you sitting in the house that is essentially his bad mouthing him in front of a stranger because you are jealous of her! What are you thinking?"

Marie sat back down and looked up at Pam. "I loved him." Was all she said.

"Well, it's not about you, is it? It's not even about me anymore. Now it is all about the baby—Jack's baby. Sandra is going to have this child whether we approve or not. It will have the legacy of Jack as its father. Furthermore, Jack left his business to Sandra. That's right," responding to the look of astonishment on Marie's face, "one more piece of news. I hope to God that the last of it was your bomb. I don't think I can take anymore."

Whether or not Marie heard a word her sister said remained to be seen, because the next thing she said was, "You are going to support her in this? What the hell happened to your pride?"

Pam laughed and sat down again. *Pride? You are kidding, right? What pride?* But she only said, "Yes, I am going to support her." She got up from the chair. "I'm going to go find her to see if we can't talk about some things I want to talk about. If you don't want to, get up and go to your room. You aren't dictating what the conversation is anymore." She walked back into the house and called for Sandra.

The next morning, a haggard Pam got up out of her bed and went to the bathroom. She reached for the knob on the tub faucet and then pulled back. She was going to go without showering and doing her hair and makeup that day. She'd wash, comb her hair, and put eyeliner and lipstick on, but that was all. She was going to take the day off. *To hell with the dinner tonight.* She would order pizza if there was anyone left to eat it. She tried to remember the last time she went without makeup and could not. *Who am I primping for anyway? All the time I spent taking care of my*

Suzanne Jenkins

appearance to please a man who was screwing another woman in this very house. Could it be true? Was he such a monster?

She walked out of her room into the hallway and looked out the doors that lead to the veranda. The sun was just at the horizon. It was going to be a hot, bright day. She suddenly felt like she wanted to sit on the beach. She might even wear a bathing suit and get her legs wet.

Back in the kitchen, she got the coffee pot ready. Something was happening to her. She felt comfortable in her house. The restlessness she had encountered during the past week or so was gone. She laughed at herself, thinking what a fickle woman she was! *Hearing the worst news a wife can hear and my response is peace? Fickle was a nice word for what I am!* Pam laughed out loud.

It was the weekend. She wanted to talk to her kids even though it was early. They both worked on Saturdays, so they should be up. Taking a cup of coffee back to her bedroom, as she wasn't ready to chat with her guests yet if they were even still there, she sat on the chaise overlooking the ocean and picked up the phone. She dialed Brent's number first; he was a man of few words. Lisa would keep her on the phone longer. He answered on the first ring.

"Mom! How the heck are you?" he asked her.

Pam told him she was doing pretty well and asked when he could come back for a visit. They chatted for five minutes and then she let him go, Brent promising her that he would let her know the following week when he would come home.

Lisa was just getting up and talked with her mother while she fixed her breakfast, brushed her teeth, did her makeup, and got dressed. Pam didn't mention any of the negative garbage that had taken place or the baby. But she fully planned on telling both kids about it when they came home next.

After Marie's revelation the night before, Pam went to Sandra and asked her to please keep what she had heard to herself, which Sandra promised to do. Sandra said she had something important to discuss about the business, but Pam was just too raw to take one more thing in. They promised to talk before the weekend was up.

With the morning and her newfound peace, Pam was anxious to hear what Sandra had to say. She probably wished she had never come to the beach.

The truth was, Sandra was feeling more disgusted with Marie than anything else. *Her timing sucked!* The day out of the city stretched out before her. She wanted to tell Pam about an idea she had for the business, which might change a lot of the angst she was having over Jack's decision to give it to her. She planned on lying on the beach, eating inappropriate foods, and ignoring Marie for the rest of the weekend. She came down the stairs into the kitchen after a glorious night of sleep. Nothing that had happened bothered her. She thought she may be becoming callus, but the truth was, Marie's entire ethic was based in jealousy—jealousy of Pam and now of Sandra. It was horrible that she was molested for all those years. Sandra felt there had to be something underlying. Nothing would make it okay to molest a child, but there was something else. She wouldn't spend time trying to uncover it this weekend, but when they got back to the city, she fully intended on trying to find out what it was.

She and Pam got to the kitchen at the same time, Pam ready for a second cup of coffee, Sandra going to pour her first.

"When you are ready for more brain work, I'd like to talk to you about an idea I had that would include the children in their father's business. I know it is early for business talk."

Pam pointed to a glass pedestal covered cake plate that was filled with danish.

"Let's eat first. My brain is still foggy from sleeping," Pam replied. "What a beautiful morning! I can't wait to get outdoors!" Pam got the butter out of the refrigerator. Butter on a danish—she was living dangerously.

"I am lying on the beach today if it is the last thing I do." Sandra was in her comfort zone with Pam. They had weathered last night. Sandra knew where she was to blame. She made a horrible moral lapse in judgment. The payment was huge, raising a child she bore of a married man alone. She needed Pam, so she would do what was needed to maintain a relationship with her. If it meant groveling, she would grovel. She wasn't above any act of contrition to make this right. The fact that Pam seemed okay this morning after the terrible revelation of Marie's proved that she was a powerfully strong woman. Sandra wondered if she knew that. She doubted it. "Did you have anything you wanted to do today? You had mentioned the flea market." Sandra looked at her.

Pam laughed. "I think the beach sounds wonderful. I'll go find some shorts to put on." She grabbed her coffee cup and plate of danish and went back to her room. If she seemed like she was fleeing from the scene of a crime, it was because she didn't have anything to say yet, especially not wanting to discuss business with Marie in the house.

Sandra didn't seem to notice and took her own coffee and breakfast out on the veranda. The air was warm, and there was a soft, ocean breeze. She pulled out a chair that faced the water and sat down. Sipping the coffee, she thought, *I could live like this so easily. I love it here. The house is comfortable, the property beautiful, what could be more wonderful?* The Danish was fabulous, flaky pastry with a marvelous filling that was part cheese, part almond paste. The one thing Sandra had going for her right now was that she needed to gain some weight, and there was a good chance this Danish would help her out. If she could figure out a way, she would live here indefinitely with Pam. For now, she would be content with this weekend, and maybe every weekend in the future. Laughing to herself, she bit into the Danish.

Marie slept until eleven a.m. She woke up in a sweat, the sun beating in through her window. Her hair was wet, stuck to her face and neck. She had a headache. The icing on the cake was that she feared she had started her period, cramps traveling from her belly down to her knees. She stumbled out of her bed and through the bathroom door. She confirmed her fears when she pulled down her pants. Back in the bedroom, Marie went through her suitcase and pulled out the most comfortable clothes she brought, baggy shorts and a long-sleeved T-shirt. She took a cool shower, washing her hair and conditioning it with expensive stuff Pam had left for her. She dressed and wrapped her hair in a bath towel. Pam and Sandra were out on the

Suzanne Jenkins

beach, sitting in folding chairs under a huge beach umbrella. Marie was glad for the solitude, but happy that
her sister was within yelling distance. The coffee pot was
empty, a full thermos left for her. She poured a cup for herself. Taking the cup, and the entire covered cake plate of
pastries, she headed for the veranda. The Saturday edition
of the *New York Times* was on the table. She would read it
from cover to cover, eating what was left of the pastries.
The sugar made her feel lightheaded. She drank another
cup of coffee. *This was what Saturdays at the beach were all
about.*

When she finished with the paper, she got up and
went into Jack's den. There, she would find shelf after
shelf of fiction. She chose a couple of books that were unfamiliar and took them to her room, throwing them on
the bed. Then she went back to the kitchen and picked
snacks out of the refrigerator and the pantry. A can of diet
soda completed her stash. She would lie in bed, propped up
on pillows, eating and reading all afternoon. She couldn't
remember the last time she gave in to laziness. *Years and
years ago*, she thought, *and it was long overdue.*

Sometime after two p.m., she must have fallen asleep.
There was a soft knock on her door, but she slept through
it. Pam opened it and peaked in at her baby sister to make
sure she was okay. Seeing the snack bags and fruit peels,
she smiled and thought, *Good.* The empty cake tray had
already been discovered. Marie needed to rest.

Marie woke up at four. Her cramps were better, and
with the nap, she finally felt refreshed. She rolled out of
bed and sat at the edge of it for a few minutes. *What would
the rest of the day bring?* Everything about her and Jack was

on the table. *There couldn't possibly be any more surprises, could there?* She knew that she, for one, was not going to try to rationalize her behavior or that of Jack's, make excuses, apologize, or expect apologies. She was finished with it. What was done was done. Sandra being pregnant was inconsequential, as far as Marie was concerned. What Pam chose to do with that information was up to her. The day had shown Marie the truth; she only had herself to blame. She had possibly attempted to gain some sympathy by blasting out her story as she did. Now, she was only regretful. She assumed that she had destroyed the relationship that she had with her sister, and rightly so. *Jack could only be blamed for the part of their relationship that took place when she was underage, correct?* The adult phase had to be shared. She thought of the nights he slept at her apartment. He'd call Pam on his cell phone to say good-night from time to time. She remembered Pam saying on one occasion that he rarely did that. *Was it only when he was in her apartment that he called, possibly for her benefit?* To say, "See, I'm still married to your sister, although I am here, with you." She would love to ask him, but it was too late.

Marie got up and left her room. Sandra was sitting at the counter, eating a piece of fruit, reading a take-out menu. Pam was puttering at the sink. They looked up when she came into the kitchen.

"Well, good afternoon! I was beginning to wonder if you were alive in there!" her sister said. Pam seemed chipper. Marie wondered how she did it. *Was she daft? Maybe that was it. Whatever quality made her able to stay so upbeat in the face of so much garbage was pretty amazing.* "Oh, just to warn you, Mom called, and she is coming here for dinner tonight." Marie's heart sunk. *Had Pam called her? Were they going to confront her?* She didn't even want to go there with her sister.

"Oh. Why? If I may ask," Marie said. "Hasn't there been enough drama around here? Thanks to me, of course." She smiled to show that she was taking the blame, not accusing.

Pam looked over at Marie. "I sort of thought you might be able to tell me why."

Marie shook her head no. "I have no idea. I'm not sure I will survive it, of that much I am certain." She slumped onto a counter stool. "What was the reason again we got together this weekend?" She looked quizzically at Pam. "I did not plan to throw that bomb out last night. I wasn't even going to mention it, but I apologize now. My timing sucked."

Sandra looked at Pam. She started chuckling. "Yes, Pam, what was it we were going to do?"

Pam shook her head in honest confusion. "I can't really remember now. I just thought that Jack's death would bring the three women who loved him the most together. Yes, Marie, you too. I know you loved him, not as it turns out how you loved him, but that really doesn't matter now. There is something about the three of us that seemed worth pursuing to me—almost three generations, all focused on the same man. Now I wonder if he was capable of love, although Marie seemed to think he loved you, Sandra."

The two sisters looked at her. She flushed.

"He told me he loved you, Pam. We know he did. But it was Jack's brand of love. Love with strings. Love with pain. I said yesterday that I thought Marie was selfish. But the truth is, Jack was selfish. And because of the women around him, let's include Bernice in this; he got away with it. He took what he wanted and didn't deny himself anything. He was so charming!" The three women all smiled at that.

"Granted, he was a charmer, all right," said Pam, thinking of her devotion to him, waiting on his every word. But then she stopped coming into the city. *Did he move her out to get her out of the way? So he could play?* She kept her doubts to herself. She cared enough about herself to refuse to stay where she was and be unhappy. That, at least, was a plus.

"But what about Mom? I really don't think I can deal with her now." Marie was struggling to keep the whine out of her voice.

"Well, she is on her way, my friend, there is nothing you can do about it now." Pam turned her back to fill a pitcher with water. She could feel her patience waning. "I want her to meet Sandra anyway. Let's keep the intrigue out of the conversation tonight, okay? There is plenty of time for that later.'"

"I think I would like a Philly cheesesteak," Sandra said, getting back to the take-out menus.

"They smell so awful! We all better get them, then," Marie said.

So they ordered cheesesteaks, fries, Greek salads, and bread sticks. When the food arrived, they took it out on the veranda to eat. Marie was going with the flow, trying to stay relaxed and not lose it in the face of Sandra's revelation, her mother coming, and having to go back to work on Monday. What the point of the weekend really was had eluded her. *Had Pam planned it to give Sandra a platform for her announcement?* She might get the courage to ask later.

The food was handed around. Pam was obviously trying to say something; she kept pausing and looking at her guests. Finally, she spoke up.

"I don't want to start a conversation about this, but I have something to say that I want said before my mother shows up. From now on, my motive in life is to facilitate the children—Lisa, Brent, and now the baby. Those three beings are the purpose of us staying civil. It has to be all about them, especially the baby. Nothing is more important than the baby. If it weren't for my two children, then I wouldn't have to worry about the baby. But it is their sibling." She looked over at Marie. "Can you agree with this? What happened to you was awful. But you are an adult now. Get some help if you have to. But don't make it about the children or about me. I am sorry my husband did what he did to you."

Marie was chewing on a mouth full of food. *What did Pam expect of her?* She swallowed.

"I guess I can agree with it. What do you want from me?" Sandra's head swung around to Marie. *What a bitch!* she thought. "What I meant was, how can I help you achieve that?" she said, looking directly at Sandra.

Pam answered for her. "We can achieve it by thinking of the baby first, not of ourselves. Marie, if I can get over what has happened to my family, you can get over it, too. Let's stop now before Mom gets here."

At seven p.m., Nelda arrived. She was looking forward to spending the evening with Pam. They hadn't been together since the funeral. Although only two weeks had passed, it felt much longer.

Pam greeted her at the door, and Nelda was slightly taken aback by her appearance—no makeup, hair pulled back in a banana clip, bathing suit cover-up.

"Good beach day?" she inquired.

Pam led the way to the veranda.

"Fabulous. I can't remember the last time I spent all day reading under an umbrella."

When she stepped over the threshold to the veranda, Nelda grabbed her shirt at the neck. *Didn't I just see Marie? Oh God, was she anorexic again?* She was literally grey, and although she was sitting there eating a cheesesteak, of all things, she was skeletal. Nelda kept her mouth shut, trying not to purse her lips.

"Good evening, Mother!" Marie said. Nelda bent down and kissed her. She smelled of soap and water. At least she was bathing.

"Mom, this is Sandra Benson. She holds an important position at Jack's company."

Sandra stood up and reached over the table to grab Nelda's hand.

"Nice to meet you!"

If things could just stay pleasant, or otherwise superficial, like this, Pam would be happy—no in-depth conversations, no psycho-dramas. She noticed her mother's concern at Marie's appearance. She would take her aside later and tell her that she had been eating pretty much nonstop for the past twenty-four hours. Maybe she has just been lonely, or reverting from anorexia to a binge-purge cycle.

The evening went well, although Nelda wasn't herself. Later, Pam used the expression "bright" to describe the way her mother looked. Her eyes were glazed over, and she was smiling inappropriately.

Pam whispered to her sister, "Maybe she's been drinking."

Marie ended up asking her mother to stay; she offered to drive her home in the morning. She had a drawer in Marie's room with clean pajamas and underwear, and there was nothing pressing waiting for her to get back to Brooklyn.

The next morning, Sandra came down with her suitcase. She was going to leave, too. She had a long train ride home and wanted to prepare for the week. Pam offered to drive her to the train station, but Marie had already said she could drop her off. They stayed for coffee and croissants and then left together. Pam felt the anxiety building. She thought she might be nervous about being left, but then realized she wanted them to move on. She wanted to be alone again.

29

The three women left, cordiality swirling around them. Pam walked them out to Marie's car and stood at the curb waving good-bye as they pulled away. The moment she was alone, she started thinking of what she could do next. She had a list of things that needed to be done that week. She was going to take Marie's room and make it into a nursery. She was thinking that Sandra would enlist her aid in childcare from time to time. Of course, before she did anything permanent, she would ask her. Then she was going to move Marie upstairs. The rooms had great views up there and private bathrooms. It would be enough to keep her busy for a while.

And, lastly, there was Jack's den. Although it was the place the family gathered to watch TV or play games, it was really his room. It had a huge desk and chair and his books and papers. He didn't want to be isolated from the family in a private office. He liked being part of the action. She thought about Jack. He was a dichotomy. Of course, she always thought he was so transparent, loving his kids and family, such an attentive son to Bernice, so many friends all over the country that loved him. And, if it were all true, adulterer, child abuser, and all the adjectives to describe someone who would molest his own sister-in-law for years and years and years, force her to have two abortions, and physically harm her. *Could it really be?* Although Pam had no intention of ever again discussing him negatively with either Marie or Sandra, she knew she had barely begun psychoanalyzing his behavior for herself. She didn't know where to begin.

She stood in the middle of the den and slowly turned around. *Where to start?* The apartment on Madison Avenue came into her mind. *Oh boy*, she thought, *I have to deal with that as well.* She walked over and sat at his desk. It was a gleaming monstrosity of a desk, with three big drawers down each side and three slim drawers across the top. She thought maybe she would start with a drawer that held paper. Paper was always so difficult to deal with. *What was important? What was being saved as a memento? What was trash?* She opened and closed drawers until she came to the second drawer from the top on the right. It held manila file folders, lying face up, stacked to the top. She would get a box from the garage and place the folders in the box and start going through them.

The first folder contained letters from an organization that supported sports for teens on the island. She knew Jack was involved with the group and occasionally sponsored the lacrosse games. That he was active in children's groups was scary, knowing what she did now. She set that folder aside; it might hold information that would be needed at tax time.

The next folder held a spreadsheet and receipts pertaining to his expenses in the house. He rarely worked from home. She flipped through the receipts. It looked like he was using a portion of the apartment in the city as a home office. Folder after folder held nothing of interest to her. She wondered what she was looking for. Her motive of cleaning out his desk fell flat. She was simply searching for something to help her understand who he was.

Thinking of the apartment again, she remembered the folder filled with the evidence of his birth. Maybe she needed to get in touch with Bernice. The idea that Bernice knew of Jack's infidelity and the baby unnerved her. She wondered if Sandra was on the phone with Bernice this very minute, filling her in on the weekend. She doubted Marie's shocking story was dinnertime conversation between Sandra and Bernice.

At the bottom of the drawer, tucked away in the left corner, she eyed a strip of paper. It appeared to be stuck there. She pulled on it, and it was more than a strip. She stood up and pushed the chair away. Bending over, she pulled the drawer all the way out of the desk and let it drop to the floor. At the back of the outside of the drawer, a whole sheet of paper, the edge stuck in the drawer, had fallen out of a folder that was hidden in the body of the desk, behind the drawers.

Pam was having a hot flash. She thought of the saying "curiosity killed the cat" as she reached for the folder. It was newer, not dust covered, so she felt it may have been put there purposely, recently.

She put the folder on the desk, looking at it, not opening it. Her stomach rumbled. She was empty. It was time for more coffee and something to eat. Walking into the kitchen, she turned around and went back to the den and picked up the folder. She took it with her and placed it in the pantry. Then she locked the pantry door.

30

Sandra was suffocating in the backseat of Marie's car. Nelda was obviously confused by her presence; she made that clear last night when she repeated five or six times, "Now, how do you know Jack?"

Marie tried to talk Sandra into coming all the way into the city with her, but Sandra knew she would die first. She insisted that she be taken to the train stop; her excuse was she had a ticket that needed to be used or it would expire. Marie wasn't buying it, but Nelda was relieved that she didn't have to spend the next hour with a stranger.

The train was on time, and Sandra found a seat with legroom so she didn't have to struggle with her suitcase. She put her head against the headrest and closed her eyes. When she opened them again, the train was pulling into Penn Station. *Oh, to find a cab,* she prayed. There was a lineup of cabs when she stepped outside.

It was hot in the city, and hotter in the cab. She dug through her purse for a tissue. The driver was a maniac, slamming the brakes at red lights, speeding off at green, and screeching the brakes when he went around corners. She screamed at him to slow down. At the corner of Broadway and Seventy-ninth, she told him to let her out. She threw the fare on the front seat and slammed the door. She'd walk the rest of the way before she would let that jerk see where she lived. When she got to H&R, she went in and got half a dozen bagels and a pint of vegetable cream cheese, her lunch for the next six days. With each step toward her apartment, her suitcase rolling behind her, she relaxed a little more.

She wondered what she was thinking when staying at the beach seemed like such an enticing idea? There was nothing like the security of her own house. She unlocked the door and pushed it open, and the cool, dark safety enveloped her as she stepped over the threshold. She was home.

Marie found a place to park the car on her mother's street so she could go in. It had been weeks since she was in the house. They walked side by side down the street, talking about the evening at Pam's. Marie was itching to tell her mother the news that Sandra was pregnant with Jack's baby and, worse, that he had willed her his controlling interest in the business. It hadn't occurred to Marie until she was in bed, unable to sleep, that Jack hadn't remembered her in his will—the final slap in the face. Her mother had always been Pam's champion. She would have to work her announcement carefully to illicit the most sympathy for herself. It would be intolerable if Nelda started ragging on her and praising Pam.

She stood on the stoop while her mother struggled with the lock. Marie noticed the paper-thin skin on her mother's hands and the way they shook. *When had she gotten so old?* At Jack's funeral, her mother took charge. Pam had put her in control of Jack's family, the kitchen, and calling friends and family. *Had she aged like this in two weeks?*

Maybe hearing about the baby would be too much for her. *Tough, it had to be done,* she decided.

They stepped over the threshold. Marie involuntarily gasped when she saw the interior of her mother's house. Always compulsively neat, it was trashed. It smelled like garbage, and worse, there was food and dirty dishes all over the kitchen. Marie paused and took it in, finally addressing her mother. At first, she wondered if the place had been vandalized. And then realized what could be happening.

"Mom, what the hell is this? Why aren't you cleaning up?"

Nelda put her purse down on the counter. She sat down in a kitchen chair.

"I haven't felt up to cleaning. I guess I got used to it looking like this," she said.

Marie stepped forward, doing a three-hundred-and-sixty-degree turn.

"Well, this is not acceptable. Go change your clothes and then make us a pot of coffee. I'm glad we left Pam's when we did because this is going to take all day to clean up, and I have to go to work tomorrow."

She literally rolled up her sleeves. Moving over to the sink, she fished through rank-smelling water and found the plug, lifting it so the foul mess would go down the drain. She started running the hot water while she rummaged through the cabinet under the sink for some kind of detergent. Replacing the plug, she squirted in a generous amount of the stuff and let the sink fill up.

She yelled to her mother, "Is the dishwasher working?"

Nelda yelled back, "I think so."

Marie thought to herself, *Oh, for God's sake. What next?* She would handle this mess, but it was evident that something was going to have to be done for her mother, either Pam or her keeping an eye on the house or a cleaning lady coming in once a week, probably a combination of both.

Marie worked for a few hours, washing up, throwing trash away, running the vacuum, and dusting. She tackled the bathroom downstairs, but was afraid to go up to her mother's room. She didn't think she had the energy for it. But when she was done with the public rooms, she went upstairs anyway, concentrating on her mother's bedroom and bathroom, changing sheets, picking up dirty towels and clothes for the washer, and emptying trash bins.

She hauled several loads of dirty clothing down to the basement and got the washer going. She went back up to the kitchen and got herself a cup of coffee. She picked up her mother's phone and dialed Pam's number. Pam answered on the first ring.

"Mom?" she answered. "No, Pam, it's Marie. I decided to come in with her, and you would not believe the mess I found. I don't think she has been doing dishes or cleaning for a couple of weeks. I am just starting the laundry now." She described the filth and smell.

"Oh my God! I wonder what is going on? What is she doing now?"

Marie looked in the living room. Her mother was sorting through magazines, dusting bookshelves as she went. She looked pale, ill.

Marie yelled in to her, "Mother, sit down and re-lax, will you? She looks like shit. Did you notice? I didn't! Guess I was too wrapped up in myself. I wonder if she had a stroke?" Marie whispered into the phone.

They planned for Pam to visit her on Monday and, if she thought it was necessary, bring her home. They were both concerned about leaving her alone, but she would hate being in the city with Marie, left alone in the apartment while she went to work.

Marie checked the pantry and the refrigerator to make sure there was food there. It was adequate. She went in and sat down in her father's old recliner.

"Mom, what should we fix for dinner?"

"Oh, is it that time already? I'm not really hungry," she said.

Marie got out of the chair and went into the kitchen again. She opened the pantry door and started listing what they could have.

"Chicken noodle soup with a tuna sandwich," she said. "Or beef stew? Yuck, never mind." Opening the fridge door and assessing the contents, she said, "Okay, Mom, I know what you would like. How about a grilled-cheese sandwich?"

"That sounds good," she said. She walked into the kitchen, unsteady on her feet.

Marie couldn't believe she didn't notice this before. She suddenly felt overwhelming love and compassion for her mother. Turning her back so her tears wouldn't show, Marie busied herself at the stove. *What more could go wrong? All of the shit with Jack and now this? My mother failing?* Pam would say, "This is just life." She prepared the sandwiches and took them to the table.

"Come, Mom, let's eat together." At least she would have a meal tonight, and then Pam would take over tomorrow.

She felt convicted about her own nutrition, about the way she didn't care for herself. Forty-five was pushing it. She wasn't a child anymore, with years ahead of herself to make amends for the damage done to her body. She wondered what was happening to her family and what else would happen before this downward spiral would end. The thought of the impact her eating disorder could have had on Lisa. Embarrassed and shame-filled, she made the decision to do better.

She waited while Nelda had her shower and got clean pajamas on. She was lucid, but so frail. Marie was worried about her while she bathed. She tried to imagine how day after day, the woman lived alone, managed the stairs, took the bus to the train, did her own shopping, and it had come to this—her daughter standing outside of the bathroom door, just in case.

Nelda promised Marie she would stay upstairs until the morning. She didn't want her mother walking up and down the stairs at night. Preparing a snack for her, Marie gathered up everything her mother could possibly want in the evening. She put crackers and cheese on a small plate, a package of cookies, and a glass of milk. Watching her daughter, Nelda asked if she could have tea, too. Marie put the kettle on and found an old china teapot. She took the tray of snacks up to the bedroom and then made another trip with the teapot, a mug, and cream and sugar.

She got Nelda situated in bed, sitting up, the remote on the night table, the tray of food and tea things on a small folding table she had dragged in from her old room. She poured the tea and placed the mug on the night table. Her mother, a statuesque woman in her youth, looked like a small bird propped up in bed.

She went downstairs and made sure the door to the garage and the backyard were locked, that the windows down there were closed. Remembering the basement, she went down there, the creepiness factor multiplied by the darkness, and made sure the windows were closed and locked there as well. *What am I worried about?* Her mother had lived in that same house, raised her family there for sixty years, and never had a problem. She felt as though she were leaving a small child to sleep in the house alone.

Suddenly, Marie knew she couldn't leave her mother. She would spend the night, make sure she was okay in the morning, and go in to work late. She called Pam to tell her the plan so she would feel at peace about her mom and not make herself crazy trying to get there in the morning. They talked for an hour. They had their mother's best interests at heart. And it was wonderful to have something to talk about that didn't revolve around the sin of Jack Smith.

Pam took the news of her mother's decline in stride. She didn't notice it when they were together the night before. She was too worried that Marie would slip and say something about the baby. It was just another thing to deal with. She would devote her life to her mother, if necessary, driving to Brooklyn every day to care for her and moving her to live at the beach when she would submit.

Suzanne Jenkins

She walked into the wing of the house that the children and Marie had shared. It was going to be the nursery wing soon. It would be a suitable place for her mother to live, if need be. Maybe because of what the past two and a half weeks had been to Pam, she was thinking more rationally about Nelda. The first thing she would do tomorrow would be to take her to the doctor. *What if she did have a small stroke, as Marie had suggested?* It was too late to do anything about it. That was one of the drawbacks of living alone.

31

Although it was late, Pam wanted to take a look at the folder Jack had hidden away. Looking around her kitchen, she knew she was alone and unobserved, but irrationally, she needed to be certain. Unlocking the door, she opened the pantry and reached for the folder. She looked into it and saw odds and ends of paper and what looked like random notes. It wasn't Jack's writing.

Sitting down on a stool, she took the top note and unfolded it. It looked like Marie's writing. There was no date or any reference to time. It was crisp, so she didn't think the paper was old.

"Jack, I can't deal with you anymore. I'm not coming to the beach tonight. If you try to force me, I am telling Pam. Marie."

Pam put the note down. *Why would he have saved this?* She tried to remember a time when Marie didn't come to a planned visit. There were a few over the years—Marie not feeling well at the last minute, a flat tire, a leaking toilet.

The next one was also written in Marie's hand, on nondescript notepaper: "Jack, Everything you said to me was lies. I don't believe any of it. You are purposely trying to make me look crazy, and it won't work." A third note said, simply, "Jack, I'm sorry about last night. It won't happen again. Marie."

Wow, Pam thought, *a lot of drama. How did he juggle everything and still run a business and be a husband and father?* She would never know. She thumbed through the rest of the notes, and they were all the same genre—two or three lines and no date or identifying marks to tell when they were written.

She put the folder down on the counter, knowing that she would destroy it. There was no point in saving something to back up Marie's claims, just in case. She didn't know what Marie was going to do once it sunk in that Jack didn't leave her anything in the will. They bought that apartment for her, her car, paid for her education. There wouldn't be anything else from Jack. And nothing she could say about him would be substantiated by these notes.

Jack had installed a fire pit on the veranda the year they moved to Long Island. Pam didn't want it. She was worried about the children getting burned, about the fire leaving the confines of the pit and catching the roof and burning the house down. Now she was happy it was there.

She went out with the folder in her hand. There was an automatic start mechanism. With a twist of a knob, she turned the gas on and the fire started. She took the notes out, one by one, all but two unread, and tossed them in the flames. Pam realized the strength and self-control it was taking not to read all the notes. Still confused as to why Jack would save such incriminating stuff, she had a wave of fear and regret. *What if I needed them suddenly?* But could think of no reason and continued to throw them on the fire until the folder was empty.

She wondered if he had written notes to Sandra, and worse, to Marie. She hoped not. However, if he had, they were no reflection on her. There was nothing she could do about it if he had left a record of his misdeeds.

The rest of the evening stretched wonderfully out before her. The contrast of her feeling of joy and the empty, anxiety-ridden nights prior to that night made no sense at all, but she wasn't going to question it. Figuring it was just the aftermath of having too much drama, she decided to just go with the flow and enjoy it. Putting her pajamas on, she went out to the veranda, lowered the screens, and read. There was a comfortable sitting area out there, with a sofa and chair and ottoman. The screen made it possible to turn a reading light on and not be bothered by bugs. She lost herself in a novel that had failed to hold her interest just a few days ago. Alone in her house, everyone else in her life accounted for, all was well with the world.

32

Sandra put her bagels away, one in a baggie for the next day and the rest in the freezer. She put the teakettle on for a cup of tea. She had to have it. While she was waiting for the kettle to whistle, she unzipped her suitcase in the hall and lifted her clothing out of it. That thing had been through some filthy streets today and would not roll through her house.

The list of tasks to accomplish threaded through her mind. Reaching for a pen and paper on her table, she started writing. There were a few checks to send that week and a call to make regarding her health insurance. Sometime soon she would have to run into Jersey City to go to a discount department store there. She was ashamed to admit, but it was the only place she could get a hair product she liked at about half what it cost in the city.

She remembered Jack's office. Pete had said on Friday that he wasn't going to rush Pam. He figured she would want his belongings sooner or later. Sandra was concerned about that for some reason. There was nothing to make her think he had left anything incriminating behind. But it was still unnerving. She thought she might mention it to Pam, just to get the ball rolling. Seeing his things in there made her sad, and she avoided it whenever possible.

Her phone rang. She picked it up and, as if she were reading Sandra's mind, saw Bernice's phone number. *Oh*

God, not now, she thought. She just didn't know if she had
it in her today. She let the machine pick up and then un-
plugged the phone. Thinking quickly, she tiptoed to the
door and placed the chain in its socket. Then she closed
the shade in her bedroom, just in case someone was on
Eighty-second, peering between buildings to try to determine if she was home and just avoiding a call. Her paranoia
validated, she picked up her tea and went down the stairs
to her den. She plopped down in the overstuffed chair and
reached for the remote. An afternoon of mindless television would help her recover from "Jack Family Overload,"
or JFO.

Bernice wasn't the only one trying to reach Sandra.
Jack's younger brother, Bill, spent an upsetting morning
with his mother. Their usual Sunday brunch was a peaceful family tradition. Anne and Bill and their two sons took
a weekly cab ride uptown from their Greenwich Village
brownstone to spend the morning with Bernice, eating a
lavish spread and reading the Sunday *Times*. Anne enjoyed
going, in spite of her overbearing mother-in-law. It was
a treat to be served a delicious meal in such a beautiful
home. In the nice weather, like today, they often sat in the
courtyard. The high brick wall and several water features
buffered the noise of the street. Out-of-season plantings
and rare specimens told a story of wealth and indiscrimi-
nate spending.

If asked, both Anne and Pam never knew quite how
to explain what it was their husbands did for a living. Bill
ran the family business, which Harold started long before
he married Bernice. He had a little money from a trust
that matured when he turned twenty-five. He bought a

block of apartment buildings that needed renovation. Harold discovered that he was good at pinpointing what tenants wanted who would ultimately live in that neighborhood. His real estate venture segued into a demographic research company. He had a knack for figuring out exactly what should go where and who would end up there. Jack worked for him out of college and found that he was good at it, too, or more specifically, knew where to find people who were good at it. Bernice often said that it was with Harold's blessing that Jack left and formed his own company, Harold fielding clients to Jack's downtown office and keeping the uptown clients for himself. If only it had been that easy.

This Sunday brought what was left of the Smith family together again. Bernice had some news to break to her son. She had mulled over Sandra's situation all week. And unbeknownst to Bernice, the will had been read. Pam had the good sense to call her and tell her that Jack had given his half of the business to his girlfriend. Bernice was sure she had an ulterior motive. Pam wanted her to know she knew about Sandra. But Bernice knew about the baby. She smirked into the phone while her daughter-in-law droned on and on about the wisdom of her dead husband's choice. Evidently, Sandra had made a promise to include Pam's two children in the business and draw up papers, if need be. *We'll see*, Bernice thought, *we'll see.*

After they ate, Bernice made a great fuss about showing the boys a new electronic game she bought them. They went into the den, and she unveiled it. They would be occupied for some time. She went back out through the

Suzanne Jenkins

French doors, closing them behind her this time. She rang for Mildred and told her she was not to be disturbed.

"Mother, what is it? You look as white as a ghost." Bill was sitting at the glass table, drinking his third cup of coffee, and reading the sports page. Anne was leafing through a stack of gardening magazines Bernice had saved for her. They were both looking at her.

"Well, I have some news. News that may be shocking to you, but I think once you accept it, it will be good news." She was pacing on the cobblestones, her flats smacking the rock with each step. "Come over here and sit down, won't you, Anne? I don't want to have to speak too loudly." Anne got up from the stone bench and came back to the table.

Bill was clearly concerned. "Get on with it, Mother! You're scaring me." *Was she getting married again? That would be the worst.* Bill was used to taking a backseat. *But another man? No fucking way.*

"Calm down! For heaven's sake, you're making me nervous now." She came back to the table and sat down. "I am just going to say it. Jack was having an affair with a young woman who worked for him, a researcher. She is pregnant, very early. Jack didn't know. She is keeping the baby. And Jack willed her his share of the business." She exhaled loudly and fell back in her chair. There, it was out.

Bill was bright red in the face. He made a fist and slammed it down on the glass. Coffee cups jumped.

Bernice, startled, yelled, "Bill!"

"No way!" he yelled. "No fucking way! There is no fucking way my brother was having an affair!" He had jumped up and was yelling this, with Columbus Circle right on the other side of the wall. The boys had heard, too, and were looking up and walking to the door to see what their dad was yelling about. Anne stood up to reassure them, to make sure they stayed in the den. She walked over to her husband.

"Bill! Let your mother finish." She looked at Bernice. *Was there more?* Anne knew that, secretly, Jack had alluded to sharing his clients with Bill. They needed the business desperately. The city was changing, and things were not what they used to be uptown. Harold had died at the worst time, and some clients left then, nervous about losing someone they trusted.

"That's all," she said. "The young woman is lovely, poised and educated. Evidently, even Pam has embraced her."

"Pam's nuts!" Bill yelled again. "What the hell is she going to live on if the business goes to a stranger? And a baby? How do you even know it's Jack's? Oh my God, I can't believe this." Bill sat down then and with his head in his hand, repeated, "This is crazy. No way." Then he got up and pushed his chair in. "Come on, get the boys, Anne. I want to go home." He was agitated. Bernice understood that some line had been crossed, and he didn't understand how she could possibly be accepting this. His wife didn't argue, and Bernice didn't try to get him to stay. They went into the den and told the boys to gather up their toys. "I need a ride home. There is no way we are going out there to look for a cab." Bernice rang for Mildred. They were told the car would be around in a minute.

No one spoke. Bernice knew her son was livid and doing the best he could to control himself. Anne was petrified. The car arrived, and everyone got in. The boys said good-bye to their grandmother, Anne kissed her cheek, but Bill, in a daze, said nothing, looking straight ahead. They traveled downtown in silence.

When they pulled up to their house and got out of the car, Anne corralled the boys and whispered that their father had just gotten some bad news, and they had to be quiet, go to their rooms, and play for the afternoon. They understood and took off up the stairs. Bill seemed unaware of where they were. He walked into their library and closed the door. Anne breathed a sigh of relief and went to their room.

Once Bill was in the safety of his own home, locked away behind closed doors, he began to shake. He paced back and forth. He was so angry. He knew that his mother didn't have anything to do with it, but he was pissed at her because she was giving this whore the time of day. *And Pam? Was she crazy? Pam was a fool, but this was even a lot for her.* He was going to call her, but he would wait until Monday, when he was in the office. He wasn't going to let Anne hear what he had to say.

He realized he didn't know the name of the woman. That changed things. No one was going to give him any information about her in the state he was in. He needed to pull himself together and get ready to do an acting job like he had never done before. He was good at it. His entire life had been one big acting job.

33

By Monday, a quartet of human beings, all related by Jack Smith, woke up with one thought on their minds: how a tiny, unborn baby would change their lives.

Marie Fabian went to work late, coming in to the city from her mother's house in Brooklyn. She knew that her mother's care was a blip on the screen, that in the big picture, it wouldn't change much of how she lived her life.

Pam Smith left her house to make the forty-five minute drive to her mother. She made the decision that Nelda was coming home with her. She had too much to do to spend the day in Brooklyn. Her excuse for coming was that she needed her mother to help her choose paint and paper for the baby's room. She was going to drop that bomb today.

Sandra Benson had one thing on her mind as she made her way downtown: She was going to tackle Jack's office. She thought about it all night. Although she was fairly sure that Jack was meticulously discreet, Marie's disclosure Saturday night made her faith in him waver. If anything was uncovered in her search, she already had a speech ready for Pam, to whom everything contained within belonged. She wanted to protect Jack's dignity. If Pete were to discover anything, there was no way of knowing he would be discreet.

She got off her train at the Wall Street station. The walk to her office was only a few blocks. She was going to delay her task until the end of the day, when everyone left at five p.m. But when she got in, she discovered that Pete was taking the day off. She would have the freedom to go through Jack's office first thing.

When she went through the door, her anxiety level increased dramatically. Her heart began to pound so that she could feel it knocking on her chest wall. Her hands were sweating, and she felt nauseated. She closed the door behind her. The shades were already drawn to the corridor. She stood with her back against the door and looked around. The credenza, bookcases, conference table, and desk were all stacked with folders and papers. *Where should I begin looking? What am I looking for?*

She walked around and sat on his chair, facing the desk. The top was piled with client files. She quickly determined that there was nothing there that could incriminate him. Rolling the chair back, she slowly swept the room. Her eyes stopped at the credenza. It was long, about six feet, with four eigthteen-inch doors across the front of it. She rolled over to it and opened the first door. It contained the contents of a minibar. Closing that door, she opened the second one. It held a box of promotional gifts—caps, pens, T-shirts, mugs. The third door held stationary and computer paper. The fourth door had to be the one, but it was more boring office stuff.

She rolled back to the desk and began opening drawers. The top one, in the center of the desk, was a shock; in it was a gun. She had never touched one before, had no idea how to tell if it was loaded or not, and was afraid it would go off if she did picked it up. He had gum, aspirin, tissues, mints, Tums, and a styptic pen in the same drawer. *Everything he could possibly need.*

Opening all the drawers down the left of the desk revealed nothing. On the right side of the desk, she found his business checkbook, personal checkbook, folders containing season tickets to the opera, theater, museum openings, and ballet. Jack was a supporter of all the arts.

The last drawer she opened was filled with client files on hold. She leafed through them, recognizing names and places. She didn't think there was anything relevant there, so pushed on the drawer to slide it back into place. It resisted, so she pushed a little harder, and she could hear the crinkling of paper. Pulling the drawer out as far as it could go, she got down on her hands and knees to try to see behind it, and hit pay dirt. There was a stack of envelopes, folders, and papers. She pulled on the drawer, and it slid out of its opening. Reaching back into the hole, she pulled out the stack of hidden documents, stuffed them in her briefcase, and replaced the drawer.

Taking her briefcase back into her own office, she set it on the floor and worked on regaining her equilibrium. The possibility of getting caught had increased her blood pressure and pulse, and she waited for them to return to normal so she could get back to work.

Not so many blocks north in Midtown, Marie was just getting to work. Her mother was docile and in good humor when she left her, interested that Pam was coming, but a little confused as to why. Marie told her that Pam would explain everything when she got there.

Thankful for a full workload that week, she would be unavailable for anymore parental interventions. She wasn't left with a huge trust fund and had to work for a living. Pam didn't do anything worthwhile all day, so she could take over. Marie was surprised at her change of attitude, but wasn't going to psychoanalyze it. She was doing the best that she could.

Farther uptown, in a beautiful prewar building, the fourth person in the quartet was in a foul mood. Bill Smith's secretary was giving him a wide berth. Having been instructed to put no calls through and allow no one near him, she was having a busy morning juggling unhappy callers, mostly his mother. Bill had been clear, not even his wife was to be put through, unless it was life or death. Bernice was sick at heart hearing the verdict; she was not going to get to speak to her son until he called her back. She was tempted to call either Sandra or Pam, but resisted the urge. That would backfire, surely.

Bill started calling his sister-in-law at 7:00 a.m. without success. Finally, at 10:00, she answered with a breathless hello.

"Pam, it's Bill," he said. When there was no response, he repeated, "Bill! Your brother-in-law!" *For God's sake, she was a moron!*

"Bill?" Pam had never, ever heard his voice on the phone. He had never called her before. "What's wrong?" she said, concerned. In the next breath, she shouted, "Mother, sit down! I'll be right with you."

He calmed down, realizing she had a visitor there. "We need to talk soon—like today. He waited, and when she didn't respond right away, he went on, "Bernice tells me we are expecting a new member of the Smith family."

Pam breathed into the phone. *What did he expect from me?*

"Pam! Are you listening to me? For God's sake, what the hell is going on? Did you have any idea that Jack was fucking around on you?"

"That's enough, Bill! First of all, you have never, in all the years I was married to your brother, called this house. I am shocked to hear your voice over the phone! Secondly, that Jack got someone pregnant is not my fault, and you will not speak to me as though it were. Thirdly, it is none of your business what Jack was doing, or what I was doing, or what anyone in this house was doing."

He sat at his desk, one hand holding the phone, the other holding his head.

"I'm sorry. You're right. It's just such a shock," he said. "He was going to field some clients our way."

"Is that all you are worried about, Bill? Business? She'll honor whatever Jack was planning. She's a lovely woman, a professional business woman."

"Of course, that isn't all! It's so complicated; I can't believe this has happened. And a baby? Are you sure it's his?" Pam didn't answer him. He went on, "It's just not like Jack."

"You didn't know your brother then, because it was just like him. Bill, I can't go into anymore now. Evidently, my mother has had a stroke or something, and I have to get her some medical help today," she lied. "We'll talk later, okay? I'll call you tonight." She hung up not waiting for him to respond. *What a jerk!*

"So, Mom." Pam walked to the table and pulled a chair out to sit next to her mother. "What's going on?" She reached out to take her hand.

"Thank you for your concern about me, dear," she said. "I'm not sure what's going on with me. I didn't feel good all week." She looked down at her hands and then up at Pam. "I feel better today."

"Mom, I need to tell you something. Are you up for some news that may upset you?" She took her mom's hands in hers. She needed to tell Nelda today. She didn't want any more loose ends. Her kids were the last to hear from her.

"What now?" she said, frowning.

"Jack had an affair before he died, and the girl is pregnant." There, she said it. It was out. Her mother knew the truth. *What could be more embarrassing than having your critical mother know that her daughter was married to someone who wasn't satisfied with her? What could be worse?* Hopefully, her mother would never find out.

"With who?" Her voice was up an octave, not shrill, but on its way.

"Do you remember Sandra? The girl who was here yesterday? Her." Pam realized how lame that must sound.

"Why...why in God's name did you have her here, Pam? That doesn't make any sense." Nelda was clearly annoyed.

Why is she annoyed? Pam wondered. *How did Jacks' behavior affect her?*

"I think I need to be involved with the baby, Mom. I can't explain it, exactly. Something about it being part of Jack. The baby will be the kids' sibling. I need to facilitate that." She was getting depressed. Her mother was acutely lucid for having had a stroke. Perhaps if she were still acting like a lost child, this would have been easy.

"The baby doesn't mean anything to your children, Pam. Stop being such a ninny!" She pushed her chair away from the table and slowly got up, her body not in agreement with her mind. She thought about what a wimp her daughter was. *She let that ass run her life while he was involved with another woman.* She never liked him. "Am I staying here? Why did you bring me here?" Her voice was higher now, like a child who was not getting her way.

"Mom, could you just relax? Sit down, okay? I know you must be so disappointed in Jack, in me. But what else can I do? I can't deny the baby. The children would never forgive me. So everything I am doing is for them and, ultimately, the good of the baby." Again, she realized how lame that sounded. *Her whole life boiled down to this; the illegitimate baby of her late husband.*

"Pam, maybe what you could do is focus on yourself and those two lovely children you gave birth to. Do you really think they are going to be happy about this? How are you going to tell them? 'Lisa, Brent, your dad had an affair, and the girl is pregnant,' like you told me? Really? I don't see them jumping for joy." Nelda was pacing now, the way she did when her own girls were young and she was trying to reason with them.

The realization brought tears to Pam's eyes. Her mother may be failing, but she was still a formidable woman, someone who knew her mind.

"For some reason I have never been able to understand, you have always put yourself last. Even as a little girl, you would relinquish what was yours to your sisters. Your father used to get so angry with me. He said that my self-deprecating behavior was destroying your self-esteem. I didn't know any other way to be. He would yell at me for being a wimp in front of our girls, and then he'd yell at me to bring him a beer. Oh boy, it was a losing situation.

"When you were a newlywed, and that spoiled brat Marie threw such a horrendous temper tantrum that we thought she would hurt herself, your dad gave in that time. I'll never forget, you came home to pick up the rest of your wedding gifts, your little cake topper probably not even frozen yet, and you left with your sister. I knew that I was in trouble then.

"Having spent the weekend with you, she would be miserable on Monday after school and having to come home to Brooklyn. She started the anorexia then. I know, you thought it happened later, but that very first week she refused to eat. Dad slapped her so hard across the face that she fell up against the wall in the kitchen. I screamed. When I tried to go to her, to help her up, she clawed at me, screaming that she hated me."

"Mother, I knew she was giving you a rough time, but I had no idea it was that bad!" Pam was appalled. "How long did she act like that?" she asked, almost afraid to hear the answer, but knowing what it was, knowing that she was partly to blame for her mother's difficulty with Marie.

"She hated us, Pam, especially Dad. At least she treated him with hatred. I wondered if he was abusing her because that is how violent she reacted to being around him. Did she ever mention anything like that to you? Did she ever suggest that he might have molested her?"

Pam reeled. "Never! Mother! Never! She never even hinted at it!" Pam's heart was beating so hard. *What could this mean?* Jack was molesting her, not our father. She would have wanted to get away from him, not Dad, unless she was lying, unless it was consensual, unless she initiated it. *Still wrong, Jack, still wrong. Oh God.* She put her hands over her face. *What did this mean?* She remembered the letters, the few she read, threatening Jack, begging him. Now she was glad they had been destroyed.

34

Sandra locked the door to her office and, once again, requested that she not be bothered for an hour. She returned to her briefcase, the contents spread out on the table. The folders she set aside for later. It was the envelopes that she wanted to open first. They weren't actually sealed, but the flap was tucked in.

She picked up the one on top of the pile. It was a business-sized envelope with a privacy liner. She carefully pulled the flap out, and inside, she saw a thick wad of cash. *Why would Jack stash cash in his desk? It didn't make any sense.* She took the money out and counted it—one hundred twenty dollar bills. She put it back in the envelope and picked up the next one in the pile. It was the same thing. There were seven envelopes in total, each with two thousand dollars in twenties. *Why?* Piling them back up, she stuck them into her purse. She'd give them to Pam. It was not a huge amount of money, but enough that it might tempt thievery. She was already taking possession of her business.

Pam and Nelda sat at her kitchen table, drinking coffee for the rest of the morning, while the phone rang over and over again. Nelda agreed that the time had come for the house in Brooklyn to be put up for sale. She also agreed that coming to live in Pam's guest quarters above the garage would be very nice, the original idea of her staying in the children's suite discarded.

The discussion about Marie ended with both of them agreeing that they would never know the whole story, and if they did, it would be horribly one-sided. Pam was certain that her father didn't molest Marie. She just knew it in her gut. Marie didn't want to be away from Jack. She was in love with him, even as a teenager. Pam tried to push those thoughts out of her mind. The despondence was creeping in when she had been doing so well.

It was best if she concentrated on her mother. But, eventually, she was going to have to answer the phone. She picked up the receiver and thumbed through the caller ID. Sandra called twice, and Bill called again. She didn't want to talk to Bill.

"Mom, do you think you will be okay if I leave you alone for a while? I have to make some phone calls."

"I have never needed entertaining in the all years I have been coming here, and I don't need it now."

Pam didn't hear her, busy dialing Sandra's office number.

While on the path to Pam's house, Sandra was reluctant to break the solitude of her journey to Long Island. She knew in her heart of hearts that the sooner she revealed her findings the better for everyone, especially Pam.

To the right of the walkway, there grew a tortured mugho pine. Pam loved the pines on the New Jersey shoreline, and when they bought this house, one of her first purchases was the pine. She had placed all of the plantings herself. People laughed at Pam, made fun of her, and called her the spoiled wife of a rich man, but the truth was that she did her own decorating and gardening, and although she had given in to trying to clean the place herself, she rarely asked her cleaning ladies to do more than the basic cleaning. Sandra noticed the yard, its simple beauty, with gravel and sand, some hardy perennials clumped together, lychnis and black-eyed Susans, and lamb's ears. She didn't know the names herself but would ask Pam about it. She wanted her own house with a yard. There was a momma Cardinal sitting in the pine, watching her. She was so lovely, not at all plain, a soft Chinese red, with that perky little spike on her head and a bright orange beak. She cocked her head to the side to look at Sandra and then flew off.

Sandra looked to her left and saw Nelda looking out at her from the kitchen window. She looked annoyed. *Oh great!* Sandra thought. She smiled a big, fake smile and waved at her. The old lady just frowned and walked away, a few seconds later opening the door.

"Hi, Mrs. Fabian!" Sandra said. She decided to forgo the "How nice to see you."

"I'll get Pam" was all she replied. Sandra stood in the hallway, waiting. *Oh fuck*, she thought, *maybe I should have called first.*

"Hey! I was just trying to call you!" Pam said as she walked toward Sandra with open arms.

Sandra was grateful for the response.

Without waiting, Sandra whispered, "I need to talk to you—now."

Pam led her out to the veranda.

"Mom, we need to talk privately."

Nelda didn't respond. She was washing vegetables in the kitchen, scrubbing radishes with a little brush, each one, even the tiny ones, given a thorough going over.

Sandra put her briefcase on the chair next to her while Pam closed the French doors. She started to pull the envelopes and folder out of her briefcase.

"What's going on?" Pam said. She sat across from Sandra, looking at her, thinking for the fourth time in as many days, *What more could happen?*

"Pam, I'm going to come right out and say this without making excuses. I was up all night, worried about Jack's office. Pete told me to let you take as long as you wanted to come to get his things, and I completely agreed. But then I started to think that he might have left something in there that would further hurt you. Oh, I don't know what, we never wrote letters to each other, not even an e-mail. I was more worried about Pete or one of the others finding something. I mean, you know all there is to know about us. I promise you that."

"Go on. I understand that. I appreciate that," Pam urged.

"So I went in this morning and locked myself in his office. There was nothing there, really, just piles of work, nothing clandestine, nothing underhanded. I did find a gun in his top drawer, right next to the gum and mints. That was weird. I never imagined Jack even knowing how to use a gun."

"Jack hated them" was all Pam replied.

"I didn't go through the filing cabinet, but I did want to go back to his desk. It was compelling. I can't explain it. The lower right hand drawer—I squatted down and pulled it out, and there it was." She pointed to the pile she had pulled out of her briefcase. "Seven envelopes, each with two thousand dollars in one hundred dollar bills. Not sealed. That was strange enough, but this is worse." She waved the manila folder toward Pam, inviting her to take it.

Pam visibly pulled away from it.

"What's it about? Tell me! I don't want to read it!" She was shaken now. *What could this all mean?*

"I'm not sure myself what the impact of this will have, if any. Jack was filing a civil suit against his father when the man died. A suit that charged him with sexual abuse and battery." She opened the folder and began reading from the documents prepared by Jack's lawyer. " 'From my client's earliest recollection, until the age of seventeen, he was beaten with fists, and also belts, wood paddles, and plastic pipe, by Harold Smith, his father. He also charges that Mr. Smith fondled him, sodomized him, and forcibly raped him during this time.' " She stopped. There didn't seem like any point in going further.

Pam was stricken. She was pale and shaking.

"I wonder if the money has anything to do with it. I mean, it's a small amount, but why both things in the back of the drawer? I don't get it."

"Can I tell you what I think it might be?" Sandra asked.

Pam looked at her and nodded yes.

"I think he was paying this money to your sister. It's just a gut feeling."

Pam thought of the notes she had burned. *Oh, why did I do that? What if Marie was blackmailing him? But for two thousand dollars a month? It didn't make any sense.*

"The civil suit is harder to explain. There is a statute of limitations in New York State, but child protection groups are fighting to lift the statute for cases of violence and sexual abuse of children." She rifled through the folder and pulled out a letter from the attorney to Jack. "Here, this explains it. It looks to me like Jack wanted to shake things up, for some reason. He knew it wouldn't go to court. Why the attorney even agreed to file it is a mystery."

They sat together in silence, the waves crashing on the sand, a storm out to sea mirroring what was going on here, on the veranda. Children were screaming with pleasure, running up and down the beach. The smell of the salt air and coconut suntan oil filled the senses. It was all too much. Pam put her head in her hands, a headache beginning just on the periphery. She looked up at Sandra.

"He filed this in August, and Harold died in September. Jack would have found out the following month that he wasn't really his father."

"But I wonder if he found out before Harold's death?" Sandra asked. " Do you have the letter the woman, Beverly Johnson, wrote? Do you have the letter she wrote Jack? What was the date on that letter?"

"It's at the apartment," Pam said. She remembered Marie's notes. "I found a folder in the same place in Jack's desk here yesterday. It was filled with notes threatening Jack. I couldn't read through them. I burned them."

"It doesn't make any difference, Pam, don't worry about it," Sandra told her. "We just need to come out and ask her if he was giving her money. I mean, it is okay if he was. He was her brother-in-law. But why like this? Cash? There are seven envelopes, one for each month left in this year. Oh, I wish I had found something else to explain all of this."

They sat, there listening to the sounds of summer. Pam got up.

"Poor Jack. If this is true," she said, "he had a horrible life. Tortured like that by a man who was supposed to be his father. I'll never forget Bernice gushing about what a fabulous father Harold was. We would take the kids there for Thanksgiving every year. Harold was right there with all the kiddy toys. Did you ever see that den? Oh my God! They did that so the grandchildren would want to go there. Jack was always reluctant and refused to let Brent and Lisa sleep over at their grandparent's house. 'I like my family under one roof,' he used to say. Once, when he was away on business, I got sick. I mean, I was bedridden, probably pneumonia, after I had the flu. Bernice came and got the kids for me. Marie was in school. When Jack found out, he flew back the same day. I thought it was for concern about me, but now I wonder if he didn't want those children under the same roof as his dad, as Harold," she corrected. Shivering, "Poor Jack," she repeated.

They sat in silence for several minutes. Then she thought of Bill. Had he been abused as well? She wondered if she should warn Sandra. Always the peacemaker, this time she would stretch herself.

"I almost don't want to tell you this, Sandra. But I think I better, about Jack's brother, Bill." Sandra nodded to her to continue. "Evidently, yesterday at brunch, Bernice decided to drop the baby bomb. Why is beyond me. But, evidently, he is enraged. He called here, and I refused to discuss it with him. I don't understand what the impact will be for him. It doesn't make any sense. I know he was expecting Jack to field some business his way, and I told him you would probably do the same thing. But he was so upset about the infidelity. I kept asking him what difference it made, as it had nothing to do with him."

"Jack actually told me that his father's business was in trouble. Just in passing, he mentioned it, no details. I know he was sad about it, but I got the impression that he wasn't losing any sleep over it," Sandra said. "Can I ask what Bill said to you?"

Pam wasn't ready to relate that horrible scene.

"He is angry, but it doesn't seem rational to me. I will not discuss it with him or my mother-in-law." Pam hoped Sandra would take a hint from that and stop her dialogue with Bernice. But her role in this wasn't to control anyone. She wouldn't turn her back. But if Sandra chose to take Bernice into her confidence, she might have consequences. "I wish we could just toss all of this crap into the trash," she said with a sweep of her arm toward the pile of paper.

She wondered what she was supposed to do now, if she should try to see the attorney Jack retained. *Would he be able to say anything to her? Did attorney-client privilege apply after the death of the client?* She decided right then that she would see the attorney and find out what she could from him.

Sandra left the envelopes and file with Pam and headed back to Manhattan. *What a hell of a day.* She felt empowered by her actions, by being honest with Pam. Uncovering those things in Jack's office saved them from potentially being a real nightmare if gotten into the wrong hands.

She was tired. The train was hot and stuffy. Someone was eating take-out fried chicken; she could smell it, and she could hear them smacking their lips with each bite. A small child, really just a toddler, was fussing, his parent losing patience and smacking him in the face. A shrill cry, the fried chicken smell, and she was ready to barf. She thought of Pam. *What would Pam do?* The parent had the child in a grip, holding on to his arm so that he was barely touching the ground.

She called out to him, "Sir, if you don't stop hanging that kid by his arm, I am going to dial nine-one-one right now."

He glared at her, his intent clearly to frighten her. She turned her head and chuckled to herself, thinking, *Buddy, if I haven't been scared by now, you sure aren't gonna scare me.* But the man did loosen his grip on the child. She hoped he wouldn't beat the kid once they were out of sight. She couldn't save the world, but she would make sure it behaved when she was around.

Pam shut the door after Sandra. She peaked into the kitchen; Nelda wasn't there. Maybe she had gone to lie down in Marie's room. Pam wasn't going to investigate. She needed to recover from what she had just learned. She also wasn't sure that anything more needed to be done about it. *What would be the point of uncovering such horrible facts, if they were true?* Harold and Jack were dead. Bill, if he had been abused as well, had to make the decision for himself if anything could or should be done. It would mean revealing something so painful. And then, of course, there was Bernice. *Was it fair to her?* She understood something of what Bernice had been through. If you so choose, you can remain oblivious to anything that goes on under your roof.

The thought of her children, of Lisa especially, crossed her mind. Beginning with her birth, Jack was mesmerized by her. He didn't like to be alone with the children when they were infants, clearly terrified by their size and how fragile they appeared. He never changed a diaper. He didn't have any trouble cleaning up poop from accidents, just not off their bodies. She wondered now if it wasn't an attempt to avoid contact with their genitals.

And with Brent, there was almost a reverence about him. Jack was stern with his children, but there was such love there, nearing worship. No, she couldn't imagine him ever touching either of their kids inappropriately. Instead, he had taken whatever it was out on Marie.

Pam remembered the first time they got ready to go to the beach when they had rented a house in The Hamptons. Marie wasn't more than twelve years old. She came out of the kid's bedroom wearing a tiny little bikini. She was completely undeveloped, the bathing suit like two bandanas wrapped around a pole. Jack was appalled. He took Pam in the pantry and admonished her for allowing her sister to walk on a public beach showing her body. Pam looked at him like he was nuts. There was nothing to see.

So to keep peace, she asked her to put a T-shirt on. Now she wondered, *Was he acting like a father would act? Or was he trying to protect himself from too much stimulation?*

She couldn't help herself now; her imagination had taken off like a bird in flight. Marie's accusations swirled around her. She really believed that her sister provoked Jack. No matter what, he had been wrong, that much she knew. And not seeing her sister as a seductress didn't mean a thing. Only a man could really know what tempted him.

She walked out to the edge of their walkway. The beach was crowded. School was out, and that meant that the season could start in earnest. Unless it rained, every day would be like this, a mass of colorful umbrellas, the smell of suntan lotion, soft music from someone's radio. She loved living at the beach. Walking back toward the veranda gave her a fresh perspective. She remembered the file folder of information about Jack's real dad in the apartment in the city. She was sorry that she hadn't given the key to the apartment to Sandra. She'd give her a few more minutes to get home and then call her.

Sandra had to stop by the office before she went home, which meant getting another train downtown. It was only during hectic days like this, days where she ran all over the city and back, that her pregnancy was evident to her. She was exhausted. She did what needed be done at work and then got a train back uptown. It was hot on the train, but she was sitting down and was close to the air-conditioning vent. *Eight months of this. How am I going to do it?*

She walked from the station to her apartment instead of getting a cab, hoping the walk would revive her. At the last minute, she stopped in a Zabar's and got something for dinner that she could heat up in the microwave. There was no way she was cooking, and she hadn't eaten all day.

She saw him when she turned the corner on Eighty-second. Bill Smith. Remembering him from the funeral, she was surprised how unlike Jack he looked. But, of course, she knew why; they were stepbrothers. Sandra wondered if Bill knew. She was not in the mood for any confrontations and could feel her anger building. She'd stay cool, unless he crossed her. But she wanted someone to know she was there, just in case. She got out her cell phone and keyed in Pam's number. She didn't answer, but when the voice message came on, Sandra simply left the message that Bill Smith had come to her home, and she wanted Pam to know that information. She hung up.

He was tall like Jack, but there the similarity ended. Where Jack was handsome in a dignified, graying-at-the temples way, Bill was dark, more muscular. He was intimidating. But if he thought he would intimidate Sandra, he was in for a surprise.

Bill was waiting for her at the end of the walkway to her apartment. He'd gone to the office to see her and found out she was on her way to Jack's house. A few keystrokes on the computer and he found her address. Not sure what he was going to say to her, he just wanted her to know that not everyone in his family would tolerate her shenanigans. As she got closer to the apartment, he started to get a little nervous. He remembered her from the funeral now. *Of course, she couldn't be missed. She was beautiful.*

But if she thought her beauty would allow her to get away with ruining his family, she was wrong.

He stood up straighter the closer she got. She was tall by comparison to Pam, who was so short. Tall and dark. Her legs were long. He imagined them wrapped around his brother's waist. He felt some heat in his groin. It pissed him off. He wanted to frighten her a little, but he felt like smiling at her. And so smile he did as she approached him. He walked a few steps toward her, hand outstretched to take hers, but she ignored it.

"I've had a really long day. Can't this wait?" If he thought he could show up on her doorstep and push her around, he was wrong. She opened her purse to get her keys out and then fumbled with the lock. He was following her close behind, like a dog.

"I won't take up your time, but I need to talk to you." She turned around to look at him.

"I don't even know you! Why should I let you into my apartment?" He dug in his back pocket for his wallet. He was going to get his license out. "Oh, for God's sake," she said. But she did take it out of his hand and examined it. Handing it back to him, she had to force herself not to stamp her foot. "Let's get it over with then." She led the way to the back of the hallway. Thankfully, her apartment was clean.

He stepped through her doorway and was surprised. It was cool and light in there. Simply decorated. The furniture was, well, just useful furniture. There wasn't a lot of clutter, knick-knacks, or artwork.

"I can see why Jack liked it here," he said.

"Jack was never here," she said. "Nor did I ever go to his place." Suddenly, defeated, she couldn't take anymore. She dropped into a kitchen chair, letting her purse hit the floor. "Please, please, leave me alone. I'm not going to cause any trouble for you. I don't know what you think I am going to do." Even in this posture, with her head in her hands, begging him, she was in charge.

"Can I sit down?" He had his hand on the back of a chair, ready to pull it out.

Was this guy kidding? She looked up at him through her fingers and shrugged her shoulders.

"Do whatever you want," she said. He sat down across from her.

Neither said a word for a few minutes. Sandra needed tea and she needed something to eat. Pulling together what little energy she had left, she got up and went to the kitchen.

"I'm going to make some tea. Do you want a cup?" She had coffee, but there was no way she was making it for him.

"Okay, that sounds good." He was clearly comfortable. *This was such an imposition*, Sandra thought. She did her best not to bang things around and, slam doors, but it took all her willpower not to.

"This is a great apartment," he yelled. When she didn't respond, he asked, "How long have you lived here?"

Clenching her jaws, she pretty much growled the answer. "Four years." She walked out of the kitchen. "Look," she suddenly forgot his name, "Jack's brother, or whoever you are, I am not in the mood for small talk. Why can't you just tell me what you want and leave?"

He looked at her with his dark eyes and smiled, friendly, unthreatening. Totally the opposite of what he had been planning.

"It might be easier if you were sitting down," he said. "Not because it is going to make you faint or anything, but because we need to be eye to eye."

"Well, I am starving and need tea." She turned back to the kitchen and prepared the tea. She took her premade Zabar's meal out of the paper bag and put it in the micro-wave. She needed to eat. When the water was hot enough, she poured it into the pot, threw two tea bags in, got mugs and spoons, and put everything on a tray. "You'll just have to excuse me. I am eating this now because I am about ready to faint. If I knew you were going to be here, I would have bought one for you, too." Preparing her own tea, she pushed the extra mug toward Bill.

He seemed happy and relaxed, in spite of being an-grier than he had been in a long, long time just a few hours ago. Sitting in this tidy, cool, comfortable place, across from this gorgeous, self-assured, intelligent woman, he couldn't stay mad. *No wonder his brother had messed around on his wife. Sandra was worth it!*

He picked up his tea. It was hot, but didn't have much taste. He was not a tea drinker, but to be in her company, he'd drink whatever she offered him.

35

Nelda got up from her nap and didn't know where she was. The room was completely unfamiliar to her. She pushed the shade aside to look out the window, but the view of a fence with plantings in front of it didn't register. She went to the closet and opened it. It was empty, except for a robe and a garment bag. There was an attached bathroom; that also didn't provide any clues. The mirror above the bathroom sink reflected an old woman with brown-dyed hair, grey eyes, and too much makeup. *Is that my face staring back at me? When had my skin gotten so wrinkled, the creases of the pillowcase still evident on my cheek?* Her eyes, once large and hazel, had gotten so much smaller, old eyes that had shrunk. *That nose was the nose of a clown!* Long and bulbous, her little upturned pixie nose was gone as well. Slowly, as she examined herself in the mirror, her place in the world was returning to her. She was a wife, or had been a wife, and a mother. Her children were all successful, every one of them. Susan was a dentist in Connecticut, Sharon a physical therapist in New Jersey, Marie an editor in Manhattan, and Pam—Pam went to school to be an art teacher. But although she never taught, she married rich.

This was Pam's house. It was a big house—a cape, they called it. It was wooden shingled, painted white, and had green shutters. *The furniture was nondescript*, Nelda thought. Marie one time tried to explain to her mother that the furniture was called cottage style. It was over-stuffed and comfortable. The dining furniture had six styles of chairs, all painted white. The only room that appeared to have been thoughtfully furnished was Jack's office.

Nelda walked back to the bed and straightened the spread. *This was Marie's room.* Pam asked her to stay there until they could shop for new bedding for the guest quarters. Their conversation of the day was coming back to her. She sat on the bed. What had she agreed to? It was still foggy, bits and pieces of information returning, but nowhere complete.

She stood up, smoothing the wrinkles out of her slacks. *I should have taken them off before I had laid down.* Walking to the door, she turned around one last time and looked at the room. It still looked strange to her.

Pam was sitting on the veranda drinking coffee, looking out over the ocean. Nelda was proud of the way her daughter had lived her life, but now wondered if she wasn't the dumbest of her four girls. The news of the day flooded over her—Jack's indiscretion, the baby, moving to the beach, putting the Brooklyn house up for sale. She felt a little shaky. Pam turned around when she heard her mother's footsteps in the kitchen.

"Hi, sleepy head! I was just thinking about dinner. Did you have a good rest?" Nelda walked through the French doors and sat down next to her daughter. She lowered herself into the chair.

"It took me a few minutes to pull myself together. I wasn't sure where the heck I was when I woke up." She was surprised at her need to reveal this to Pam. Usually, she'd rather not admit to her failing memory. But that had gotten her into trouble. This was a new beginning. She didn't mind leaving that house in Brooklyn. It was lonely there. She trusted her daughter to protect her, but she would have to be honest about what was happening to her.

"Are you okay now?' Pam asked, concerned for her mother. Maybe the apartment above the garage was too far away for safety if she was feeling confused right across the hallway in Marie's room.

"Yes, I just didn't recognize the room." She paused, thinking. "Will I be able to bring my furniture here?"

"Of course, Mom! I already called a moving company to empty out the apartment, and then we will decorate your room together. We'll go to the house tomorrow if you are up to it, okay?" She reached out for her mother's hand and gave it a squeeze. "What should we have for dinner? I don't feel like cooking tonight," Pam said.

"Oh, I want to cook. I love cooking in your kitchen." Nelda got up to rummage through the refrigerator.

Pam sat back and picked up her book again. Her mother in the kitchen was a good thing. She would be busy for an hour fixing dinner for them both, killing two birds with one stone. Pam would gladly relinquish that task to her.

Sandra was not having as much success at being left alone. She ate her meal from Zabar's, barely tasting it. But when she was through and had sipped her tea, she felt better, less anxious.

"Okay, you have one more chance to speak. If you don't hurry up here, I am going to boot you out or call the police, whichever comes first."

"You won't have to do either. I'll tell you why I came here." He straightened up, pushing his tea mug away and looking at her nose. He was afraid if he looked her in the eyes, he would be unable to say to her just what he had come here for. He wondered what he *had* come to her apartment for. He laughed a soft, friendly laugh. "The truth is, I came here to read you the riot act about flaunting a baby of my brother Jack, all over the city. Now, I don't see what I was so worried about. I do need your help regarding my business. That hasn't changed. But your personal business... the baby...well, I guess I was a little crazy there for a day." He leaned back in the chair.

Sandra looked at him. She didn't know how to respond to that. She thought if she kept it about business, it would be easier to get rid of him.

"What kind of help?" she asked.

"Jack was going to field some clients my way. He said he had some old Upper East Side clients that I could take over. I need the business. We are having an off year since my dad died."

"I'll look at the files on his desk in the morning. Do you know whom he was referring to? We have a lot of clients uptown." She stood up, pushing her chair back and reaching for the tea things.

Bill grabbed her wrist as she went to take his mug.

"Don't get up yet," he asked of her. She looked down at his hand on her wrist, and pulled away.

"It's time for you to go." She left the mugs and her dinner there on the table and walked toward the door. Turning her back on him felt dangerous, so she stepped aside and motioned toward the door with her hand.

Bill got up and walked to the door.

"I'm sorry" was all he said, turning the knob on the door to let himself out. She didn't say anything to him, but when he was gone, she locked the door and made sure the chain was on and then ran downstairs and double-checked the door to the patio and the locks on the window. She hated it that he made her feel frightened. Not knowing what to do, she called Pam. She told Pam about the encounter, and then at least someone knew that he had been there, in case anything happened.

Pam was angry. She thought Sandra would be safe, but if she felt uncertain, she told her to get a car and come to the beach. They talked for an hour, rehashing the afternoon, still undecided about what information to reveal to what was left of the family.

She began to understand Jack's wisdom of placing the business in the trusty hands of Sandra Benson.

The next morning, the first thing Sandra did when she got to the office was go to Pete and ask him if he knew anything about Jack's offer to his brother. He said it was the first he had heard of it. They went to Jack's assistant, Jenny, who also didn't know anything about sending clients to Bill Smith.

With Jenny's help, Sandra and Pete spent the next three hours going through every file Jack was working on. There wasn't one client that Pete was willing to release.

Sandra didn't feel in a position to do it without his approval. So that ended it. Sandra stayed behind in Jack's office to straighten up the mess they had made with files, when another envelope, this one under the gun, caught her eye.

36

In Hell's Kitchen, Marie was beginning her day by getting to work on time. She felt some relief that her mother was at Pam's; it meant that she didn't have to travel to Brooklyn every night to check on her. She had a pile of technical reports to edit, which were boring and monotonous. What had seemed a full and exciting week the day before she now loathed. She went to her little office, almost a cubical, and closed the door. She contemplated how many more years she would have to do this. She was forty-five years old. *Twenty? Twenty-five? Fuck! Eight hours was too long to do it, to sit on this uncomfortable chair, in this stinking office, in a horrible part of town.* She got up from her desk, picked up her purse, and left her cubical. She passed by the receptionist and told her she was leaving for the day for a family emergency. *Fire me*, she thought to herself. *I don't give a shit.*

The sidewalks were relatively empty at this hour; the unfortunate people who would be down there at that time of day were either looking for a job or lost. There were no coffee shops, no chain stores, not even a McDonald's. There was no place to shop and nothing to buy.

Why did I ever agree to live down here? Jack told her again and again that she would grow to love it. *He was so full of shit.* He wanted her here so he could come and go without being observed by anyone who knew them. She had lived there for eight years and still hated the neighborhood. These exact thoughts went through her head every day as she walked to work and again in the evening when it was time to go home. The only way she could tolerate it was by going a few miles uptown and shopping or going to movies or visiting her only friend, a guy lucky enough to live on West End Avenue. Digging her cell phone out, she pressed his number and put the phone to her ear. He picked up on the first ring.

"Shouldn't you be typing or something?" he said without saying hello.

"Thanks, Arthur," she replied with a tinge of sarcasm. "Actually, I left for the day. Do you want to do something?" She stopped walking toward her apartment, hoping he would tell her to come uptown and spend the day.

"Oh, sweetheart, I can't! I would love it, but I have a date! After all this time, I have a date!" Arthur, at the end of a long-term relationship, would sooner cut off his hand than cancel.

"Great! Who is it?" She didn't care and was disappointed he wasn't available to her.

"Someone I met on the Internet, where else?" he said. "Look, sweetheart, I have to hang up. We'll get together Friday night, okay?" She agreed, and they hung up.

She did not want to go home, but didn't have anywhere else to go. Her life was ruined. She had no friends to speak of and had betrayed her sister beyond forgiveness. *Who was left?* She turned back to the sidewalk and continued her walk home.

Pam woke up to the smell of coffee brewing. She took her time getting ready, returning to her old routine of primping to perfection. She chose a white pique shorts set with a short-sleeved shirt and white leather sandals. The weather was reported to be warm and sunny, a good beach day. She had the rest of the week to get through, and then her darling children would both be home for the Fourth of July weekend. She wanted to get her mother situated up in the guest apartment so she could have some privacy with the kids. They would have to put some boundaries in place in order for this to work. It would be so much better if her mother were the one to suggest it.

She went out to the kitchen to see that her mother had made coffee and also pancakes. Pam, who rarely ate more than a piece of fruit in the morning, decided to just eat and be grateful. She'd start back at the gym that day.

"Good morning, Mother! Look at this! I'm going to be as fat as a pig if this keeps up."

"This is a special day, our first day together! I won't cook like this once I'm in the apartment." Was she reading minds now? "Do you have anything that needs doing today?"

If Pam scurried, Nelda bustled. How her house got into the state it was in was a mystery to her daughter. Unless loneliness was to blame, Pam wasn't seeing anything that would have made her mother give up as she had at home in Brooklyn. After breakfast, with a false sense of security, she got her purse and left for the gym and grocery shopping.

Bill Smith arrived at his office early. He was confident that Jack's girlfriend would call today. There was no reason for them not to honor Jack's wishes. He spent the first hours going over a spreadsheet that clearly illustrated that he either had to increase their incoming revenue or face bankruptcy. The humiliation of that, the pure terror of having to move his mother out of that house, sell it and the contents, and possibly lose the house he and Anne lived in brought a physical response that dictated an immediate run to his private bathroom.

When Sandra hadn't called him by one, he called her. He'd given her the morning to locate the clients or files or whatever the hell it was Jack was working on. But she wasn't in the office, and the receptionist wasn't giving out any details.

"Can you just tell me, is she out for lunch?" But, no, she wouldn't even reveal that. Bill was furious.

"Goddamn it!" He shouted after she had hung up. He searched for the paper that he wrote her address and phone number down on. But there was no phone number. He wadded up the paper and threw it on the floor. He'd call Pam. Nelda answered the phone. *Oh shit.* The last thing he needed to do was talk to that dotard.

"Hi, Mrs. Fabian, its Jack's brother, Bill. How are you?" He was gritting his teeth, trying to hold back.

"Bill? Bill? Is that Jack's brother's name?" She was clearly confused.

He raised his voice, thinking yelling would help her understand him. "Is Pam home?" He demanded.

"No...no, she just left for the gym. What do you want?"

He contemplated asking her if she knew Sandra and then just hung up the phone. He had no patience left for talking to an old lady. He'd go back to Sandra's house. He had to know now. They were in serious trouble. He had mortgaged the mansion last year and used the money to keep things afloat. Dad had already driven the business into the ground. He didn't understand the concept of change. There was nothing left, no clients and no revenue. They were broke. Jack had given his mother a couple thousand dollars a week to pay the staff, buy food, and keep up appearances. Now that was gone. If he could prove that the business was still viable, that they had clients, he could last another month, maybe two. He had to know. He grabbed his car keys, choosing to drive himself to Sandra's apartment, which was just few blocks from his office, rather than getting a cab. Illegally parking in front of her building, he ran to the door and pushed her buzzer. There was no answer.

That bitch was not going to hold him back. His brother told him he'd see what he could do. *Did he forget? Or was Sandra trying to hold out on him? She wanted Jack's clients for herself.* If Sandra wouldn't help him, Pam would. Pam was a pushover; everyone knew that. The way she was handling this whore was a perfect example of what a wimp she was. Pam would give him the money he needed; she wouldn't allow Bernice to lose the house or he and Anne to be thrown out on the streets. He got back in his car and headed toward the Fifty-ninth Street Bridge.

The child Bill Smith spent the evening hours after school hiding. He wasn't going to accidently run in to his father. No chance encounter with Harold Smith had ever been good. He would either grab his son and beat him with whatever was at hand; he had welts from tennis rackets, fishing poles, and the Sunday Times, or drag him off to his bedroom. Once over the threshold, Bill blacked out. He had some memory of sexual abuse, but he brushed that off as being childish drama, replication of what he had overheard his older brother pleading with their mother to intervene and stop. She never did.

Bernice was usually drunk by the time her children got off the bus each afternoon. The horror that was her life began shortly after she married Harold, when Jack was a baby. She spent her waking hours protecting her son from Harold's brutality. Slowly over time, Bernice learned that if she began drinking when she got up, just one or two cocktails, what Harold did wasn't so horrible after all.

At first, Jack went willingly to him. But after a few times alone with him, the child screamed in terror when his step-father approached him. It fueled Harold's anger to be rebuffed by a child like that. By the time Jack was talking, and Bill was born, the damage had been done. Jack put himself into a trance during the abuse, hardly acknowledging it after a time. When the boys were teenagers, their goal was to protect their friends from their father. Jack did what he could to save Bill from the worst of the abuse by taking his place. He went to college in the city so he could continue intervening. And finally, both boys were old enough to put a stop to it. Jack was the first, brave enough to confront Harold.

"Dad, your games are stopping today." He had approached Harold while he was sitting in the den, reading the financial section. He put the paper down, bending forward in his chair, and looked up at his son with a grimace on his face.

"You'll do what I say. I'll tell you when it is over," he growled. Jack stood tall in front of him with his fists clenched at his sides.

"I will go to the police if you ever lay a hand on Bill again. And you aren't coming near me."

"You'll go to the police, will you now?" Harold chuckled. "Why do you think they will believe you?" But he had gone white.

"I have physical evidence, that's why. Do you really want to take a chance?" He turned and walked away from Harold. He moved out of the mansion then, never to return as an occupant. The House of Horrors, he called it. As far as Jack knew, Bill remained safe. They never, ever discussed their life with Harold, until the fateful day Beverly Johnson's letter arrived.

He got it before Harold died, but just barely. He wanted to confront his mother first. If it were true, if he had spent his entire childhood being beaten and molested by someone who wasn't even his own father, well, he didn't know what he would do. He walked to the mansion from his Madison Avenue apartment. Bernice met him at the ornate front entrance, smiling, with her arms outstretched as she always did when she saw her son. But it was apparent when he refused her embrace that something was wrong. She had lied for so long about his parentage that it was the last thing on her mind.

"Where's Bertram Albert?" He asked after they had walked into the den together. Bernice almost fainted. She walked to the French doors that lead to the main hallway, and closed them. She took a seat at the closest game table, and pointed to a chair across from her.

"Sit down, Jack. I'll tell you everything, but you must sit." But Jack wasn't hanging around. He was pissed, and he wanted her to know it was her fault.

"I won't be staying, Mother. You allowed me to be punched, kicked, fucked up the ass, by someone who wasn't even my father. At least if it had been my own dad, I could continue rationalizing it. It was just something that happened in my family. My 'father' was a pervert. A fucking maniac. And now I find out he isn't related to me at all. Is Bill his?" Bernice sat there, silent, her face a mask of anguish. "Answer me mother!" He yelled.

"Yes," Bernice whispered. "Bill is his. But he did love you!"

"Shut up!" Jack screamed. "Are you a lunatic? Did the alcohol finally ruin your brain?" He wasn't even going to argue with her. His love for his mother couldn't have been real after all; she was incapable of returning it. He left the beautiful room for the last time. He wouldn't even bother confronting Harold. But he knew he was going to do something better.

The next day, Jack met with a team of lawyers downtown. They prepared a statement that would probably never be reviewed in a court of law. He hoped serving his step-father the brief would aid in the redemption of his youth.

What it did was precipitate a heart attack in Harold that no amount of heroics could overcome. His death had the exact opposite effect on Jack as was expected. He was overcome with grief. So Harold had gotten away with it after all. And to make matters worse, he left behind a financial mess of gargantuan proportions. Jack knew business was slow, but it was much worse than that. He worked out a budget for his mother. He would give her two thousand dollars a week. If she couldn't make it on that amount, she'd have to start firing some of her staff.

Shortly after Harold died, Bill started in on Jack, hounding him for clients, asking for money. Jack had compassion for his brother, but he wasn't going to bail him out. He gave him one loan, then another, finally mortgaging his house and the mansion for him. Although it was legal, drawn up by their lawyers, Jack didn't want to have to foreclose on his mother or his brother. And he made damn sure Pam didn't know about it. But if the day came that Bill no longer could make the payments, Jack would foreclose without hesitation.

Then the threats started. Jack continued to give the money to his mother, but he was not going to be bullied by his brother. Bill found out from Bernice that Jack had intended on going public with the abuse charges, even confronting Harold with it. Bill threatened Jack with death if he exposed them. Once Harold was dead, the brothers should have found a way to deal with their feelings of betrayal. But it wasn't going to be that easy.

After Jack died, Bill missed the first payment. Before long Pam would be getting yet another surprise.

As Bill drove to Babylon, the image of his brother dying, collapsing to the floor of the train appeared in his mind. He broke down crying twice, out of regret certainly, but more out of fear. *What was he going to do once he got to Jack's house? He needed to force Pam to lend him money before it was too late.* And then the reality of what he was planning hit him. *She would soon know that she held the mortgage to the mansion; to his house in the village. What would be the point of lending money to him and he in turn give it back to her? Oh God, what a mess!*

Marie got home and knew she couldn't stay there. She couldn't stand being alone; she didn't want the memories of Jack to haunt her one more second. Oddly, it was safer in the beach house; there was less horror there than in her apartment. She grabbed her car keys and left the apartment for Long Island.

She got there in time for lunch. When she pulled into the driveway, she could see her mother in the kitchen. They waved to each other. Marie felt like it was old times; there was happiness there now that there hadn't existed in a while, since the kids left. It was never really just about Jack. Her grief and guilt would make it about him, but it was more about Pam and the kids, the warmth and love they gave her. Jack had appealed to some perverse pride, a conquest gone wrong. She was so sorry she had allowed it.

Her mother opened the door for her. She looked so good, having taken time with her hair and makeup and wearing a nice outfit. She said she would be happy to make lunch for Marie, but she and Pam just missed each other. Pam had to go into the city for some business, but would be back in time for dinner.

They had a lovely lunch out on the veranda. Then Marie went into her room and put her swimsuit on. She would go to the beach for an hour or so and then come back in and take a nap.

She spent a little longer on the beach than she had planned because she met a man! One of Pam's neighbors, a retired lawyer, was walking his dog. They started talking, and before she knew it, he asked her to have coffee with him after dinner. They set a time and said good-bye. She gathered up her beach stuff and headed back up the walkway to the house. She wasn't invisible after all.

Nelda was puttering around the kitchen, assembling what looked like baking ingredients for something fattening.

"I'm going to lie down for a while, Mom."

Nelda said, "Okay." She was distracted by her recipe.

Marie went into her room in the children's wing. It was cool and dark, perfect for sleeping. She went into her bathroom and pulled off her suit. She took a shower and washed her hair. The water felt good on her hot, sunburnt skin. She stood out of the protection of the umbrella, talking to the neighbor for at least on hour. But it was worth it. It was the first time in recent memory that she felt happy and excited. *It was just for coffee*, she reminded herself. But it was a start.

She fell into her bed, completely relaxed and refreshed. She fell into a deep sleep. Suddenly, she was awakened, hearing a scuffle. Her first reaction was to run out of her room, but she was stopped by the voice of a man. She didn't recognize the voice, but it was definitely a male. She tiptoed to her door and slowly and carefully turned the knob.

"Don't hurt her!" Pam screamed!

Suzanne Jenkins

When had she gotten home? Marie closed the door and locked it. She crept back to the bed and got her cell phone, keying in nine-one-one. She whispered into the phone that she thought there had been a break-in, that someone was hurting her aged mother. The dispatcher said they would send two cars out right away. She hung up and went back to her door. She could hear Pam's voice, low and pleading, and her mother whimpering. She didn't know if she should go out to help them or stay locked in her room. *What would make things better? Worse?* She chose staying put. In less than five minutes, she heard the whoosh of cars out front and then a loud "Bang!"

37

Earlier in the day, Sandra was in quandary, needing to get back into Jack's office. She looked out in the hall. No one was coming, and Jenny was at lunch. She quietly closed the door to Jack's office. *Was the envelope there, under the gun, all along?* She didn't remember seeing it when she was searching through his drawers. She didn't want to touch the gun. She wondered what else she had missed.

Walking, tiptoeing, she came around to the desk and sat in Jack's chair. Very carefully, she pushed the gun off the envelope with the tip of her finger, afraid it might go off. The envelope wasn't sealed, and the return address was printed with the address of the New York City Police Department. *What?* She pulled the flap up and peeked inside; it was an official-looking form. She pulled the paper out and, looking up to make sure she was still alone, unfolded it.

It was a restraining order! *For Jack?* She read through the form, a combination of typewritten and handwritten information. Jack had taken the order out against someone; it wasn't against him. *Of course, what was I thinking?* Her heart was beating wildly in her chest. And then she saw the name William Smith.

Jack had taken a restraining order out against his own brother. The form didn't reveal the details, the reasons. Jack had felt threatened enough by Bill to get the

Suzanne Jenkins

order and keep a gun in his desk. *Did he carry it?* She wondered if he had left the gun in his desk because they would
be together that Friday night? She was stymied. *What was
going on?*

She got up from the desk and shoved the form back
into its envelope and stuffed it down the front of her shirt.
Then she took the gun out of the drawer and carefully
put it in the pocket of her skirt. She didn't know if it was
loaded and didn't even know how to check for bullets. She
wondered if he had a permit for the gun; it was probably
in his wallet, the one that was stolen. Her office was just
down the hall. She wanted to call Pam right away. Pam
picked up on the second ring; she was in the grocery store.

"I'm glad you called," she said. "I forgot to cancel
Jack's credit cards and someone just called to tell me that
there has been a lot of activity on two of them. What's
wrong with me that I would forget such a thing?"

"You've had a lot on your mind! One of us should
have reminded you," Sandra said.

"But that's not all," Pam continued. "I have to come
into the city this afternoon. The police finally looked at
the security tapes from the train the evening Jack was
mugged. They think he knew who took his wallet! They
want me to look at the tapes to see if I recognize the man.
Jack was talking to him before he collapsed, and then this
person, whoever it was, bent over him and took his wallet!" Pam's voice cracked. "I feel so badly for him. To have
that final betrayal."

Sandra could her muffled sobs.

"Oh Pam, I am so sorry. But I have to see you right
away. I was going to catch a train to you, but if you have to

Pam of Babylon

come into the city, we must meet. I think I want to come home with you, too. I was going to ask you. I think you are right; it's not safe for me to stay here."

"Oh my God, what happened?" Pam exclaimed.

"I can't tell you over the phone. Where can I meet you?"

"I'm getting ready to pay for my groceries, and then I'll drop them off at home and drive in. Can you meet me at the downtown station at two?"

Sandra agreed to do that.

After Pam looked at the pictures they had for her, they would drive up to the apartment and get the files Jack had there and come back to the beach. Pam felt she needed to make a list of everything that needed to be done, all the loose ends that were dangling. *The file about Jack's real father? Did anything need to be done about that? Or the civil suit against Harold? Do I need to confront Bernice?* She was of the mindset to burn everything and never speak of it again. But the problem was that there were still victims alive. It didn't die with Jack. Marie, poor Marie. The baby. And her own children, she would have to question them somehow, just in case there was something they had been hiding.

She said good-bye to Sandra, and no sooner did she hang up from that call did her phone beep again. This time it was Marie.

"Hi, Pam, I'm on my way. Whether you want me or not, here I come!" She was chipper; Pam could hear joy in her voice that she hadn't heard for a very long time.

"Well that is great, because I have to drive into the city. You will be here with Mom. See, everything has a way of working out!" She waited for the backlash from her optimism, but none came. *Was Marie all right?*

Pam took the bag of groceries in to her mother, who was preparing to go on one of her legendary baking sprees. They would all regret it when it came time to put bathing suits on that weekend.

She didn't know if there were any papers she needed to bring, but just in case, she grabbed her passport, a file containing Jack's birth and death certificates, and a copy of their marriage license. While she drove, she couldn't stop thinking about Jack. After hearing from the police, the vision of him lying on the filthy train floor kept shimmering before her eyes. She hoped they had stills for her to view and not the video. She didn't want to see him alive and talking right before he collapsed.

Traffic wasn't bad going into the city at that hour, and she arrived with enough time to go to the apartment first. She was happy to get that over with. Once those files were out of there, she could call the rental office and ask them to list it furnished. She wasn't about to worry about emptying it out at this point, maybe in a few months, but not today.

She parked in the garage and took the elevator up fifteen floors. When she stepped out onto the carpeted hallway, she was reminded once again way she didn't like it there. It was airless and dark. Compared to their place on the West Side, this apartment building was depressing. The plastic box was in the same place she had left it on their bed. The files were still spread all around. She gathered them up and put the top on the box. It was more cumbersome than heavy. She pushed it across the carpet with the toe of her shoe. Right before she locked up the apartment, she took one last look around. She'd call the cleaning service to come in, empty it, and take Jack's clothes to charity. She was never going back there if she could help it.

Traffic heading downtown was terrible. She just made it with enough time to park her car and get inside. The receptionist called the detective working the case. He didn't make Pam wait. Extending his hand, he thanked her for driving all the way into the city to help them out. He acknowledged the death of Jack.

"Please accept our condolences for your loss," he said. He led Pam through a maze of desks into a small room. Offering her a chair, he took one next to her, opening up a large folder on the desk. The folder contained six grainy pictures of a man walking toward the camera and then going through the open doors of the train. It was Bill.

"It's my brother-in-law. I don't get it." Pam was more than confused; she was totally baffled. *How did he end up on just the train Jack was taking? In just the car? It didn't make any sense.* The detective didn't say anything to Pam, letting her work it out on her own, without his prompting. "So does this mean my brother-in-law was with Jack when he passed out? He's the one who is stealing from me? I can't believe this!" She shook her head back and forth. "A restraining order against Bill was filled by Jack."

The detective perked up at that.

"You're sure?" he asked. "It should be easy enough to find out." He stood up to go in search of more information, telling Pam, "I'll be right back. Would you like a coffee?" She shook her head no.

What was going on? Why was Bill bothering Jack? She wondered if it had anything to do with Harold and Bernice.

The detective came back a few minutes later with some faxes in his hand, leafing through them and reading them.

"You were right, here is the restraining order. Your husband filed it in late April. Here's the court record. He handed her a thin sheet of paper, the type that used to come from old fax machines.

What she was looking at were copies of handwritten letters Jack had received from his brother. She read out loud.

" 'Jack, I need your help here. Mother is going to lose the house if you don't come through. Why are you playing games with us? You've got the money. I've seen your bank account. If you can't help me and the business, then help our mother. Bill.' "

" 'Jack, I know what you are up to. I'm going to expose you if you don't come through for mother.' "

And finally, " 'Jack, don't test me. You think I won't carry out my threats, but you are dead wrong, emphasis on dead.' "

Pam thought of the letter Marie had written him. *Were they even from Marie? Had Bill found out in some way about the relationship between Marie and Jack and threatened to expose them?* "Read this," the detective said, handing Pam another piece of paper.

" 'At midnight on March tenth, my brother, William Smith, came to my apartment on Madison Avenue. I allowed him access so he wouldn't disturb the other tenants. He appeared civil at first, but quickly deescalated after I refused to give him money. He pulled out a small handgun and threatened to kill me. He also stated that he would come to my place of business and shoot my employees.' " Pam looked up the detective. "What does this mean? Was Bill blackmailing Jack for some reason?"

"Your brother-in-law is nearly bankrupt, Mrs. Smith. Here's a copy of a financial statement from your late father-in-law to your husband requesting a transfer of clientele and another asking for a loan of four hundred thousand dollars. I don't know if your husband made the loan or not, but judging by the sound of the subsequent communication, I doubt it."

"My husband was generous to a fault, but he wasn't stupid. If his family lost all of their money because of poor business practices, Jack would be the last person on earth to bail them out." She added silently, *and look what that got him.* There didn't seem to be anything else to say. She stood up to leave. Offering her hand to the detective, she said, "Thank you for solving that mystery. It's one less thing for me to have to worry about." They shook hands then, and he showed her the way out.

Sandra was waiting for her on the steps.

"Well, did you know who it was?" she asked.

"Bill" was all Pam said.

"No way!" Sandra said, stunned. "He stole his own brother's wallet? Left him to suffer on the floor of the train all alone? Her voice, getting higher, was a giveaway to her anguish.

The final indignity. Bill could have saved his brother's life. He could have called nine-one-one. They would have stopped the train and someone would have performed

CPR. He took his wallet with his identification so that the only way his loved ones would know what happened to him was by the last numbers on his cell phone. She broke down right there, unable to go on.

"Let's get to the car, dear. I'll take you home, and we can have a nice dinner on the veranda tonight. You'll feel better as soon as we get out of this godforsaken city."

Pam held Sandra's hand as though she were a small child and led her to the parking garage. They rolled the windows down and let the breeze blow their hair around. When they were going over the bridge, the air changed from hot and stagnant to fresh and warm. There was a hint of brine in the air. Pam turned the radio up. The Mommas and the Poppas were playing "California Dreaming." Sandra fell sound asleep.

She woke up with Pam whispering her name and shaking her arm. They were on Pam's street.

"Sandra, I think Bill is here! Wake up!" Sandra was alert immediately.

"How do you know?"

"There is a strange car parked behind Marie's. I think it's Bill's." She pulled up in front of the next-door neighbor's house. "Don't slam the door," she whispered.

They held on to each other as they crept up the walk. Sandra held on to Pam's arm and squeezed it. She whispered in her ear, "Do you know how to use a gun?' Pam nodded yes. Sandra opened her purse and pulled out Jack's small handgun. "Here, take this. I don't even know if it is loaded." Pam took the gun without question.

She put her hand on the door, and it was unlocked, swinging open. She grabbed the knob before it hit the wall.

But it was too late. He had watched them pull up in front of the house. Nelda was slouched in a kitchen chair. Bill stood behind her, with his right arm across her shoulders and a knife, one of Pam's big carving knives, in his right hand, the blade pressed up against her neck. For one second, Pam could see nothing but the frailness of her mother. Then she saw her perfectly applied makeup, her hair styled and sprayed so every hair would stay in place. She was wearing her usual "ladies who lunch" attire, stockings, and high heels. The old Nelda had returned. She wasn't making a sound, but every so often, he would choke up on her neck with the knife, and she would yelp. You could expect it with his movement. It was making Pam crazy.

"Bill! What's gotten in to you?" Pam said, repeating a phrase Bernice often used with her children and in-laws. "This is no way to solve your problems. You'll only make them worse."

"Shut up! Shut up! You worthless wimp," he yelled. "Go right now and get your checkbook. I want a check written out to me for forty thousand dollars. Go!" he screamed.

Pam kept the gun close to the side of her leg. She went to the desk in the kitchen, pulled out a checkbook, and starting writing the check. She tore it out of the book and placed it on the kitchen table.

"There, Bill, there's the check. You can have all the money you want, but let go of my mother! Please!" Instead of releasing her, he tightened up on his grip, pressing the blade in further. Nelda yelped again. Pam brought the gun out in front and held it steadily in her hands. "Get the knife away from my mother's throat!" she calmly said to Bill.

All of her life she had been discounted by those around her as fluff, silly, a wimp, and empty-headed. She saw her mother flinch as Bill pressed the knife more firmly against the soft, crepey skin of her neck. Pam squeezed the trigger then, and the bullet hit him right at the tip of his elbow, throwing his arm back and releasing her mother. They dove toward her, Sandra grabbing her. Bill hit the floor. Pam kicked the knife away from Bill's hand. He was yelling, holding onto his shattered arm, in pain, crying out for mercy. She stood over him, restraining herself from kicking him in the head.

At that moment, Marie came running in from the children's wing, and the police rushed in from the front door.

"Now who's a wimp, Billy?" Pam said to him.

38

It took a while for the police to sort out what had happened. They handcuffed Bill and called an ambulance to take him to the hospital. His injuries weren't life threatening, but painful. The gun was harder to deal with. They were able to determine that Jack had a permit for it, but until Bill owned up to where he had put the wallet, the police would have to take the gun. They asked Pam to stay in town until it could be determined whether she broke any laws or not. Nelda was sitting down at the kitchen table while an EMT examined the small cut from Pam's carving knife. Bill would be booked for attempted murder if the cops on the scene had anything to say about it. Jack had been a good friend of the DA's office.

Sandra was making a pot of coffee. Her head was still spinning. What would have happened if they had come home later? She asked Marie how she knew to call for the police. Not that it ended up making much difference, thanks to sharpshooter Pam.

"I could hear Pam telling him not to hurt Mom. It was the scuffling that woke me up! My God! It shocked me out of sleep! You know something isn't right, but the confusion of just waking up makes it impossible to figure out. I didn't know what the hell was happening. When'd you figure out he was here?"

"Pam saw the strange car in the driveway and then the door was unlocked. I took the gun out of my bag and gave it to Pam. We tried to be as quiet as we could be, but he was waiting for Pam. He already had Nelda sitting down with the knife pressed to her throat." Suddenly, Sandra lost it.

"Oh my God, Nelda!" She went over to Pam's mother and knelt in front of her. "I am so sorry you had to go through that!" Nelda took Sandra's hand, patting it. Her own hand was so soft, the skin like a baby's.

"I was glad to see you and Pam walk through that door! He had me by the throat. I thought I was a goner!" She laughed. "You think you are tired of living, and then something like this happens, and it makes you grateful to be alive. I need to stay alive for the new baby." She looked up at Sandra, their eyes connecting. Marie moved nearer, and the three of them talked about what had just happened. It was a moment of peace and of bonding.

A detective arrived to question Pam. She recognized him from Jack's funeral, a handsome, older man of medium height, dressed in slacks and a white shirt with a gun in a shoulder holster.

"I had just returned from seeing the police in Manhattan," she explained when he asked her to tell him everything she could. "I identified Bill as the man who stole my husband's wallet after he had a heart attack on the train. My friend here, Sandra, found a restraining order that Jack had taken out against his brother. It was Bill who has been withdrawing money from my account using credit cards I forgot to cancel." She looked at the detective, embarrassed for the oversight. "Go ahead, you can say it. What a stupid move."

"No, that's not what I was thinking. You just lost your husband. There is no one else to pick up those pieces, is there? My wife died two years ago. She had some kind of automatic plan that sent her makeup and hair products every month. After about a year of getting this stuff in the mail, it finally occurred to me to have it discontinued. My daughters cashed in! Things get missed and forgotten. It's human nature."

"I'm sorry about your wife," Pam said. "I can't believe how fast time is going. Did you feel the same way?"

"It did go fast. The urgent stuff will come to the surface to be dealt with, like your credit cards. He'll be charged with theft, by the way. Later on, the less important things will be revealed, like my wife's makeup. It was sort of therapeutic to get those boxes every month. It was difficult to have them stopped." He looked down at his hands. "However, I didn't have the drama you obviously are having. My life was quiet, almost boring."

"I could use a little boring right about now," Pam replied. "We were just saying that enough is enough in the excitement department."

"I think I have everything I need." Then he paused, clearly struggling with his thoughts. "Listen. I know it's just been a few weeks since your husband died. And I only mean this in the most respectful terms. But would you have coffee with me sometime? We could talk about the case." He smiled at her.

She was thinking, *Boy, if he knew what had transpired here this week, he would run in the opposite direction.*

"Wow, you are really rushing me," Pam said. But she was smiling.

39

Bernice called Pam early Tuesday morning. She saw the number on caller ID and knew she would have to get whatever was about to happen over with. She was ignoring the obvious, avoiding the painful.

"Pam," Bernice was barely able to get the name out. Pam could hear her attempts to control her sobbing. But she wasn't feeling much compassion for her mother-in-law.

"I'm here, Bernice." Seconds passed, almost a minute. "Bernice, I'm going to hang up."

"Don't! Please. Why'd you do it? Why'd you shoot my only son?" She didn't try to cover up her crying now. "We took you into our home, gave you love, showered you with gifts. The way you pay me back, us back, is by aiming a gun at Bill! No wonder Jack cheated on you! You're horrible!" Pam could hear Bernice breathing heavily, exhausted from the tirade.

"You're kidding me, right? Did you read the charges, Bernice? Did you know he was with Jack when he had the heart attack? That he stole Jack's wallet?" Pam knew she was getting shrill, her voice getting higher and louder. "It's not bad enough that he betrayed his own brother, but then to break into my house and try to cut my mother's throat! By shooting him, I prevented him from committing a murder. I bet you didn't think of that, did you? Why'd you call here, Bernice? Hurry up and get whatever it is off your chest because I am hanging up. And then I never want you to call here again, do you understand me?"

Pam wanted to talk to Sandra about keeping the baby away from the Smith family. Starting with the abuse of Jack, they were the source of the trouble that had filtered down to Marie. Bernice finally yelled out at Pam.

"I need money! You know the truth; you know we are in serious financial trouble. Bill told me everything last night. He told me Jack was helping him, giving him money to put in my personal account. I'm down to ten dollars now."

"Wait! Let's see if I understand what you asking of me. You are calling because you want me to give you money? You just accused me of betraying you!" *Boy, talk about nerve!* Although not one to dwell on past slights, Pam thought she was gaining some strength, some self-respect she hadn't known existed previously. "Bernice, be honest with me. For once, try to have some respect for me as a human being, the mother of your son's children." She waited, listening to the silence on the other end of the line, wondering if she had hung up.

"Okay, you're right. I'm sorry, Pam. I have had so much to deal with lately; this has pushed me to the edge. You deserve respect. But I am desperate! Bill was hiding how bad things had gotten, even before Harold died. I'm at my wit's end. He mortgaged the mansion! This house has been in Harold's family for almost one hundred and fifty years, did you know that Pam? It's your children's legacy! Everything in it, the piano, all of the artwork, are priceless things, treasures. A place like this would take millions of dollars to replace. I only need a fraction of that to keep it, less than four hundred thousand dollars." She stopped, whether she was crying again or just waiting for a reply, Pam wasn't sure.

"Let me think about it, okay, Bernice? If I do help you, how will you keep it going? Bill said himself that all of their clients are gone. I can't force Peter, or Sandra, for that matter, to give Bill work. I have to think about this, what would be the best thing for everyone." Bernice was silent.

Pam felt certain that bailing Bernice and Bill out would be a huge mistake, a waste of money. She needed to get some advice. Jack had an entire office full of consultants and financial advisers that she would talk to.

"Please, whatever you can do for us! If Jack were alive, I know he would continue helping us," Bernice said. "He owed it to me! Harold got him started in the business. He paved the way for him!" Pam was losing patience.

"What Jack would or wouldn't do has nothing to do with me anymore, Bernice. Please don't call me again and attack me. If we can't communicate civilly, there is no way we can resolve your financial problems." Bernice agreed, groveling and asking forgiveness.

Pam hung up the phone. She'd have a cup of coffee and then go into the den and call Peter. He would know whom she should call. There was one thing she was sure of; she wasn't giving money to anyone.

She took her coffee out to the veranda. The sun was up and burning the dew off the sand. It would be a good beach day. She had three days before her beloved children would be home. They were meeting in Chicago and flying into JFK together, making logistics much simpler. She looked forward to cleaning their rooms and getting food ready for them.

She thought of the people in the house; Marie was in her room in the children's wing, Sandra upstairs in the guest wing, and her mother above the garage in her apartment. Soon, every room would be occupied. She felt an old peace returning. Before, she was deluded into thinking all was well; now it really was. She felt sad that Jack, her strength and purpose for living for most of her adult life, had been the source of anguish and uncertainty. A woman knows, subconsciously, if her partner is betraying her, hiding part of himself from view. She would suffer in strange ways, lowered self-esteem and its many components just the beginning. Pam definitely was the victim of Jack's deceit. Now that he was dead, she was starting to relax. It was amazing how she had lived her life on the edge, wound up tight, ready to jump into action if necessary. She remembered Lisa saying to her years ago when she was trying to talk to her, "Momma, could you stop for one minute and listen to me?" Pam had to forcibly slow down and focus.

Before the children were born, Jack controlled Pam's life by enlisting the aid of his mother, suggesting his wife needed her help entering their social circle. And after their birth, Bernice interfered in their care just enough to undermine Pam's self-confidence.

Even after the move to Long Island, Jack kept his hold on his wife. He would show up unexpectedly in the middle of the week, albeit infrequently, but just enough to make Pam wonder every day if this would be the day he would come home. She was ready for him so that he could never come home and say that he found her without makeup or hair fixed, in a messy house or one without food to prepare for him.

Did he hate her? She wondered how he could have a long-term sexual relationship with Marie, and God only knew how many other women, and feel anything for her. It was too painful to dwell on.

The vision of Jack on the train floor, possibly writhing in pain, continued to haunt her. She needed to find out how Bill knew Jack would be on the train. Suddenly, she thought of Jack's cell phone. *What had happened to it?* She got up and went back into the house and headed for Marie's room. Maybe she'd remember where it ended up.

"Jack's phone?" she said, sitting up in bed. *Was her sister having a rough morning?* She never came in and woke Marie up. "I have it. The nurse gave it to me when we were at the hospital." She reached for her purse on the floor next to her bed, digging through it, hoping the phone was still there. "I'm pretty sure the battery must be dead," she said, handing it off to her sister.

Pam took it without saying anything else and left to go into the den; she saw the charge cord in the top drawer when she was searching through his desk the week before. She found the cord and plugged it into the wall and the phone. The phone came on; 'six voicemail messages' flashed on the screen. Pam didn't know how to retrieve messages from this model phone, but she was determined to figure it out. After two false starts, she heard a familiar voice. A wave of heat, starting at her forehead, spread across her body. It was Jack.

"Hey, this is Jack, leave a message." He sounded so young; the message was juvenile, unprofessional. So like

Jack, trying to impress, trying to connect with young people. *Who besides Sandra and Marie were calling him that he felt a message like that was necessary?* She would never know. She pressed more buttons and found what she was looking for—the unfamiliar voice of her former brother-in-law. "This is Bill. It's Saturday. Jack, get back to me. I need to talk to you today. I am going to the beach house in one hour if I don't hear from you by ten."

Pam replayed the message twice. She was faced with the knowledge that she didn't really know what Jack had done Friday night, if he was really in his own bed in the apartment or if he was with Sandra. Marie said he stopped coming to her apartment months ago. What had he been doing Saturday morning? Marie said she saw the two of them on the street. Where were they coming from? Sandra said he had never stayed at her place. She wasn't sure if she could believe that. Pam was in a quandary. *It didn't really matter if Jack had arranged to see Bill on the train, did it? What difference did it make now?* He was dead. Nothing she could learn now would change that. Maybe it was some closure she was looking for. So many senseless mistakes added up to chaos. Bill had threatened Jack, said he was going to come here. *What would have happened if he had?* Pam would have been here alone. She didn't have the gun yet. Bill was desperate; there was no telling what he would have done to her. Putting a knife to Nelda's throat may have been just the tip of the iceberg.

But, if it was feasible, she would probably end up helping out Bernice and Bill; Anne and the boys were part of this, too. She couldn't see making them suffer because Bill was a jerk. Plus, she didn't have anything to lose. She was wealthy and could afford to be generous. It would be good karma.

40

The morning unfolded. Pam could hear Nelda opening windows in her new apartment. The shower was running in the guest bathroom; Sandra must be up. She'd be going back into the city today; with Bill incarcerated, she was safe now. Marie was hiding out in her bedroom. The phone encounter may have scared her. *Good!* Pam laughed to herself. She didn't feel like talking to anyone. As that thought floated through her head, the house phone rang. The thought to let it ring crossed her mind, but it might be the kids. She walked to the phone and looked at the caller ID. *It was the police station! What did they want?* She picked it up and said hello.

"It's Detective Andrews, Mrs. Smith." Pam smiled at the phone.

"Hi, Detective Andrews," she said. "Call me Pam."

"Okay, Pam. Call me Andy," he replied. "So, are you busy? Is this a bad time for you?"

"No, this is actually a great time. What do you have in mind? Do you want to talk about my case?" she said, tongue in check, surprising herself. *Witty? That was not usually a word she would associate with herself.*

"We could do that. I actually just need a cup of coffee, and I am parked in front of your house." He hesitated, adding, "If that isn't too forward."

"I have a house full of women here today. Can I take a rain check?" Pam said.

"You may, but how about we go out for one? We can go around the corner."

Pam thought for a moment and then agreed. No one would think anything of it if they saw her with a man. It could be her insurance guy or a relative.

"I just need to grab my purse, and I'll be right out." She hung up the phone. Her purse was in the bedroom. She went in the bathroom to check her lipstick and hair; everything was perfect. Having taken good care of herself was paying off.

She'd have coffee with Detective Andrews. She was hopeful her guests would occupy themselves until she got home. Her life was stretching out before her, more interesting than she could remember. There would soon be a new baby to play with. Her own children would be home in just a few days for the rest of the summer. She was making a friend and going to have coffee with him right now. *How was it possible that I had the worst news a woman can get just a few weeks ago and be looking forward to my life already?*

He was standing next to his car, waiting for her. *She is a gorgeous woman*, he thought to himself. The most attractive woman he had seen in a while. He was going to be careful with her. She was worth it.

"So, Mrs. Smith, shall we walk?" he said, smiling at her.

"It's Pam, remember?" Pam said, smiling. "Call me Pam."